I0708345

A Familiar Family Connection

A Familiar Family Connection

The Ryan D Ryder Series

ESKAY KABBA

4 Horsemen
Publications, Inc.

A Familiar Family Connection
Copyright © 2023 Eskay Kabba. All rights reserved.

4 Horsemen Publications, Inc.
1497 Main St. Suite 169
Dunedin, FL 34698
4horsemenpublications.com
info@4horsemenpublications.com

Cover by J. Kotick
Typesetting by Autumn Skye
Edited by Kris Cotter

All rights to the work within are reserved to the author and publisher. No part of this publication may be reproduced, stored in a retrieval system, or transmitted in any form or by any means, electronic, mechanical, photocopying, recording, scanning, or otherwise, except as permitted under Section 107 or 108 of the 1976 International Copyright Act, without prior written permission except in brief quotations embodied in critical articles and reviews. Please contact either the Publisher or Author to gain permission.

This is a work of fiction. All characters, organizations, and events portrayed in this novel are either products of the author's imagination or are used fictitiously.

Library of Congress Control Number: 2023940385

Paperback ISBN-13: 979-8-8232-0221-3
Hardcover ISBN-13: 979-8-8232-0223-7
Audiobook ISBN-13: 979-8-8232-0220-6
Ebook ISBN-13: 979-8-8232-0222-0

DEDICATION

To Jojo—A familiar connection.

Table of Contents

Chapter 1 1
Chapter 2 20
Chapter 3 38
Chapter 4 50
Chapter 5 76
Chapter 6 91
Chapter 7 105
Chapter 8 123
Chapter 9 146
Chapter 10 170
Chapter 11 189
Chapter 12 204
Chapter 13 219
Chapter 14 235
Book Club Questions 259
Author Bio 261

Content warning: Explicit Langauge,
Explicit Sexual Situations, and Drug Use.

*N*icholas woke up on Monday morning and stretched over to the empty pillow next to him. He rubbed his eyes and looked around. It was still dark out; the sun's rays were just beginning to peek through the curtains. Only his tuxedo cat, Izzy, was looking at him from the bottom of the mattress. He rolled over to the edge of the bed and looked out. The bathroom door was open, so he knew Rion wasn't there.

"Ree?" he called out. He didn't hear a response.

Nick climbed out of the bed and went to search for him. He opened the second bedroom, which was also his home office, and his boyfriend was not in there. Nick made his way down the hall to the living room and spotted Rion. He couldn't help but smile. Rion was lying down with his back on the floor, a pillow behind his head, his legs on the couch, and his laptop on his thighs, and he was typing furiously. He was also murmuring, and it took Nick a moment to realize he was singing. He had his Bose headphones on, and murmured every other word of whatever song was playing loudly in his ears. Probably something by Lil Nas X or Imagine Dragons, Nick assumed.

Nick came closer, careful not to startle Rion while he was in a zone, or hibernating, as his sisters called it. He had learned that lesson before, almost getting his head ripped off last month when he touched Rion's shoulder, pulling him out of his stupor. And Rion had given him the silent treatment for a full twenty-four hours because he had lost his train of thought for the scene in his newest novel.

"You have to treat him like a scared animal in the woods," Gabby, Rion's sister, had told him once. "If you move too quickly, you're going to startle him, and he'll show his teeth and claws. Tread lightly."

Nick took her advice to heart. This time, he slowly walked around the coffee table to the other side of the couch and waved.

Rion sensed the movement and looked up. He smiled. "Hey, Nicky."

Nick came all the way down to the wooden floor and put his face next to Rion's. He kissed his lips softly and pulled the headphones from his ears at the same time. "Good morning, Ree. How long have you been up?"

"I don't know... 3 a.m.? Four, maybe?"

Nick nodded. "You've been like this for a week. Maybe get some sleep?"

"Yeah, yeah, I will," he said unconvincingly. "But today's my first day at Deep Strokez, so I need to be up."

He flipped his legs down from the couch seat and tried to rise, but Nick held him in place with his hand on Rion's wrist. "You can start tomorrow," Nick said, kissing up Rion's pen tattoo, the ink drops in rainbow colors on his arm. "I'm the boss, and I can change your start date, just like that."

"But I want to start today," Rion replied and kissed his shoulder.

Their lips met again, softly, repeatedly, then became more intense, and Rion moved, flipping down. Nick shifted to lay on his side as Rion pulled his length out through his boxer briefs. He got right to it, putting Nick's barely hard cock in his mouth. Nick moaned but returned the favor since Rion's groin was also in his face. They pleasured each other, taking their time and moving slowly, not wanting to cum too soon. Rion began to move faster, pushing Nick deeper into his throat. Nick felt his climax coming and, conscious not to use his teeth, pressed his lips down hard, losing track of time and space as he released warm semen into his lover's mouth. As soon as Nick was able to move again, he stroked as Rion continued to swallow his cum, until he felt Rion's thighs tense up.

Nick covered Rion's cock with his lips as he began to cum, too. Nick continued to suck until Rion pulled off Nick's cock yelling, "Stop, fuck, stop, too sensitive!"

Nick laughed as Rion rolled onto his back, his body still trembling. Nick leaned over and took a small bite of his thigh, making him yelp.

"Ready to go to work?" asked Nick.

He didn't wait for a response. Instead, he jumped up and went into the shower, making the water temperature just the way his boyfriend liked it, knowing he was on his way.

Rion made the decision to not go into the office with Nick, who typically went in as early as 7 a.m. He waited until 8:30 a.m. to walk the twenty minutes to the office building on Columbus Circle and took the elevator to the 34th floor. Once the doors opened, he stood before a large glass door with the words *Deep Strokez Publications* on it. It was already buzzing inside. Rion opened the door and stopped at the front desk.

"Hello, Mrs. Anne. Nice to see you today," he greeted the receptionist.

"Hello, Rion," she replied happily. "Welcome aboard, officially."

"Well, not officially. I'm still just freelance," Rion reminded her.

"And if you do well, maybe your friend could give you a full-time job?" she said with a wink. She handed him a keycard for the front door and a folder of papers he needed to sign.

"I have a full-time job, Mrs. Anne, you know this." He winked back at her.

"I sure do, Mr. Ryder," she said with a smile. "Still waiting for part two of Jet Lagged." Then she got down to business. "Go see Martine at the third desk to the right. She'll prepare your ID card and set you up with payroll."

"Thank you," he said to the older woman and crossed through the low swinging doors into the large open space.

Rion loved Nick's flat organization structure. It was organized chaos in the large room. Desks were turned every which way, some toward the picture windows, some against. A few people were busy, hard at work, with their headphones on, typing away. Others were huddled in conversations or simply hanging out. If it wasn't for the lone office at the back of the room, Rion would have had no idea who the CEO was. Not that Nicholas was ever in his office. He worked the floor with the team throughout the day and worked later nights. Nick was already at a meeting with his editors at the conference table in the middle of the room. He looked up briefly mid-conversation and gave Rion a head nod, but continued talking to his staff. Rion nodded back and did not glance his way again.

Martine happily waved him over. "Hi, Rion! I'm so glad you made it through the group interview and joined us. Those boys were a little tough on you, weren't they?"

She motioned with her chin over to Edgar, Eddie, and Dion, who were in an intense game of table football on Edgar's desk. They were Nick's three top reporters and wrote everything from traditional news articles to the latest sex-related news nationwide. Eddie was the reporter who interviewed Nicholas after his infamous scandal last year.

"Yes, they were, but I'm tougher." He playfully pulled up his sleeve and showed his bicep.

Martine's eyes went wide. "What a gorgeous tattoo," she said and reached her hand out to touch his forearm.

Rion stretched his hand so she could get a better look at it. As she stroked his arm, he could feel Nick's eyes on him from the side. But when he turned his head, Nick had turned back to his team. It made Rion smile.

He brought his arm down, and she took the hint. "Let's get to work."

Martine took his picture for his ID and talked to him as she made his lanyard. She walked him through the ins and outs of the office and showed him to his desk. "There are about thirty staff altogether, we're a small operation, but at least eight of us are in the office every day: myself, Ms. Anne at the front desk, Nguyen, who is our lead digital manager but also troubleshoots our IT issues, the three stooges over there," she pointed at Edgar, Eddie, and Dion again, "Marcel, the executive assistant and general manager, and of course Nick. The reporters bring the stories, but they have to go through the editors for selection, accuracy, and proofreading before they make it in. The others filter in and out, but everyone is required to have at least one office day a week and to attend their individual department meetings, which are held monthly. We come together for the staff meetings, also once a month. Today is the editorial meeting, but it also happens to be the full staff meeting." She walked him over to Marcel, whose desk was right next to Nick's office.

Marcel was all business. A flamboyant man with an eye for fashion and a nose for bullshit, Marcel's first words were, "I need to know when your 'In' day is, and I need to know that you're going to stick to it."

Rion nodded. "Okay... Monday."

"Thank you." He immediately wrote it down. "I expect you to be in the office every Monday for at least six hours, not including your lunch break. The rest of your time, you do from home. Don't forget to add the hours you worked into ADP. Do it daily, I check.

And use your Outlook calendar to communicate your meetings and personal days out."

Rion nodded again as Marcel continued. "Our full staff meeting is at 10:30 a.m., so you'll meet everyone then. During the staff meeting, you will introduce yourself and let everyone know that you have openings on your team for book reviews. No more than four people and yourself. That's five, and that's enough. Any more than that, you have to get it approved by Nick. Then we have lunch. After that, Nguyen will set you up with our Microsoft Office 365 login codes so you'll have access to your files from anywhere. At 1:30 p.m., you will meet with your team. Plan to do so once a month for a minimum of forty-five minutes. At 3:10 p.m., you will meet with Nicholas in his office to discuss your first day. You are his last meeting so do not be late. Any questions?"

"Erm... nope. Not right now."

"Good." Marcel brushed his cat-like glasses up his face and said, "If you need anything, find me. I'm always around."

"Thank you, Marcel. I already feel part of the team," Rion said sincerely.

That got a smile out of him. But just as quickly, Marcel turned to yell at the three full-time reporters who were getting loud and a little rowdy. "Don't you have anything better to do!?" They quickly dispersed their table game and went to their separate desks.

Rion smiled and picked an empty desk to sit at. He pulled out his computer and opened it up, not really sure what he was supposed to do except hang out. He noticed that when Nick's meeting was up, he called Marcel to his office and closed the door. Rion looked around and decided to get up and begin introducing himself to people, starting with Nguyen, the Vietnamese digital manager. He learned a little about his family, his girlfriend, and his IT background. As people filtered into the office, he learned not only who they were and their positions—journalist, editor, graphic artist, financial analyst—but also how they started working at *Deep Strokez*. Everyone had great things to say about Nick. And while Rion already knew Nick was a great guy, hearing others tell him how much they loved working *with* him—not *for* him, he noticed that, too—gave him a sense of internal pride at having a well-respected partner.

At 10:25 a.m., the office door opened and Marcel and Nick walked out and sat at the table. Others took their cue and began to grab seats at the conference table or on a nearby desk. Rion counted at least twenty-six people in attendance, including himself. He opted to sit at the table directly across from Nick. They glanced at each other, and Nick glanced away first when Aspen, one of the graphic artists, approached him with a question. At exactly 10:30 a.m., Marcel blew a small whistle, and everyone quieted.

"The March 16th meeting is called to order. Please don't forget to sign in. Agenda for today: Nick is going to update us on the strategic plan, Nguyen has IT updates, new staff member Rion is going to recruit for the erotic book club reviews, and Ms. Anne has housekeeping items. Any other items to consider for today?"

"I got one!" Edgar raised his hand.

"If it's about a stipend to travel internationally, no," Nick said with his eyes narrowed. Edgar slowly put his hand down, and the others snickered.

"Okay then," Marcel said, unamused. "I turn it over to Nicholas." He nodded at him.

"Thanks, Marcel," Nick began, "and thank you all for checking in. I want to officially introduce some of our newer staff: Aspen Markle started two weeks ago as our graphic designer, Duncan Lopez, a part-time journalist who is going to focus on Caribbean- and Hispanic-related content, and Rion Matthews, a free-lance editor who will be heading the erotic book club, a brand-new feature you'll hear about later." Rion clapped with everyone else.

"Now, updates on where we are in our timeline to go completely online. As you know, our timeline sped up a bit thanks to unforeseen circumstances—"

Eddie coughed loudly. "Ahem, ahem, sex tape, ahem!"

Nick's team snickered again, and Rion found himself smiling. Nick cringed and said, "I'm docking your pay for that," making everyone laugh out loud. Marcel was the only one that rolled his eyes in impatience.

Nick continued, "As I was saying, thanks to unforeseen circumstances, we have officially sold out of our November, December, and January prints and have no need to continue printing March copies. But thanks to the genius idea from Barry to sell older copies for a dollar, we are quickly selling out the prints from the previous year, too. I've been meeting with Nguyen, Archer, and the rest of the marketing team almost weekly, and it seems we could be ready to launch the new graphics by July 1st, right in time for summer." The whole staff cheered. Nick quieted them down and continued, "We still need volunteers to monitor the chat rooms and add volunteers as time goes on, but we will work that out in the April meeting. We also need a European-based reporter—"

Edgar cut him off again, throwing his hands in the air. "I told you I'm willing to move!"

"And I told you I'm not paying for your expenses that will include receipts to the Red-Light District, so again, no," Nick said with a smile.

Everyone laughed loudly at that. "Jeez, you're an awful boss," Edgar said playfully.

Nick ignored him and continued to talk about the upcoming plans for the rebranding of their website. He took questions and comments from his staff and then handed the meeting to Nguyen with a head nod. Nguyen talked about moving staff meetings from Microsoft Teams back to BlueJeans temporarily until they could figure out the kinks in the server for videoconferencing, and about adding a two-step authorization process that everyone would need on their phones. "I'll reach out to each of you individually in the next two weeks."

He quieted and turned to Rion, giving him a head nod. Rion nodded back, but as everyone turned to look at him, he realized it was his turn to speak.

"Oh. Right." He cleared his throat, glanced at Nick, whose face was unreadable, and turned to the others, looking around as he spoke hesitantly. "So, yeah, I'm Rion. As some of you already know, I'm a writer, under the pen name Ryan D. Ryder. Nick... erm... came up with this great idea to add erotic book reviews to the website, which I think is great, and asked me to head the... erm... reviewing of the books... so yeah, erm—"

Dion cut him off. "Dude, are you sure you write eroticism? Because you sound like someone who doesn't get laid very often."

Others around the table laughed loudly. Nick said abrasively, "Hey! Lay off the new guy, jackass."

"Ohhh," some said loudly as others cackled.

"No, it's okay, it's okay," Rion said, waving his hand around, realizing who he was dealing with. "Because I know for a fact that I came this morning, and the day before that, and the day before that, while you look like someone who jerks off to his own reporting. And considering the word count of your last story, you're definitely *short* on minutes," Rion said smugly as people laughed loudly again. "But don't worry, I could teach you a few things." He winked at him and smirked.

"Hooooly shit!" Edgar said loudly and laughed a loud belly laugh.

"Sorry, bud, I don't go that way," Dion said with a smile that didn't reach his eyes.

"Oh, you would if I ever get my hands on you," Rion said and puckered a kiss at him.

The staff went wild with laughter as Dion gave him the finger, and Marcel rolled his eyes again. Nick yelled, "Hey, hey, HEY!" They quieted down, giving their boss respect. "Before this turns into a dick-measuring contest that I'm pretty sure Rion would win, let's jump into the book club idea, shall we?"

Everyone snickered again. Rion's mouth opened slightly as Nick looked at him with a straight face. He stared a little longer than intended, then found his voice and spoke more firmly than the last time, looking around again. "So I plan to have a team review three books a month to start, see how the traction goes. If we get good feedback, we will step it up to five books a month. I'm looking for four others here that would want to join in."

"We get paid for this?" a woman called out from the wall.

"You already know you get paid for the hours you work, Carli," Marcel said dryly.

"Then I'm in!" Carli said.

"I'm in, too," Eddie said. He grinned at Rion.

Nick said, "Rion, I have asked Aspen to work alongside you on what you want your landing page to display. Aspen has expressed interest in also reviewing books."

She nodded profusely. "Definitely. MM Romance is my thing."

"Sounds great, Aspen. I can't wait to work with you on this," Rion said.

Mrs. Anne raised her hand. "Is it only for the main staff?"

Before Nick could answer, Rion said to her, "I would love to have you on my team, Ms. Anne. You have a good eye for erotic novels."

Barry, the financial analyst, asked, "Does it have to be a reporter? I like sex."

"We all like sex, Barry. That's why we're here!" said the skinny redhead a few paces down from Rion.

"I think it would be good to have three men and three women on the team, so please, join us," Rion said sincerely. But then he remembered and looked over at Marcel, who had an eyebrow all the way up. "Oh, I think... erm... we only should have five..."

Nick glanced at Marcel and then back at Rion. "Six is fine, five plus you. Marcel, make a note of it." Marcel dutifully wrote it down. "Anything else, Rion?"

"Erm... yeah... I mean, yes," he spoke more firmly again. "We'll meet this afternoon at 1:30 to go over logistics and then plan a virtual meeting a couple of weeks on ... BlueJeans?" He looked at Nguyen to confirm, who gave him a thumbs up and a smile, happy that someone was listening to him. "BlueJeans. Right."

He turned to Nick. "Okay. That's it." He smiled proudly at him. Nick tried very hard not to smile back and gestured toward Ms. Anne. "Oh, right! Ms. Anne, you can... You can talk now."

Dion and Edgar shook their heads in disappointment that Rion did not know all the nuances of their office culture in the two hours he'd been there. Eddie, on the other hand, watched him intently with a smile. Ms. Anne began talking about keeping the office kitchen space clean and remembering to show their badges at the front desk downstairs as security was tightening up in the building. A bit of bickering happened between a few staff over leftovers getting dibs by other people that Nick had to quell, right as the Subway sandwiches were delivered for the staff meeting. Marcel read off the highlights from the meeting, asking if he had missed anything important. No one disputed the minutes, ready to eat after the hour-and-forty-five-minute meeting. Once done, he adjourned the meeting, and people began to move around again.

Nick wandered over to Rion but refrained from touching him. "You okay?" he asked quietly.

"Fine," Rion replied. "Dion is a douche."

Nick smiled. "Yes. But you handled yourself just fine."

"Yeah, about that," Rion started, and spoke even quieter. "Try not to defend me so much. You went real alpha male 'don't fuck with my boyfriend' kind of angry at him."

"Was I?" Nick asked. "Hmm... I would have called him a jackass if he tested Aspen, who is also new. But for the record..." He leaned in and whispered in his ear, "Nobody fucks with my boyfriend."

Rion blushed, then looked around to see who noticed, but everyone else was in their own conversations or getting food. He looked into Nick's blue eyes as Nick winked and stepped away to join the food line. Rion stood there a moment, then turned around to come face to face with Eddie, who he knew saw the whole exchange.

"Hey," Rion spoke first.

"Hey," Eddie said. He grinned again. "Where did you say you were from again, Rion?"

"Fresno," Rion answered him. "But I lived in San Francisco for the last six years before moving here."

Eddie nodded slowly. "Cool. So, how did you and Nick become friends?" They walked over to the line together.

"We, erm... met a couple of months back. I was researching a new book, and I struck up a conversation with him, found out that he owns a magazine, and he offered me a freelance job."

Not completely untrue, Rion reasoned with himself, but it still felt weird leaving out a major part of who Nick was to him. It was moments like this that made him want to yell from the rooftops, "I'm in love with Nicholas!" But he also wanted his privacy, and being linked to the infamous Nicholas "Mr. Deep

Strokez" Highton was about as private as whoever Leonardo DiCaprio was dating at the moment.

"Yeah, same thing, kind of. Nick was a guest lecturer at NYU three years ago at a workshop around fundamental journalism, and I found him interesting. We got to talking, and he asked if I wanted to come on as an intern for my senior year. Once I graduated, I came aboard full-time. I guess you'll be looking to do the same at some point?"

"Me? Nah." Rion shook his head. "I just want to help Nick jumpstart this book reviews idea and then pass on the torch. I don't plan to stay on Nick's payroll."

"Yeah? Why is that?" Eddie asked curiously.

"Because I have a career. I'm a full-time writer now and an author."

Eddie smiled widely at him and chuckled. "You sure that's the only reason?"

Rion kept a straight face. "Is that not reason enough?"

Eddie chuckled again and grabbed a box of roast beef and provolone. "Yeah. Yeah, it is. Especially since you guys are so close. You don't want money and position to ruin the *relationship* you have."

He caught Rion's eyes and winked at him. He patted his shoulder and turned around to move farther down the line, grabbing a coke and moving on without another word to Rion.

Rion sighed internally, then grabbed his own box with an Italian sub in it. He glanced at Nick, who was in a conversation with Carli and the redhead from the meeting earlier, and opted to sit at his desk. He was surprised when Barry and another guy whose name he didn't know came over to him.

"I already know the perfect book to start with!" he said excitedly. Rion focused all his attention on his new colleagues.

After his meeting with his book club and finalizing the books to read for the month, he made his way to Nick's office; as usual, the door was wide open. Aspen, Nguyen, and Carli were discussing changing the color themes on one of the landing pages when Rion knocked.

"Hey. I'm supposed to meet with you to discuss my first day."

"Oh, okay. So, how was your first day?" Nick asked.

All four eyes were on Rion. "Fine... I ... guess..."

Nick nodded. "Good. Are you in the office tomorrow?"

Rion nodded slowly. "Yeah, I'll be in all this week to get a feel of the office, and then I'll start my new schedule next week."

"Sounds like a plan," Nick agreed. He looked at his watch. "We can check in tomorrow again if you want, but otherwise, you're free to head out for the day. I'm sure you have a special someone to get home to."

Rion kept his face as neutral as Nick did. "I do, actually. Got to get dinner ready for him. I'm making quesadillas."

Nick smiled. "Good job today at the meeting. I'll see you tomorrow, Rion."

Rion nodded and hit the door twice on his way out.

"Eddie knows," Rion said as they sat next to each other in the living room, eating dinner with their feet on the ottoman and food on a large tray between them on the leather couch. UCLA and Duke were playing on the big screen, trying to make it to the Elite 8, and naturally, Rion and Nick were rivals.

"Knows what?" he asked with his eyes glued to the sixty-inch TV. "Aaaah, toss the damn ball!" he yelled.

"About us," Rion said as he shoved another triangle of chicken and cheese into his mouth.

Nick glanced at him, then back at the screen. "He doesn't."

"He asked me if I've ever been to London during our book review meeting."

Nick didn't flinch. "So? What did you say?"

"I said I had. Then I asked casually if he's ever been. Then went around the table asking about other countries others have been to. Thank God Ms. Anne had been to London before, too. She started talking about landmarks, and I was able to change the subject."

"He's just fishing," Nick said, then yelled again as UCLA took control of the ball again. "He's an investigative reporter. That's what they do."

"Face it, Duke is doo-doo right now. UCLA is taking it," Rion said and grabbed a handful of chips from the bowl.

"Fuck off. We have half a third quarter and all of the fourth quarter. They just need to get their rhythm." Rion laughed. Nick looked at him again. "So what if he does know? Is that the worst thing in the world for people to know about us?"

Rion sighed and looked back at Nick. "No, it's not the worst thing, except we lose our privacy and end up being in celebrity news and tabloids. You may be used to all that, but I'm not. That's why I use a pen name, to remain anonymous." He paused, then said casually, "Oh, and don't forget that your uber-rich parents will try to destroy me."

Nick was frustrated with Rion's decision to be his hidden Stedman to his Oprah-like status, but understood it. More than anything, Rion didn't want Nick's parents to know. He was afraid of how they would plot to end their relationship as they had done with every serious relationship Nick had ever been in. Madeline Highton, Nick's mother, had gone out of her way to try to arrange relationships and even a marriage engagement for her son, but to no avail; he always found a way out of it. Nicholas knew that Rion had valid reasons for wanting to keep their relationship hidden from others, but it had been harder and harder for him to not want to show Rion off as the number one guy in his life over the last couple of months.

Nick reached his thumb out to touch the side of Rion's lip. "You have a little cheese there." He gently brushed it off and brought his thumb to his mouth to suck slowly, keeping eye contact with his lover.

They stared at each other. Rion asked, "You don't want to finish the game and watch Duke get spanked?"

"I think I'd rather spank you," Nick said seductively.

Rion lifted the tray from between them, moving his feet off the ottoman to put the tray there. As soon as he turned back, Nick was already on him, pushing him down onto his back and pressing his body against him. They kissed, food particles still in both of their mouths, tongues tasting of cheese and salsa. Nick took off Rion's shirt and made his way down, kissing and licking his torso.

He leaned back up and said, "Take off your clothes."

Rion began to get naked as Nick got up and quickly went to the room to grab the lube and came back. He commanded Rion to "Get on your knees and face the couch." Rion did without another word.

Nick came behind him and kissed his back as the basketball game played behind them, both forgetting about it for the moment. He put lube on his fingers and got Rion ready before he lubed himself, then entered him. Rion moaned and held onto the seat cushion. Nick started out slow but quickly heated up, holding onto his shoulders and thrusting hard. As he started to feel his orgasm, he slid his hands down Rion's arms and held onto his wrists. He pumped until Rion cried out, and he knew his lover came. Nick came right behind him, filling up Rion's bottom.

Nick slowly pulled out and sat on the floor. Rion slid backward and sat between his legs, his head against Nick's shoulder. Nick reached around him and played with the hair on his chest.

"Don't worry about Eddie," he said softly. "You're still my Stedman." He leaned Rion's head to the side and kissed him on the neck.

*R*ion dreamed of Hyde Park. It wasn't often that he remembered his dreams, but he remembered that one. He could feel the grass beneath him and rubbed the palm of his hand back and forth on it. He could feel the heat of the sun on his face, but his eyes were closed, giving his eyelids a reddish glow from the inside. Children played in the distant background, just close enough to hear their laughter. He could tell he was alone, and he was fine with it. Rion was used to being alone.

Rion woke to the faint sound of buzzing, slowly taking him out of his dream. It was his phone dinging with a text, and it was probably Gabrielle, his sister. He opened his eyes, and the room was dark. Nick had closed the blinds so the sun wouldn't wake him before he went into the office. He rolled over onto Nicholas's pillow and breathed in deeply, feeling satisfied. Rion had not thought he would love being with Nick as much as he did. But they were a perfect combination. Nick worked long hours, giving Rion the space that he wanted to think and write. Even the few hours he went to work, it was cordial and professional. And when they were home, Nick gave him the attention and affection he needed. On the weekends when Rion wasn't buried in his writing, they would go on long walks together, exploring museums and art and all that the city had to offer. One thing Rion still couldn't get used to was how cold it got during the winter months, so when the temperature dropped too low, they would stay in bed, make love, eat, and make love, watch movies, and make love, sleep, and make love again. Rion couldn't believe his life was this perfect.

He stretched and rolled off the bed to take his morning leak and jump into the shower. Today the temperature was going up to the high sixties, and he ached to be in warmer weather, his dream reminding him of how much he missed being in the warm sun. When he stepped out of the shower, he looked at the beard that he had grown out; his face was almost completely covered. He understood why Nicholas let his beard grow for the winter months. It kept his face warm. His sisters hated it, saying he looked like an extra from *Planet of the Apes*. He laughed to himself, then grabbed the electric shaver. He trimmed it down until he couldn't anymore, then took the razor and shaved it all off, including his mustache. He smiled at himself, knowing that Nick would have some choice words about his new look. His curly hair had grown out enough to put it in a man-bun, so he did so.

Rion dressed in a t-shirt and threw a thin zip-up sweater over it, made himself a simple breakfast of eggs on toast, made another sandwich for lunch, and filled up his water bottle. Izzy floated around his feet, giving soft meows, so he opened up a fresh packet of

Fancy Feast for her and fed her. He packed his laptop and food in his bookbag, took an edible that he got from a local supplier since THC was recreational in New York now, then headed downstairs and stepped out of the building.

"Good morning, Mr. Matthews," the doorman greeted him.

"Good morning," he said back politely. "And thank you."

It was windy, as it always was by the river, but he could feel the warmth of the sun. He closed his eyes and stood there. The doorman let him have a moment, then asked, "Would you like me to call you a car, sir?"

Rion opened his eyes and said, "It's a great day, Adam. I'm going to go for a long walk." He started walking toward the river.

But when he got to the opening of Riverside Park, he decided it was not the place he was looking to be. So he turned around and walked in the opposite direction, ending up at Central Park instead. He entered the park and found it more crowded than he thought it would be with joggers and walkers, mothers or nannies with their young children, and college kids studying or hand-holding with their significant others. He knew it was due to the warmer weather. Rion sighed in disappointment but didn't feel like continuing to walk around until he found the perfect park. He strolled until he saw an unoccupied tree. Rion plopped down in the grass underneath a tree and sat there for a moment, enjoying the warmth still with a small nip in the air, and watched the park unfold around him. Then he opened his laptop to a blank Google Doc page and began to write.

Rion was still sitting in Central Park three hours later when his phone rang. He answered it with his Bluetooth in his ear. "Hey, Rel."

"Hey, baby bro," Muriel answered. "I was just thinking of you. What are you doing?"

"Sitting in the park, people-watching, writing."

She snorted. "Drinking your Americano Grande from the nearest Starbucks?"

He laughed. "At work?" Rion glanced at the time and it was around 10 a.m. in San Francisco.

"Yeah, first lull of the morning. Figured I would check on you," she said. Muriel worked as a general manager at a diner in the heart of San Francisco. It was always busy.

"How's the fam?" he asked.

"Missing you." He didn't respond. "Oh, don't get sad about that, Rion. You did the right thing. Aren't you happy?"

His mind went back to his thoughts this morning. "Yeah, sis. I am."

"Good. Maurese was around here asking about you. He's back in San Fran, saying he had some dealing with his brother, D.J., the one he never talks about but always has to deal with. He's also been talking with Reese, helping him stay on the right track."

"Yeah? That's good. Tell him I said 'hey' the next time you see him."

"Sure will. But he's going to end up calling you himself to check on you, too. He still can't believe you actually did it. He says he's proud of you."

Rion smiled. Muriel's father, Maurese Hollingsworth, was the closest thing to a father figure to him. "I'll look out for his call."

They talked a little about Maurese's life in Stockton and his new fiancée. She hesitated before she said, "Roslyn is still clean. In case you wanted to know."

He hesitated back and said, "Okay."

"We had a long talk, she and I," she continued. "And I was honest with her. I told her I didn't know if I could truly forgive everything that I went through. But I can see how she is trying to redeem herself, staying clean, keeping a job, making amends. And that she is okay with me." Rion didn't respond. "At some point, baby bro, you're going to have to confront her, then listen to her. And I don't mean that outburst you did at Thanksgiving. I mean, really talk to her."

"Yeah, well… I'm not ready for that. Not until she is ready to be honest with me about who my father is."

"I get it," Muriel acknowledged. "But I think she is working her way up to it. Just don't give up on her."

"I've already given up on her," he said factually.

"Okay, well, don't. Because she really is trying. She's never stayed clean this long, you know this. And if she's trying, you should try, too."

Rion didn't want to talk about his mother anymore. "How's Ava?"

Muriel scoffed. "New boyfriend, same Ava."

Rion chuckled. "She's in love again?"

"Is she?" she said sarcastically. "She's singing about how this one is the one. I was trying to make sure she stays on meds."

"Oh, is she staying with you? Not in my apartment with her friend?"

"No, I think they had a falling out. She's staying with Roslyn. Your apartment is empty."

Rion grimaced at his mother's name being brought up again. Before she could start another conversation, he said, "I have to go. Hug the kids for me."

"Yeah, me too. My break is over. Just wanted to see how you're doing."

"Well, head back to work. Love you, big sis."

"Love you too, baby bro."

Rion pressed the off button in his ear, thinking about his mother. He knew that everything that Rel said was right. He knew that she had been trying to rebuild her relationship with him. He just didn't think he was ready to forgive her for the dark days of his youth. Not yet.

He held up the phone, turned his camera on, took a picture of his bare face, then sent it in the sibling group text. He immediately received messages back from his sisters.

[Rel: ♡♡♡]

[Gabby: OMG Nick is going to FREAK]

[Ava: Oh good, I was wondering when you were going to stop looking like a 70's porn star.]

He laughed out loud, packed up his items, and walked slowly back home from the park.

Nick came home around five to the smell of roasted chicken. He dropped his laptop bag at the front entrance and walked over to the kitchen, saying, "Smells like someone was feeling domesticated toda—"

He paused upon seeing Rion's grinning face as he stirred the pasta. Nick came closer and put his elbows on the island. "Who are you, and what have you done with my boyfriend?"

Rion leaned over the island and kissed his lips. "Hello, lover."

"Hmmm... You taste like him, but still..." He reached up and touched his smooth skin. "Wow."

"You love it or you hate it?"

"I ... don't know yet. I don't hate it, that's for sure. You look amazing. I think I'm just used to you with some facial hair." He reached up and touched his curls. "Don't ever cut this off, though. We're over if you do that."

Rion laughed, kissed his lips again, and moved back over to the stove. "Dinner in fifteen."

Nick's phone rang to the tune of *Addams Family* as he walked home from work. He groaned, then put on a calm voice and answered. "Hello, Mother."

"Nicholas, darling. How goes the day?" Madeline Highton asked.

"It's been a good day," he replied. *Until now*, he thought. Nick's mother used to call him every Friday morning but since his incident at The Masquerade Gala last fall, her calls were sporadic. And nastier. "And yours?"

"Splendid. The gardeners are out today, and I picked the spring collection this year for the front of the house, purple azaleas."

"It sounds wonderful, Mother," he replied.

She continued to talk about the changes of the season and the upcoming debutante ball that she was the committee president for. She briefly mentioned his father, who was currently on a work trip, and spending time with Emma and her grandchildren the following weekend. "That all sounds wonderful," he replied again as he stopped in the nearest market to gather truffles for Rion.

"Yes, it is. Oh, I ran into Penelope. She said to tell you hello." Nick paused in the produce section of the grocery store. He waited for it. "She's been successfully dating Paul Rochel for the last couple of weeks, and it's going very well. I suspect she has gotten over that nasty breakup the two of you had."

"Uh-huh."

"She was curious if you were still with the supermodel. She could have sworn Yesenia was at a party at Le Pré Catalan in France with tennis star Charlie Caine. They were together for the French Open as well." His mother waited for his response.

Nick knew Penny, his ex and fake fiancée of two hours, asked no such questions. His mother just wanted to know these things. He answered, "No, Mother, we are no longer dating."

"Oh. Well, who is the unlucky woman this time?" Nick did not answer. "Nicholas, it is not polite to blindside me with these things anymore. For your own sake."

"Don't worry, Mother. There will be no more blindsides," he told her while simultaneously thinking about his live-in boyfriend, whom she knew nothing about. He picked up the truffles and went to the register.

"There better not be," she said sternly. "You've caused this family enough drama for a lifetime."

"Always good talking with you, Mother," Nick said dryly.

"I mean, really, Penny dodged a huge bullet being tied to you. A woman of her caliber could never be truly sophisticated being with a man who sells *sex* for a living."

"Really, these conversations are always enlightening."

"I'm just being honest with you, my son. I feel extremely sorry for the woman that ends up by your side. You'll never marry her, and you'll continue to share yourself with any vagabond whom you deem has a so-called connection with you."

"You know, Mother, it is more helpful for you to just pretend I'm five years old again and ignore me for the next decade. That way, whoever I end up with can't really be a reflection on you, and you can feign ignorance." Nick paid for his purchase.

The line went silent. Then she said, "I just need you to stop being such a fucking disappointment."

Nicholas scoffed out a laugh as he exited the store. "Why, Mother, you must really be upset. Using a swear word in the middle of the day? A woman of your *caliber*?"

"Mock me if you must, but you will regret the choices that you have been making. And when you do, I will be waiting in the wings to pick you up. After a sincere apology from you."

Nicholas had had enough sparring for the day. "Thank you for always being there for me, Mother. I have to go now. Next week, I presume?"

"Heed my words," Madeline said seriously. "But yes, next week, Nicholas darling."

"Great. Have a wonderful day. Glad to hear about the purple azaleas."

"Thank you. Goodbye, Nicholas."

"Goodbye, Mother." Nick hung up first and sighed deeply.

Nick went into his apartment and put the small bag on the kitchen counter. "Hey, thanks," Rion said from the living room. But Nick had already turned around and gone to his bedroom.

Nick began to unbutton his shirt but was having a difficult time with the buttons. Rion came into the room. He walked in front of him, pushed his hands out of the way, and unbuttoned Nick's shirt for him.

"Mommy dearest?" Rion asked softly.

Nick grunted a response. Rion got his shirt off and kissed his chest, then his face. "Got a cognac waiting for you on the counter."

He walked into the closet, grabbed the first t-shirt he saw, and handed it to Nick. "You got five minutes. Then you brush it off and play a card game with me."

Nick nodded and kissed Rion on the lips. Then Rion left the room.

Rion woke to the feel of wet kisses across his chest and stomach and a tenor voice singing softly, "Happy birthday to you. Happy birthday to you. Happy birthday, sweet Ree Ree, happy birthday to you."

Rion reached out without opening up his eyes and mumbled, "Jesus, Nicky, no. Not Ree Ree." Nick moved his way up to kiss his neck a few times and his chin and lips. "I take it you're not going into the office?"

"No," Nick said with another kiss on his lips.

"I take it you have plans for me?"

"Yes." Kiss.

"Will I like these plans?"

"Depends on how you feel about making love all morning, a quick drive, a Broadway show in the evening, then making love all night."

Rion smiled. "I think we can give that a try."

Nick kissed his lips again. "Come shower with me."

"Right now?" Rion groaned. He still had not opened his eyes. "What time is it?"

"7:49 a.m. And I promise it will be worth it. Meet me in the shower." Nick kissed his face one more time and left him in the bed.

Rion groaned, then turned over to his stomach and looked out the window at the blue sky. He wasn't a religious person, but he was suddenly grateful to the universe for how his life was turning out. At twenty-six, he was a published author and was well known in LGBTQ smutty romance circles. His family was safe, happy, and healthy. And his partner was everything he could have ever asked for. He had been taking fewer edibles, exercising more, and feeling less anxious since he moved to New York to be with Nicholas. For all of this, he was thankful.

He heard the shower running and decided to get up and join Nick. He was rinsing off and smiled when Rion entered. He grabbed a cloth, added the fresh-scented body wash to it, and began to wordlessly scrub Rion's body.

Rion didn't know what made him say it, maybe a part of him wanted to test Nick's feelings for him, but he asked, "Nick? What would you say if I decided to move out into my own apartment?"

Nick inhaled and exhaled deeply, but continued to wash him down. "I would say... I understand why you would want or need your own space. I know sometimes it can feel like this is my space, and you're a guest in it, so I get it. I would miss your daily presence, but support your decision."

Rion actually didn't feel that way. For some reason, from the moment he arrived in New York back in December, Nick's home had felt like his home, too. Maybe because being with Nick felt like home. But instead of saying his thoughts, he told him, "I appreciate that. Your understanding and support are invaluable."

Nick nodded and avoided his eyes. "So, when do you want to start looking at places? Zoey can help get the best deals, and you can use my name as collateral to get into an expensive high-rise for half the cost. You can even move into this building ... if you want to."

Rion shook his head. "I'm not moving out, Nick. My home is with you. I'm home."

Nick stopped rubbing the cloth over his body and looked at him. "Why do you do that?"

"Do what?" Rion asked innocently. Nick stared at him. Rion shrugged. "I don't know. Part of my anxiety issues is to question everything, especially if it seems too good to be true. Just seeing if you really get me."

Nick pulled him close against his body. "Well, could you find other ways instead of giving me a mini heart attack? I don't want you to go."

"Well, why didn't you just say that?" Rion whined back and held him back.

"If I had said that first, you would have run scared, and you know it," Nick said. Rion wanted to deny it, but he knew he was right. "I don't want you to feel trapped or that I'm trying to control you. But you gotta know how much I need you next to me. I felt like I was choking for five straight months last year, and when you walked into my office in December, suddenly, I could breathe again. You give me life, Rion."

"That was very poetic of you, Nicky," Rion said softly with a smile.

Nick did not smile back. "I have a present for you. Well, two, but the first one is right here."

"In the shower?" Rion asked jokingly.

Nick took Rion's hands and moved them from his waist lower to hold his butt cheeks. "Right there."

Rion took less than a moment to figure out what he was offering. His cock started to tighten against his body. He stared into Nick's intense blue eyes. "You're serious?"

"I did all three steps that you told me to do last year," said Nick. "Well, I did the first two. Here's the last one: Make love to me, Rion Matthews. I want you to make love to me."

Rion let a few moments pass, then said, "I didn't see you do the first two."

"And why would I let you see me do it?" Nick asked.

The side of Rion's mouth went up in a smirk. "So you're serious."

"You going to keep asking me that, or are you going to take what I'm offering?" Nick asked with an eyebrow raised. "You have my full consent."

"Holy, holy shit," Rion said softly. He kissed Nick's mouth over and over again. "I love you, Nick."

Nick kissed him back. "Good. Then show me." He turned off the shower and took Rion's hand.

They walked into the bedroom and fell onto the mattress together, bodies still dripping wet, rolling around, kissing, and touching. Rion slowly turned him around, kissing his shoulders and back down to his buttocks, and spread his cheeks. He prolonged the foreplay, digging his tongue into Nick's hole, spitting and licking. He put one finger in and did find him to be open, so skipped two and inserted three. Nick moaned loudly but did not tense up.

He rubbed his hump with the pad of his fingers, repeatedly asking, "Is this okay?"

"Uuugh... full consent... stop asking... ugh... keep going...."

Rion pulled his fingers back and moved on top of him. Nick turned his head to the side, and they kissed while Rion reached over to the dresser and grabbed the Pjur. They ended up kissing longer than Rion expected, never getting enough of the taste of Nick's tongue in his mouth. Regretfully he pulled away from his lips, knowing they had a further journey to go that morning.

Rion knelt between his legs and began to coat Nick's entire anus with lubricant, taking his time, watching Nick's breathing become more labored, then deeply breathe to calm himself down, then become labored again. When he felt he had done more than enough, he treated himself with the same exuberance of lubricant, his cock like steel in his hands. He moved his knees to the outside of Nick's thighs and leaned over his lover.

"I know you said full consent, but if at any time you want or need me to stop, just say it. Promise me?"

Nick's breath became labored again. After a few short breaths, he said, "Promise."

Rion kissed his cheek, rubbed his nose in his neck, and whispered, "Thank you for trusting me."

And with that, Rion held onto his cock and pressed against Nick. "I push in; you push back at the same time, okay?"

Nick nodded, unable to speak. As much as he wanted to do this for Rion, as much as he wanted this for himself, he found himself very nervous, on the verge of fear. Rion sensed it and used his other hand to run his hands through his hair a few times until Nick closed his eyes and Rion could feel him relax. Then Rion pushed in.

It took them a couple of tries and a few position changes, but Rion was finally able to get his cock head in with Nick on his knees and his chest on the bed. Rion gave him shallow pumps, pulled out to add more lube, and it went in easier the next time. So much so that he was able to slide farther in, more than halfway, before Nick balked.

Rion moved back and forth but told him, "You're unbelievably tight, and I'm not going to last long at all."

And sure enough, within minutes of actual pumping, Rion froze and his eyes rolled back as he began to cum. Nick gasped, never having experienced the feeling of cum warming him up from the inside before, and his cock responded, getting rock hard and pre-cum sliding out like a steady faucet.

Rion slowly pulled out and looked down at the redness of Nick's wet hole, completely open. "Do you trust me?" he asked.

"Completely," Nick mumbled.

Rion, who was still hard, slid back in, this time all the way, and bottomed out. He figured between the lube and the cum, Nick was open enough to receive all of him, and he was right. Nick let out a loud moan as Rion's cock pressed against his prostate. Rion's eyes almost rolled back again, and he said out loud what he was thinking.

"Oh my God, I've never been inside someone so tight and so wet before." Nick found himself laughing. "I'm gonna make you cum, okay? You're ready?" Rion asked.

"Yes, God, yes!" Nick almost yelled, the right side of his face buried in the pillow.

Rion held onto Nick's waist and started slowly, pulling back halfway, then sinking back fully inside, gradually increasing speed. They moaned in sync as Rion continued to move in and out, circularly, then in and out again. Nick's pain gave way to complete euphoria, and he found himself grabbing the sheets, wanting, needing this to never end. And Rion, who had already released, was happy to oblige, touching his back, hands on his shoulders and in his hair, showing him that he was right there with him. Rion always felt like sex with Nick was an emotional act, almost spiritual, and although they had traded places for the first time, this was no different. Nick's body molded to his, and Nick felt no one else could have fit him as perfectly as Rion did. They made love as one unit.

Nick's orgasm started as a growl in his belly, spread throughout his body, and cumulated at the base of his shaft. He absentmindedly reached down and began to tug. He cried out as his body trembled; his mind went completely blank, and his cock began to spurt out cum. Rion's body responded to Nick's orgasm with his own climax, and for the second time, he filled up Nick's bottom with his semen.

Nick confirmed it to himself: he had never felt anything so amazing in his entire sexual history.

Rion collapsed on Nick's back with a "Holy, holy shit." He kissed the nape of Nick's neck and asked, "Are you okay?"

"Hmm, Rion." Nick stretched upward on the bed so he was lying flat, taking his lover with him. "I am the best I have ever been. I will happily bottom for you anytime, day or night, again and again."

Rion laughed. "You say that now. Wait until I pull out. And see how you feel for the rest of the day."

"Don't pull out just yet," Nick pleaded. "Just hold me a little longer."

Rion responded by sliding his arms under Nick's shoulders, and they laced their hands together. As his cock softened, it contracted and slid out of Nick unexpectedly. Nick felt the emptiness and understood what Rion meant. He definitely felt bruised and battered. And deliriously happy.

Nick spoke again. "I don't want to move, but I feel like I need to use the bathroom."

"You do. Go first." He rolled off Nick's back.

Nick took a moment and jumped up off the bed, giving Rion the view he wanted; a trail of cum slid from his reddened anus down his thigh. Nick felt it and looked down, alarmed, then up at Rion's smirking face.

"Fucking beautiful sight," Rion said smugly.

Nick turned around and grabbed a pillow. He jumped back on the bed, pretending to smother Rion with it, making him laugh. After a few pillow hits, Rion grabbed his body and flipped him over, surprising him. They began to kiss until Nick said, "I really do have to go!"

Rion laughed and let him up, but slapped his bottom. Nick hit him one more time with a pillow, but went into the bathroom and closed the door.

Rion laid down on the bed and stared at the ceiling, even more thankful than he was two hours before.

In the early afternoon, they were in Nick's black Tesla Model X driving east. "So you're not going to tell me where we're going?" Rion asked.

"You'll figure it out when we get there," was all Nick said.

They drove to Queens, and at first, Rion thought he was going to finally introduce him to his brother Brian, who lived in Long Island, but they quickly got off at the JFK airport exit sign.

Rion immediately tensed up. "We're getting on a plane??"

Nick couldn't help but laugh. "Calm down, scaredy cat. We're not leaving; someone's arriving."

"Oh." Rion did relax but then began to ask questions. "Who? Kaleb? It's probably Kaleb. He has family in New York."

Nick didn't give him any indication, just continued driving. They parked in the short-term parking lot, and Nick grabbed a bundle of flowers and a wrapped present. "Is that for me?" Rion asked with a smile. He tried to take it, but Nick slapped his hand away. "Wait, who are the flowers for? Are Rilianne and Laurence coming too? Is it Lennox!?"

Nick laughed. "Stop asking questions and follow me."

They went to Terminal A arrivals, and there were so many planes from so many destinations that Rion could not tell. Not until he saw them and almost ran into the barricade.

"Oh my God! Oh my God!" he practically shrieked as his sister Gabrielle came toward them, holding onto Morgan, his seven-year-old niece, and pulling their suitcase.

Morgan began running toward him. "Uncle Ree!"

He immediately lifted her up in his arms, holding her tight, and spun her around. "You're so big! How did you get so big in four months?"

"I don't know, I just grow, I guess," she said factually, holding onto his neck.

"I've missed you so much, Morgan," he murmured.

"I've missed you more, Uncle Ree," she said back.

"Well, dang," Gabby said sarcastically as she approached. "I guess I should just go then."

Rion adjusted Morgan to his left side and held out his right hand to pull his sister in. "I've missed you too, Gabbs. I can't believe you're here!"

"Thank the boyfriend for the plane tickets and my boss for the next two days off," Gabby said. She let go of her brother and wrapped her arms around Nick for the first time. "Hi, Nicky. Nice to finally meet you face to face instead of over video call."

Rion watched Nick's face cringe at the sound of someone else calling him Nicky and began to laugh.

"Hi, Gabby," Nick replied, returning the hug. "These are for you." He gave her the bouquet of flowers.

"And this," he turned to Morgan, still in Rion's arms, "is for you." He handed her the package. Rion put her down, and she immediately began to tear into it. Nick spoke as she gasped. "My twelve-year-old niece said these are the dolls that pretty little girls like you want to have. I didn't know which one to get, so I got a four-pack. I hope that's okay," he said, glancing at Gabby.

But whether Gabby had an issue or not, Morgan certainly was not going to let go of her new OMG dolls. "This is like the best present ever! Thank you, Uncle Nicky!" she shrieked and threw her arms around him.

Rion appreciated that Nick did not cringe at his nickname that time. Instead, he picked her up to hug back and said, "You're very welcome, sweet Morgan."

Rion gave his sister a proper hug. "I can't believe you're here."

"I'm excited for you to show me New York," she said and handed him the handle of her luggage. He happily took it, and they linked arms to head to the car.

Both Gabby and Morgan were in awe of the New York City skyscrapers as they drove through the boroughs. When they arrived at the apartment, Rion was surprised to see that Zoey, Nick's personal assistant, was already there. The kitchen island was set with a flat birthday cake, ice cream, and drinks.

Morgan surprisingly ran up to her. "Zoey!"

"Hey, baby girl!" They hugged tightly.

Rion was confused. "How do you know each other?"

"Oh, they have been Facetiming for the last couple of weeks," his sister said. "Zoey felt it was important for the two of them to get to know each other properly, so Morgan would feel comfortable going out with her while the adults hang out."

Rion looked at Nick and smiled. "You thought of everything."

He shook his head. "Zoey thought of everything. I'm just along for the ride."

Nick gave him a kiss and walked slowly toward the kitchen. He thought about sitting on the stool but realized it would be better if he stood for a while, so he leaned against the island.

Zoey frowned upon looking at Nicholas. "Are you okay, Boss? You seem to be limping."

Rion avoided his eyes and kept a straight face as Nick felt the heat on his cheeks. But he said casually, "Yes, I'm okay. I sprained my hamstring this morning, but it will go away soon."

Zoey gave him a look, but she didn't say anything else. She turned back to Morgan. "So, are you ready to visit every single zoo in New York City!?" She raised her palm.

"Yeah!" Morgan said excitedly and gave her a high five.

"Oh man, I wanna go!" Rion said playfully.

"Nope, it's for the girls only," Morgan said smugly.

"She's right, you know," Zoey said. "Both of our birthdays are in February, so it's only for Aquarius girls."

"Yeah!" Morgan said excitedly again.

"Well, I guess we'll sit around bored until you come back," Rion teased his little niece.

"I'm sure we'll find something to do," Nick said with a smile too.

"Cake and ice cream first!" Zoey yelled.

She and Morgan raced to the kitchen. Rion turned to Nick. "She's really great with kids."

Nick nodded. "Zoey is great with everything."

After Morgan had her fill and the car service was waiting downstairs, Gabby said, "Come on, let's change your clothes so you can have your zoo day."

"Okay, Mama," she said agreeably and followed her to the second bedroom.

Rion came over to Nick and kissed his lips. "Thank you so much for this."

"You're welcome. Happy birthday, Ree." Nick kissed him back.

Rion went to the bedroom to help Morgan pick out her outfit. Nick gingerly sat on the couch and was about to turn on the TV when Zoey came over to him.

"Hey, Nick? We've known each other for a good five years now, and I've been your P.A. for at least four of them. You know you can talk to me about anything, right?" He looked up at her and didn't respond. "So tell me what you need."

She stood there and waited. At first, Nick hesitated, but then he said, "What is it that men use ... after ... having sex ... to reduce the ... discomfort?"

To her credit, she did not flinch. "Anal?"

"Yes," Nick said with a straight face.

"I don't know, but I will do some research and find out. Get you the best possible creams and medications."

He nodded. "Thanks, Zoey. For your assistance and your discretion."

"Of course." She turned around, but then turned back to him. "Also, just so you know, for women, typically, a nice hot bath with Epsom salt does the trick."

Nick felt himself growing red again but said, "Thanks."

"No problem." She paused, then said, "Also, I'm proud of you, Boss. Now your relationship is on equal footing."

Nick looked at her, alarmed. "What do you mean? Our relationship wasn't on equal footing?"

Zoey said gently, "I didn't say it wasn't. I'm saying it might feel like it is now, at least to him. I'm just saying, I don't know for sure; it's not like we talked about it. But now it seems more … reciprocal. And I am sure he appreciates that."

Nick took a moment to think about it. "I guess I should have done this a long time ago, huh?"

She shrugged. "I think if he didn't complain about it, you shouldn't worry about it. But like I said, I am sure he appreciates it now. I know I would if it was me."

He smiled a little. "Truly, Zoey, you are the best thing that ever happened to me. Well, the second-best thing now that I have Rion."

She scoffed at him. "No, you had it right the first time. The best," she said with a smile and a pat on his shoulder.

Nick had arranged for box tickets for the show *Six* on Broadway, which Rion and Gabby loved. He hadn't taken Rion to a Broadway show in the four months they had been living together, and Rion's birthday was the best occasion for it. Rion was still smiling as they came out of the auditorium, saying, "I had to pee so badly, but didn't want to get up."

"Oh my God, go pee," Gabby teased him. "I'm sure Nick has more surprises tonight."

Rion looked up expectantly, and Nick smiled. "Just one more stop for dinner, then we head home."

Rion smiled back and ran straight for the bathroom, hoping it wasn't a long line. Nick began to start a conversation with Gabby.

"So, Gabrielle, how are you enjoying my c—"

But Gabby cut him off with an unexpected hug. Nick smiled and hugged her back. "He looks so good, Nick," she said. "So happy and relaxed, smiling all day. No sign of my anxious brother. I know it's because I'm here, but I also know it's because of you. He's so happy with you."

"And I'm happy with him," Nicholas said. She raised her head off his chest and looked up. They smiled at each other.

A flash went off to the right, and they both turned. Another flash went off as a photographer took pictures of them holding onto each other.

"Oh no," Gabby exclaimed. She let go of Nick and hid her face.

Another man approached. "Topher Thompson, The City Chronicle," he said, introducing himself to Nick. "And you're Nicholas Highton, on a date."

Nick smiled easily and shook his head. "Do you have a card?" Topher took out a small card case and handed one to Nick. "Thank you. But I'm not on a date. I'm taking some friends from out of town to see a Broadway show. Sorry to disappoint you."

Topher looked over at Gabby skeptically. "She's beautiful. Are you sure you don't have a connection with her?"

"I do. A familiar family connection. But we're not sleeping together. Tell you what," Nick said, changing the subject. "I'll give you as many pictures of me as you want in all angles of the theater, and you get to ask three official questions if you leave pictures of my companions out of it. No pictures of their faces at all. Deal?"

"Really? I get to ask you anything?"

"You get to ask me anything," Nick repeated.

"Okay," Topher said. "Let's start at the top of the staircase."

Nick straightened out his dinner jacket and walked back up the stairs. The reporter and photographer followed him. As they were taking pictures of Nicholas, Rion came back from the restroom. "What's going on?"

"Paparazzi," Gabby said. "I gave Nick a hug, and they took a picture of us. So he's deflecting it."

"Hmm," Rion responded, but didn't say anything more. They waited patiently for the photographer to stop and for Nick to come back down the stairs to where they were.

Topher looked at Rion suspiciously. "He's with you, too?"

But Nick simply said, "No companions pics. They aren't here for that."

Topher nodded. He turned back to Nick. "So, three questions."

"Yup."

The photographer brought out a small recorder and began to record. Topher asked, "What's the name of your English lover?"

Nick smiled. "When he's ready to let the world know, he will." Rion and Gabby both grinned.

Topher seemed satisfied, knowing he was not going to get a straight answer. "Are you currently dating anyone seriously at the moment?"

Nick resisted the urge to look over at Rion. "Yes," he said with a straight face.

"What's her or his name?"

Nick smiled. "Now you know better."

"You said I get to ask three questions."

"I didn't say I have to answer them."

"C'mon, Nicholas—"

"Mr. Highton," Nick said with some authority. "And it would behoove you to remember that. And also to remember that John Herring is a very good friend of mine and a mentor. I can call him right now if you'd like."

Topher literally took a step back. "That won't be necessary, Mr. Highton."

"Good. What's your last question?"

Topher looked rattled by Nick's threat. So the photographer asked one. "The name Mr. Deep Strokez," he called out. "Is it true?"

Nick's eyes glossed over to the man holding the recorder. His eyes narrowed to a smoldering look, and his lips curved to a smirk. "Yes." The man grinned at him. Nick winked.

He turned back to the reporter. "Have a wonderful evening, Mr. Thompson."

Nick walked over to Gabby and Rion. He held out both his hands, and they each reached for him. They heard one last flash at the back of them as Nick walked Rion and Gabby out of the theater. They walked down Seventh Ave together for two blocks before Rion turned to his boyfriend, kissing him squarely on the lips. Gabby smiled and stepped back.

Nick looked at him in surprise. "That was not anonymous at all. What if the wolves followed us?"

"Thank you, Nicholas," Rion said, ignoring his question. "This has been the best day and the best night. I love you. But I adore you, too."

"Well, if you let me spend my money on you a little more, we could do this a few times a week. In every city across the country. Across the world. I could literally show you the world, Ree."

Rion smiled. "That would require me getting on a plane."

Nick laughed out loud. He looked around first, then returned a chaste kiss on his lips in the middle of the crowded street. "I love you. But I equally adore you." Rion responded by holding onto him. Nick returned the hug.

"I'm still here, you know," Gabby said playfully.

They turned to her and smiled. Nick took Rion's hand again, then Gabby's, and they walked together to retrieve Nick's light silver Aston Martin from a nearby garage.

After dinner and drinks at Moxy's rooftop bar, they headed back to the apartment. Zoey was sitting in the living room reading with Morgan's head in her lap, fast asleep. Rion lifted up his niece, and Morgan clung to him with her eyes closed.

"How was she?" Gabby asked.

"A perfect doll. She had the best time," Zoey told her mother. "We got so many pictures; she's going home with a full album. I have duplicates, so I'm going to make it into a picture book and have it mailed to your home."

"You're so wonderful with her. Thank you."

"My pleasure," Zoey said, stretching.

Rion said, "I'll put her down for you." He began walking to the second bedroom.

Gabby turned to Nick. "This was so great, thank you."

"There is more to see," Nick said. "We'll spend the next few days sightseeing, and if you want, we'll take in another Broadway show."

Gabby hugged Nick. "Thanks, Nick. I can't wait." She also walked to the second room.

Before Nick could thank her as well, Zoey handed him a small bag. "I was right; a little sitz bath works wonders. But just in case you need more, there is a prescription cream in there, not under your name, of course, and a muscle relaxer. You should be fine in a day or two. The more you do it, the more your internal muscles will bounce back quicker."

She left the apartment, not waiting for a response. He held the bag and looked around, then decided to hide it in the kitchen for now.

When Nick walked into their bedroom, he gasped. Rion had already stripped naked and was in the center of the bed on his knees with his buttocks high and his hands and shoulders on the mattress. Nick's cock immediately rose, pushing against his pants.

"Jesus, Ree," Nicholas breathed out. "Warn me next time."

"Cum inside of me, Nicholas," said Rion.

Nick couldn't think of anything else he would rather be doing. He quickly took off all his clothes and knelt on the bed behind his lover. Rion's entire bottom was glistening already. Nick easily slid in, and Rion moaned softly. Nick laid his body down on top of Rion's and laced their fingers together. He closed his eyes and made love to Rion for a while, quietly, not to wake their guests in the next room. Nick held on until Rion came again, then he released inside of him.

Instead of pulling out, Nick turned their bodies to the side, put his face in Rion's curly hair, breathed in deeply, then sighed.

"Happy birthday, Ree," he said softly.

Rion squeezed his hands, already falling asleep in his lover's arms.

4

Rion asked, "What's the most non-conspicuous car you own?" Nick laughed. "I'm serious, Nicholas. I want to take you somewhere for your birthday, but I can't in your Tesla or Aston Martin or Maserati, and definitely not your Spyder. We'll be robbed immediately."

"We'll be better off renting a car," Nick said. "The cheapest thing I have is a white Cadillac CT5 with chrome parts and the latest upgrades, and it was still six figures."

Rion shook his head in feigned sadness at Nick's inability to be like the rest of the poor shlubs of the world and took out his phone. "What are you doing?" Nick asked.

"Renting a car. You have Enterprise out here, right?"

Nick shook his head in feigned sadness at Rion's inability to live like the rich. He snatched Rion's phone out of his hand and took out his own phone. He pressed the number one button on his phone, Zoey's speed dial, and she picked up on the first ring.

"What do you need, Boss?" she said automatically.

Nick put the phone on speaker. "Rion wants to rent a car for my birthday weekend."

"Any specifics? Benz? BMW? Maserati?"

Rion called out, "How about a Toyota?"

Zoey was silent. Nick smiled. "I don't think I've ever been in a Toyota in my life."

"What about a Lexus?" Zoey tried. "They're owned by Toyota Motor Corporation. It can feel like you're in a Toyota."

"Yeah, that works," said Nick.

"No, that doesn't work," Rion said, irritated. "Only if that Lexus is at least ten years old and has no upgrades."

"Ten years!?" Zoey exclaimed. "Well, why don't I just send you to the auto auction in the Bronx?"

She meant it sarcastically, but Rion yelled, "Yeah! Let's do that!"

"Oh my God," she said with a scoff while Nick rolled his eyes.

"Jesus, Ree, we're not going to an auto auction. Where are you taking me? Bed-Stuy?"

"I have no idea where that is, but…" Rion sighed in exasperation. "Can you just trust me on this? Zoey, can you do it? A simple Toyota?"

"Yes, but it will be this year's version, with all the upgrades. I will not have Nicholas Highton sitting in a boxy car from the early 2000s," she said huffily. "He has a reputation to maintain, and frankly, so do I, as the best personal assistant in all of the city."

"All the bells and whistles, but go back to last year's model," Rion negotiated. "And either black or dark gray. No fancy colors that will make us stick out."

"Deal," Zoey agreed. "It will be downstairs in an hour and leased for the month. You'll have the option to buy in thirty days."

"Thanks, Zoey," they both chorused.

"Anything for my favorite guys," she said and hung up.

"Where are you taking me tomorrow?" Nick asked again.

Rion gave him a sly smile. "You aren't the only one that knows how to give a good surprise."

Rion used the built-in GPS and screen for directions to an address in Queens. They traveled through the city and ended up on Sutphin Blvd in the Jamaica section. He found parking on one of the side streets, and Nick stepped out of the vehicle.

He looked around and said, "Okay. Even though this seems a little more trendy, I can see why an expensive car would attract the wrong kind of people."

Rion smiled at him. "C'mon. It's right here."

They walked over to a restaurant in the middle of the block that said "Taste of the Island" on its awning. When they entered, it was already crowded and at full capacity, with people still waiting to get in. There were also people at the bar and seated, talking loudly over the music.

But Rion walked up to the hostess and said, "We have a table reserved under Rion Matthews."

"Sure," the woman said in a strong Caribbean accent. "Cherry will take you." She snapped her fingers at another girl, who promptly came over. "Lead Mr. Matthews and his guest to the balcony, please."

They followed the young girl through the crowd and up the back spiral staircase. At the top, she opened up the door to an enclosed balcony, but the windows were open, letting in the spring breeze. It was less crowded, and while there was a bar upstairs, too, most people were seated at tables.

"Thank you for choosing Taste of the Island. Your waiter will be here shortly," the girl said in an equally strong accent. She placed the menus in front of them.

Nick looked around. "I was right. This is a hip and trendy place. I like it."

"You better like it, mate," an English voice said behind him while placing a bottle of Chardonnay on the table, "or I'll sic my auntie on you."

Nick turned around, and Kaleb Spencer, their friend from London, was standing there. "Hey!" he said happily. They stood up and hugged excitedly. "What are you doing in my neck of the woods?"

"For your birthday, of course," said Kaleb. "I flew across the pond to be your birthday guide in your own city."

"I have definitely never been to this part of Queens before," Nick admitted. "I welcome all the fun."

"Yeah, you do, don't you? You've been having a lot of it. Maybe too much of it," Kaleb said knowingly. "I, like many others on this planet, did watch your movie; thank you very much." Kaleb clasped his hands and did a small bow to him. "Smashing work. Top-rated performance. I was looking forward to the sequel."

Rion laughed out loud and Nick blushed. "I'm never going to live that down, am I?" Nick said sheepishly.

"Of course not," Kaleb said. "And why should you? Your name will forever be in the history books as one of the most famous pornographic films ever. Right next to Kim Kardashian's, equipped with your own hashtag. But..." Kaleb moved closer. "I'll never call another man Mr. Deep Strokez, yeah. So you won't have to worry about that from me."

Nick laughed. "I appreciate it."

"So!" Kaleb clapped his hand. "We're going to do it the same way we did in London, yeah? Dinner, drinks, then party? You're ready, Nicholas?"

"I'm ready!" he said excitedly.

Rion finally stood up and hugged their friend. "I'm so glad you're here, Kaleb."

"You look brilliant, mate," Kaleb said. "Being in love works for you, innit."

Rion hugged Kaleb again. "Thanks to the universe."

When he sat down, Kaleb said, "I'm seriously your waiter, gentlemen. Rion told me that when you went to dinner in London, there was no menu. You were just served six courses, yeah?"

"That's right," Nick said, smiling at Rion, then turning back to Kaleb. "The chef's table."

"Well, I'm definitely not the chef, but you'll be getting the same treatment. First course, coming right up."

Kaleb made a little bow and walked to the back behind the bar. Nick turned to Rion. "This is impressive."

"I knew you'd like it," Rion responded.

Kaleb came back with a small tray of plantains, mini beef patties, fish balls, and fried dumplings. The two men immediately dug in. Kaleb kept the drinks and the food coming, starting with a fresh salad and then little plates of everything the menu had to offer: oxtails and curry goat, rice and peas, red snapper and Escovitch fish paired with Bammy, jerk chicken, jerk shrimp, and jerk pork.

As Nick's mouth burned happily with all the spices and flavors, Kaleb sat with them a while, catching them up on his life. "Yeah, man, still working for the Underground. I'm here for a month on holiday. Everything is on the upside in my life. I've even curbed my drinking and partying just a little."

"That's surprising," said Nick, taking another sip of wine.

"Who's the girl?" Rion asked knowingly.

Kaleb laughed. "Her name is Amirah. And she's bloody gorgeous." He happily pulled out his phone to show pictures of a brown-skinned woman in athletic gear. "She's a yoga instructor and a Reiki healer. She's been healing all my demons, so she says."

"That sounds intense," said Rion. "You're a little too laid back for someone so intense."

"Probably, but the sex is fantastic. She can move into positions you can only dream of, mate," Kaleb said slyly. Both men laughed. "So what's next for the two of you? Heading my way anytime soon?"

Rion scoffed and Nick smiled. "I'd have to drag Rion by his fingernails to get him back on a plane."

"Damn right," Rion agreed.

"Don't your folks live on the other side of America, yeah?" Kaleb asked.

"I'll drive," Rion said firmly. "It's only about a week or so."

Kaleb laughed. He patted Rion's shoulder and said, "C'mon, mate. You gotta get over your fear at some point. You seemed to have gotten over your fear of a relationship with Nicholas alright." He stood up before Rion could respond and cleared some plates from the table. "Dessert next. And then we go for a ride."

When he walked away, Nicholas turned to Rion. "My offer still stands to show you the world," he said.

"As long as we can get there by boat," Rion replied seriously, making Nick laugh out loud again.

After dessert, Kaleb's aunt Trini came to the table to meet them. Nick offered to take pictures with Trini, Kaleb, and some of the staff. He immediately sent the pictures to Marcel and told him to add them to his social media pages, tagging the restaurant with a friendly caption about him spending his birthday at the best Caribbean restaurant in all of New York. Having over twenty million followers, it was sure to boost their already booming business.

Trini was grateful. "You eat here for free, any time!" she said happily before they headed out.

Kaleb jumped in the car with them and gave directions to the South Richmond Hill section of Queens. They found parking in a nearby lot and walked over to a place that looked small on the outside but was huge on the inside. The music was loud, and it was equally crowded. Kaleb spoke to a waitress, who told them to wait there, then came back a few minutes later to lead them to a VIP section. As they sat on the velvet couch, she took their drink orders and left.

Nick noticed there were all kinds of couples around them. He said in Rion's ear, "Did you choose the place or Kaleb? Because this is certainly outside of my world in so many ways. The area, the people, the music, the..."

Rion turned to Nick's ear and finished his thoughts for him. "Sprinkles of gayness?" Nick smiled, then nodded. "Yeah, it's LGBT-friendly. Kaleb gave me a few choices, and I chose this one. I wanted to make sure you were incognito, not widely recognized in these circles like you would be at the Moxy. But I also wanted you to be comfortable."

"Thanks for taking me out of my world. I'm already having the best time just being here with you."

"Of course. Because in your world, I can't just do this." He turned Nick's face to him and kissed him. Nick gave a small moan that couldn't be heard over the music and put his tongue in Rion's mouth.

"Waaait!" Kaleb implored. "Before you forget about the little people, drinks first!" He pointed at the waitress coming toward them with eight cups of a yellow substance.

Rion immediately knew what it was. "You're shitting me!" he yelled over the music.

"What?" Nick asked, looking between his friend and boyfriend.

Kaleb answered, "Spicy poblano lemonade bombs!" He handed a cup to each of them. "I would like to think that this little number here was the reason you two ended up together that night we went dancing, yeah?"

Nick looked at Rion curiously, who smiled at his friend. "Cheers, mate," Rion said.

"Cheers!" Kaleb said happily. They tapped plastic cups and drank it down in one shot.

Rion remembered how awfully sweet and spicy the drink was as he drank the whole thing and his face contorted. Nick watched him in amusement and then sniffed his drink first, before he took a small sip.

His face also scrunched up. "God, that's awful," he murmured to himself.

"Again!" Kaleb yelled happily.

Kaleb and Rion drank two more together while Nick still nursed his first one. Then Rion turned to Nick and kissed him again, with all passion. Nick did not resist, tonguing him right back. They kissed until the actual drinks they ordered made it to the small table in front of them. Nick lifted up his Manhattan and Rion lifted up his mojito. They tapped glasses and drank, not taking their eyes off each other.

Kaleb cleared his throat. "I see you two don't need me anymore," he said sarcastically. He stood up and exited the VIP section to the crowded dance floor.

The men chuckled at him. Nick leaned back and put his arm around Rion. A hookah was brought to the table, and more drinks flowed. Prosecco came toward them with sparklers and a bright neon "Happy Birthday" sign that two other waitresses were holding, and the DJ gave a "Happy Birthday, Nick" shout-out to the tune of 50 Cent's "In The Club." After that, Nick wanted to dance and pulled Rion to the dance floor with him. Reminiscent of the club they went to in London, Rion found himself to be drunker than he expected, again thanks to Kaleb and the spiked lemonade drink. When he stood up, the club lights spun a little faster, so he held Nick's hand tight and followed him to the center of the room. It was so tight you couldn't tell who was dancing with who; everyone was pushed together, hot and sweaty. Rion pulled the car keys out of his pocket and wordlessly handed them to Nick. Nick smiled and put them in his pocket. Rion put his arms around Nick's shoulders, and Nick pulled him closer by his waist. Song after song played.

They moved together, not breaking apart until Rion whispered in his ear, "Let's go."

Nick grabbed Rion's hand and spun him around, slowly making their way through the crowd back to the VIP section. Kaleb was there with two women. He stood up upon seeing them.

"We're heading out," Nick said as Rion leaned on his shoulder, glassy-eyed and smiling.

Kaleb reached out and roughed up Rion's hair. "This one is smashed. Nick's driving to the place, yeah?"

"Yeah. I gave him the keys," said Rion.

"What place?" Nick asked in confusion. "We're not going home?"

"I'll give him the address," Rion said to Kaleb, ignoring Nick's question. Nick looked at Rion curiously, but Rion just smiled at him. He said to Kaleb, "Close out the bill on my card for me and call me tomorrow. We'll hang out before you leave."

"Definitely," Kaleb said.

They gave each other hugs, and then Nick, still holding onto Rion's hand, led him out of the lounge. The night breeze felt good on their skin as they walked to the lot. He put Rion in the passenger side and got into the driver's side. He turned on the ignition and asked, "Where to?"

Rion smiled. "252 Cranberry Hole Road."

Nick slowly turned to him. Rion's grin was infectious and made him smile, too. "You're shitting me."

"I shit you not," Rion said back.

"You rented out the Highton Airbnb in Napeague?"

"Surprise!" Rion said goofily.

"You actually paid for it?"

"Of course I did," Rion said, affronted. "Three days, two nights."

"I could have just gotten the keys from Brian, you know," said Nick. "For free. His wife manages it."

"But how much fun would that have been?" Rion said back. "Because it's not just your birthday. Tomorrow is our unofficial anniversary, too. Well... today, since it's after midnight. It's the day we met on the plane, June 1st."

Nick reached out and ran his hands through Rion's hair. "Okay, Ree," he said softly. He pulled Rion's head closer to his and kissed his lips, then his forehead. "Let's go." Nick put the address into the car's GPS system and began to drive. As they got on the Southern State Parkway, Nick said, "This Toyota actually drives pretty well."

"Yeah, it does," Rion said, his eyes in slits.

"Do you want it?" Nick asked. "Anniversary present?"

"No, Nicholas," Rion said firmly. "You're not buying me a car."

"I wasn't going to buy it," he denied. "I was going to lease it in your name. And make timely payments on it."

Rion smiled again. "No, Nicky," he said again. "The last thing I want is for anyone to accuse me of being with you for the money."

"No, you'd rather people think you're with me because of my cock size and my deep strokes," Nick joked.

Rion chuckled. But the alcohol in his system was making him horny. He looked down and adjusted his bulge, then reached out and touched Nick's soft center. Nick smiled without looking at him.

"What are you doing, Ree?"

"Ever got your dick sucked in a Toyota while driving on a freeway?"

Nick laughed out loud. "You are completely drunk." Rion giggled. "And to answer your question, no. Never in a Toyota. Never while driving. Absolutely never on a freeway, which we call highways on this side of the country."

Rion ignored his snark. He unbuckled his own seatbelt and used both hands to unbutton, then zip down, Nick's pants. "You're serious," Nick said, looking down once but keeping his eyes on the road.

Rion leaned his face over into Nick's crotch. Nick reached down and adjusted the seat backward to give Rion more room, then moved his right hand and began to pet Rion's head encouragingly. Rion pulled Nick's length through the slit in his briefs and engulfed him. Nick sighed and tried to focus on his driving. Nick thickened in Rion's mouth, making Rion thicken below. Rion moved slowly, intentionally, up and down for about ten minutes until Nick groaned.

"I can't..." Nick said with shortened breath. "I gotta pull over." Rion did not respond, his mouth completely occupied.

Nick crossed three lanes to get to the shoulder and put on his blinkers. As cars whizzed past them, Nick grabbed a fist full of Rion's curls and began to move his head faster, moving his waist upward to meet him. Rion obliged, swallowing Nick completely. "Cumming," Nick said before he groaned again, filling up Rion's mouth. Nick stopped moving, but Rion didn't, not until Nick was done giving him all of it. Then Rion released Nick from his lips, closed his eyes, and accidentally fell asleep with his head in Nick's lap. Nick chuckled and continued stroking his hair. He slowly got back on the road and continued to pet his boyfriend on the long drive to the tip of the Island.

When they arrived, Nick woke Rion up. "We're here," he said softly.

Rion sat up and looked around. There were no other homes on the road as they pulled into the driveway. They stepped out into the windy, salty air and grabbed their bags from the trunk. Nick looked at Rion and asked, "Do you remember the code?"

Rion smiled. "Nope. I have it in the email." He opened up his phone and began to comb through his messages.

But Nick chuckled and pressed the numbers into the keypad next to the doorknob. "0108. It's Brian's birthday."

The pad beeped, and they heard a click. Nick pushed open the door. "Wow," Rion said, looking around. "Even your vacation homes are mini-mansions."

Nick smiled and dropped his bag on the living room floor. He went right to the accordion backdoor and opened it all the way, stepping onto the balcony porch. "I haven't been here in years," he said. "I rarely come out to the island, not even to see Brian."

Nick stared out at the sand. It was a clear night, so the moon gave just enough light to see the water lapping. He closed his eyes and smiled. Nick was happy. At twenty-eight, he was accomplished in his own right, and not because he carried the Highton name. He had earned the respect of his peers and colleagues in media circles long before his infamous sex tape emerged. And he was in love. At that moment, everything was perfect.

Rion snapped a picture. Nick turned around when he saw the flash. Rion smiled. "You look sexy there."

"Send it to Marcel for my social media page," said Nick. "He'll say something birthday related."

"Of course, Mr. Deep Strokez. Gotta keep your fans happy." Rion came closer with Pjur in his hands. "Meanwhile, I put our bags in one of the rooms upstairs. I don't even think it's the master, but it's big enough."

"The house has two masters," Nick replied, looking at his hands. "That for me?"

Rion smiled and put it in Nick's hand while kissing his lips. "Don't you mean for me?"

But Nick said, "No. It's my turn."

Nick gave it back to Rion, dropped to his knees, and unbuckled Rion's belt. Rion did not stop him as he slid off his jeans and underwear. He was soft again, but that didn't matter. Nick began to blow him, and his erection reformed quickly. Rion held onto Nick's head and guided him until he was at full attention, ready to cum. But when Nick stood up and also dropped his jeans and briefs, he turned around to face the beach, holding onto the railing.

Rion's cock immediately stiffened at what Nick was offering for a second time. "Nicholas…" Rion said softly. "It's your birthday. You get me."

"And this is how I want you for my birthday. Or a random Friday morning like today. Inside of me."

Nick bent over onto his elbows and looked out into the ocean. They hadn't switched since Rion's birthday. Nick thought Rion would regularly ask to switch now that they had crossed that line, but Rion had not. Nick wanted him to know that it wasn't a once-a-year or special occasion thing. It was a Nicky-Ree thing.

Rion came behind him and prepared him with lube. Then he slowly entered Nick. Nick winced, but knew how to push back and allow Rion all the way in. Rion held onto the rail and began to pump into him. Nick moaned softly, and Rion grunted. He wanted to take his time, but Nick was still unbelievably tight and gripped him from the inside. It did not take long at all for Rion's body to heat up. He wrapped his arms around Nick's torso and climaxed. When he came, he sighed and fell against Nick's back.

"I don't need the world, Nicky," Rion said into his shoulder. "I just need this. Right here with you."

Nick turned around and they held each other. Then they went inside to get some sleep.

A few days later, Rion was stretched on the bed proof-reading and editing his new story, hoping to submit it to his publishers in the next month. He heard the key in the door, and it opened. He called out, "Nicky?"

He didn't hear a response, but he also didn't hear any movement, not even the door closing. That made him suspicious. Rion came off the bed and opened the bedroom door wider, and locked eyes with the man in the dark green scrubs that was still holding onto the front doorknob. Izzy was rubbing her face on the man's legs, purring in recognition of him.

The man looked exactly like Nicholas but older, a maturity in his handsome features, with brown hair instead of dirty blond, and slightly shorter. Rion knew he had to be Nick's brother, Brian. Both Rion and Brian had a look of surprise that anyone would be in Nicholas's apartment in the middle of the day.

After an awkward silence, Brian spoke first. "Hi."

"Erm… Hi. I'm Rion."

"Ree-On?" Brian stretched out his name the same way Nick did when they first met.

It made Rion smile. "Yeah. Like Ryan, but fancier."

Brian smiled back. He took his key out of the door and closed it, then turned back to the stranger in his brother's apartment. "I'm Brian, Nicholas's older brother."

"Oh yeah, I figured. You look just like him. Nicky talks a lot about you…"

But he trailed off as both of Brian's eyebrows went up in complete surprise, more surprised than finding a man in his brother's home wearing nothing but a t-shirt and boxer briefs. Rion quickly figured out why: No one ever called Nicholas Nicky. It was his number one rule. A rule he had broken only for Rion.

Rion cleared his throat. "Nicholas thinks the world of you and Emma."

Brian's eyebrows slowly came down. He looked down slightly and smiled to himself, as if he was thinking. He raised his head back up and came toward Rion with his hand out for a shake. Rion immediately reached his hand out. It was firm and friendly.

"Nice to meet you, Rion. How long are you staying with Nicholas?" he asked.

"Erm… not sure yet," Rion sort of mumbled.

Brian smiled a closed-mouth smile, like he knew a secret. "Okay," he said casually. "I crash here from time to time in between surgeries. My next one is at six o'clock, so I'm just going to sleep on the couch if that's okay with you?"

"Oh yeah, it's fine! I'm just working in the ... bedroom..." Rion trailed off, realizing that his brother distinctly saw him emerge from the master bedroom. Nick's bedroom.

Brian smiled his closed-mouth smile again. "You go do that." He turned around and went toward the living room.

Rion stood in the hallway for another moment, listening to Brian get comfortable. "Hey, Rion? Is your last name Matthews?" Brian called out.

Shit, Rion thought. He walked over to the living room area to see the man closing all the blinds and pulling the muslin blanket from inside the ottoman. Brian had already taken off all his clothes and was down to his underwear.

Rion held eye contact to avoid looking anywhere else. "Yeah, it is."

"Huh," he said, adjusting the pillows before he sat on the couch. He looked at Rion and asked, "Did you rent the Airbnb from my wife, Lia Highton, last weekend for Nick's birthday?"

There was another awkward silence, then Rion nodded. "Yup. That was me."

Brian gave him another smile. "Wonderful." Brian laid down and threw the blanket over himself.

Rion discovered his feet and slowly backed out of the room, then almost ran back to the bedroom once he hit the hallway and closed the door behind him. He grabbed his phone and called Nicholas.

"Hey," Nick answered.

"Hey," Rion found himself whispering. "Your brother is here."

A momentary pause, then Nick asked, "What?"

"Your brother. Brian? Apparently, he has a key and crashes at your house from time to time—"

"Shit, shit, shit!" Nick yelled out. Rion could hear Nick move to a quieter part of the room, probably back to his office. "He hasn't done it in a year. What did he say to you?"

"Nothing, really. We introduced ourselves. He asked me how long I'm staying with you, and I didn't really answer, and he just said okay."

"Ugh, that's worse," Nick groaned. "He didn't grill you? That means he's going to grill me. Or it means he's going to tell Emma so she can grill me."

"I don't think so," said Rion. "He pretty much went right to sleep. But also... I was kind of in my undies coming out of your room, soooo..."

Nick sighed. "I'm coming home."

"You don't have to," Rion said. "It's fine. I just wanted you to know. I'll just make something up if he asks questions."

"You will do no such thing, Rion," said Nick sternly. "I'll handle it. Be there soon." Before Rion could respond, Nick hung up the phone. He sighed and put on a pair of sweatpants.

Nick didn't usually drive to work, so Rion was surprised when he heard the door open less than ten minutes later. He must have jumped into the first taxi he saw. Rion came into the hallway. Nick glanced at him, but closed the front door softly and walked into the living room first. After a moment, he came over to Rion and led him back into the bedroom, closing the door behind him.

"He's asleep."

"I told you that," Rion said as he sat on the edge of the bed. "You didn't have to come home, Nicholas. I got it."

Nick let a moment pass, then said, "I'm not lying to my brother about you."

Rion was about to protest, but the seriousness on Nick's face made him rethink it. Instead, he allowed his face to soften for his boyfriend. Nick came over to him and knelt before him, putting his face in Rion's lap and his arms around his waist. Rion began to caress his hair.

"Love you," Nick said softly.

"Love you, too," Rion said softly back.

Nick lifted his head up and Rion moved back onto the bed. Nick took off his shoes, but nothing else. He came onto the bed to lay on his pillow facing Rion. "You smell good."

Rion smiled. "You look good. I didn't see you before you left."

"Because you sleep like the dead," Nick responded. "Being up all night writing takes a toll on you. You needed the rest, so I didn't wake you. You've been going without rest for weeks now."

Rion shrugged. "When I get near the end of a story, I have to get it out of my head, or it will drive me crazy."

"Okay," Nick said. "I just want you to take better care of yourself. Eat. Sleep. Go for long walks in the park at least once a day. Then get back to it. You're a fantastic writer, Rion. The words will come out when they come out, and it will be perfect."

Rion had heard this before, from his sisters and his ex, how he didn't take care of himself when he was in the writing zone. But, somehow, it sounded better coming from Nick. He wasn't trying to control him or tell him what to do. Just expressing concern and offering advice. He appreciated how Nicholas understood him and cared for him.

He nodded and moved closer, putting his face on his chest and arm across Nick. "Okay, Nicky." They lay in silence, then Rion remembered. "Soooo, I might have called you Nicky to Brian."

Nick froze. "Shit. I'm never going to hear the end of it."

"Sorry," Rion said with a cringe.

"Don't be," he said, rubbing his back. "I'm your Nicky. And you're my Ree."

Rion smiled in Nick's brown shirt. Nick rubbed his back until he felt Rion's breath soften against him. He kissed his head and said softly, "I'm going to go work next door."

"Mm'kay," Rion mumbled.

Nick held him a bit longer until Rion fell into a deeper sleep, then slid out of the bed. He went over to the living room to check on his brother, who was snoring loudly. Brian was practically naked, with nothing but the thin blanket to cover his midsection. His scrubs were nowhere to be found, but Nick knew he must have dumped them in the washer. After Nick moved Brian's clothes to the dryer, he went into the second bedroom, turned on his computer, and accessed his files from MS Office 365. Two hours later, he closed his computer, warmed up a Hot Pocket in the kitchen for lunch, and ate it as he checked on Rion, who was still asleep. He laid down next to Rion and closed his eyes.

Nick woke up to the sound of Rion typing next to him. "What time is it?"

"A little after 4pm," Rion said, not taking his eyes off the laptop. "Brian is up; he's in the shower in the other bedroom."

"Okay." Nick yawned and stretched. "Did he stop in here?"

"No. He doesn't know you're here yet."

"Alright." He sat up and leaned on Rion's arm. Rion nudged him off and kept writing. "Ouch," he said dramatically. Rion grinned, but did not stop typing to acknowledge him. "Love you anyway," Nick said with a kiss on the cheek. Rion's cheeks became rosy, but he didn't glance at Nick.

Nick jumped off the bed and waited in the second bedroom at the desk. Brian had spread out his clothes on the bed. When his brother came out of the bathroom with a towel wrapped around his waist, Nick turned his chair around. They locked eyes, then Brian smiled widely at him and shook his head.

"What?" Nick asked with a straight face.

"You know what... *Nicky*," he said with emphasis on his name. Brian sat on the bed and started putting on his undergarments.

"Don't start that." Nick gave him a stern look.

Brian was unfazed. "Thanks for drying my scrubs."

"You're welcome."

"So where the fuck have you been hiding this one?"

"I'm not hiding him," Nick said casually.

"C'mon, Nicky," Brian said with a smile.

"Call me that again, and I will beat the shit out of you," he said seriously.

Brian laughed as he slid on his bottoms. "How long?"

"Since it's been official? About five, six months," Nick said.

"And unofficially?" Brian slid on his top and went to the dresser to comb his hair.

"It's complicated."

Brian glanced at him through the mirror. "More complicated than a European male lover?"

Nick hesitated, then admitted, "Rion was the one I was with in London last year."

Brian paused, combing. "That man is not English."

"Obviously. We met on the flight to London and spent the month there together. I never told anyone he was English. Everyone just assumed."

"Wow," Brian responded. Then he shrugged. "It all makes sense." He sat down and put on a fresh pair of socks. "No one knows?"

"Zoey. That's it. No one else knows."

"Not even Emma?" Brian asked without glancing up, sliding on his shoes.

"No. Not even Emma."

"Hmm. She knows now," he said with a smile.

"God dammit, Brian!" Nick yelled at him and jumped out of his seat.

Brian jumped out of the way of his brother's wide swing. He threw up his hands, saying, "You knew I was going to tell her! I just wanted to know if she knew before me."

"What did you tell her!?"

"That you had a boy-toy hidden in your bed," Brian

confessed. "I didn't know it was serious."

"I'm gonna get a phone call tonight, aren't I?" Nick shook his head.

"Hey, I'm surprised you didn't get one already," Brian said, making his way to the door. In the hallway, he yelled, "Hey, Ree-On!"

Rion appeared in the doorway. "It was very nice to meet you," Brian said sincerely. "Thank you for your hospitality. I have to get to work, but Nick will invite us all out for drinks soon, okay?"

"Yeah, yeah, that sounds—"

"Oh, I'm sorry, I mean *Nickyyyy*," Brian drawled but was instantly hit in the shoulder by his little brother. He howled and grabbed his arm. "Fuck! I have to work tonight, fucker!" He punched Nick right back.

"Do not call me Nicky, asshole!" Nick said with a shove to his chest.

Brian shoved him back, and they tussled a little, which somehow ended in a hug and laughter. They kissed each other's cheek, and he left without another word. Nick locked the door behind him and turned to Rion.

"Thai food tonight?"

In the middle of feasting on Drunken Noodle, Thai dumplings, and Satay over a bottle of Sauvignon Blanc, Nicholas's phone rang, and it was a video call.

He looked at it and sighed. "You ready to meet the other one?" he asked. Before Rion could respond, Nick pressed the button and held the phone up to his face.

"Hello, Emma."

"Hello, Nicholas," his sister said in a sing-songy way. She smiled at him sweetly. "How are you, my dear brother?"

"I am well, and you?" he asked politely.

"I'm wonderful. Thanks for asking. Question," she began. "Are you seeing anyone?" Her head cocked to the side, and her eyebrows scrunched together in faux confusion.

Nick's face mimicked hers. "Why do you ask?"

"Oh, well, a little birdy told me that he might have flown into your home and witnessed another little birdy in underwear coming out of your bedroom."

Rion couldn't help it; he began giggling. Nick looked over at him sharply, then back at his sister's face on the phone. "That little birdy needs to mind his fucking business."

"And me? Do I also need to mind my fucking business?" Emma asked. Nick didn't answer. "Let me see him, Nicholas."

He sighed and turned the phone around to face across the table from him. Rion looked into the face of a very pretty brunette who looked nothing like Nicholas, except for the blue eyes they shared. She smiled at him, but it was guarded.

"Hello, Rion," she said to him.

"Hello, Emma," Rion replied, not surprised that she said his name perfectly. He took the phone from Nick. "It's nice to meet you. I've heard a lot about you. All good things."

"And yet, I know nothing about you," Emma said sarcastically, making him smile. "Where are you from? Obviously not London."

He chuckled. "No, I'm originally from Fresno, California, but I live in San Francisco."

"Live? Or lived?" she asked.

Rion hesitated and glanced at Nick, who raised one eyebrow. "Lived," he said, looking at Nick. He looked down at Emma and said, "I live here now, in New York."

"I see," she said, very business-like. "Rion, would you like to have dinner with my family this weekend?"

"Emma!" Nick yelled at her.

"Shut up, Nicholas," she said in a completely calm voice. "I'm inviting your soulmate of the last year to dinner. Rion, darling," she spoke to him again. "Do you think you'd be able to make it?"

Rion glanced at Nick's annoyed face and back at Emma. "Yes. I would love to come to dinner."

"Wonderful. Have Nick schedule you a private jet to Rochester. And if he behaves, he'll even be invited in."

Rion chuckled. "I don't get on planes, but I'll be sure to tell him to drive me up."

"Wonderful. Can you tell him one more thing for me, dear? Can you remind Nicholas that secrets and lies bring nothing but flies?"

He nodded at her and looked up. "Hey, Nick? Emma would like for you to know that secrets and lies bring nothing but flies." Nick glared at him. Rion looked down at Emma, who was smiling. "I think he got the message."

"Good. I'll see you Saturday evening at 6 p.m. sharp. Do not be late."

"I won't be. Thank you for the invitation. And nice to meet you, Emma."

"Lovely to meet you too, Rion."

Rion handed the phone back to Nick. Nick stared down into his phone with a stoic face, and Emma stared back. After a few moments, Rion heard her say, "He's fucking gorgeous."

Nick immediately smiled, and Rion went pink. "He really is, isn't he?"

"Oh my God, Nicholas. Wow."

Nick chuckled. "We'll be there Saturday night, Emma."

"I'll see you then."

"Wait. Did you tell anyone?"

"Anyone like... Mother?" Nick didn't answer, and Rion held his breath. "No. I've told no one, but I do need to tell Gary. And I threatened Brian not even to mention it to Lia. You're in the clear. For now."

"Thank you, Em."

"You're welcome... *Nicky.*"

Rion laughed out loud. "Fuck," Nick muttered.

Emma let out a loud laugh. "I had to. Oh God, I had to. Good night, Nicholas. Good night, Rion."

"Good night, Emma," Rion called out.

Nick hung up and looked at his boyfriend. "You sure you're ready for this? I know you wanted to remain anonymous."

"Anonymous to the public and your parents," Rion clarified. "Not to your siblings. If you trust them, I do too."

Nick looked worried as he ate. "I trust them. I just don't know how they are going to react to our relationship."

Rion shrugged. "Cat's out of the bag now. Might as well face it head-on."

ick rang the doorbell, then took Rion's free hand. Rion held the bag of wine and held Nick's hand tighter. They stood on the steps of the stately home, and both tried not to be nervous.

A girl about twelve years old answered the door. "Hi, Uncle Nicholas."

"Hi, Blair." He gave her a one-armed hug and said, "This is my friend, Rion."

"He means boyfriend," said a voice inside the house. As they stepped in, his sixteen-year-old nephew came from the living room holding onto a Nintendo Switch. "He's your boyfriend, right?"

Nick glanced at Rion, then back at his nephew. "Right. Rion's my boyfriend. How did you know?"

"The parentals were arguing about it earlier in the day," he said with a shrug. He came over and raised his hand for a hand slap, which Nick gave. Then he turned to Rion and did the same. "I'm Robby."

"I'm Rion," he introduced himself. "Nice to meet you, Robby."

Robby turned back to his uncle. "Dad's gonna give you a hard time, but you know that. He hates you. Mom is going to give you the whole 'this isn't gonna work' spiel, but she's just worried. I overheard her and Seppani talking about it, and she's actually proud of you for following your heart. Just want you to know what you're walking into tonight. I'm gonna play along and roast y'all a little bit."

Rion snickered, and Nick smiled at his nephew. "Thanks, Robby."

"Sure, man." He went back to the living room while Nick held Rion's hand and led him to the dining room.

Emma was setting the dining room table with another woman. "Just in time, my dear brother."

She came over and gave him an air hug and kiss, then she turned to Rion and did the same. "It's so nice meeting you, Rion."

"Likewise. Thank you for inviting me into your home." He handed her the bottle of wine. "For you. I wanted to bring flowers, but Nicholas said you kind of hate them."

"I do," she acknowledged. "Don't kill flowers just to show me that you care. Send wine." She winked at him. He smiled back. She called out to her children, "Blair? Robby? Dinner."

The other woman had gone into the kitchen and came back with a big tray of lasagna. She placed it in the middle of the table. Emma said to her, "Thank you, Seppani. It looks great."

"You catered?" Rion asked. "Because you didn't have to do that. I really am a burger and fries kind of guy."

Before she could respond, Nick said, "Cater? No, no, no. Seppani, the housekeeper, cooks. Seppani cooks all the meals around here and raises the kids. That's how us rich snobs do."

Emma gave him a stern look. "Don't be trite."

Seppani touched Emma's shoulder right before she disappeared back into the kitchen, and it seemed to calm Emma down. She turned to Rion. "You sit here," Emma said, pointing to a chair. "And Nick sits there."

"Next to Gary." Nick grimaced. "Fuck."

Emma ignored his little temper tantrum. Seppani came in with a salad bowl and placed it next to the lasagna just as Blair and Robby sat down.

"I'm surprised you're both here on a Saturday night," Nick said to them.

"And miss the fireworks? Not a chance," Robby said with a smile and winked at Rion. Rion couldn't help but smile back.

Seppani came in with one last bowl of garlic bread. As they were all seated, a very tall and burly man in jeans and cowboy boots came into the dining room. He said in his booming voice, "Sorry I'm late! Calls from overseas, ya know." He walked right up to Rion. "You must be the surprise boyfriend. I'm Gary, Emma's husband." He held his hand out for a shake.

Rion stood up and shook his hand back. "Rion. Nice to meet you."

Gary turned to Nick, who did not get up. "Nicholas."

"Gary," Nick replied without looking at him.

"Play nice, boys. We have company," Emma warned as she sat down at the other end of the table.

Gary's accent was not an east coast one at all. Rion could tell he was from the southwest. He could also tell that Gary and Nick were not close.

Seppani quietly began to serve the family. Emma said, "So, Rion, how are you enjoying New York?"

"It's nice, actually. A different vibe here, for sure."

"You're from San Francisco, correct?"

"Fresno, actually. But I moved to San Francisco with my sister to help her raise my niece and go to school. Then my other sister, her kids, and my mother moved up three years ago. So we all live in San Francisco now."

"Why were you helping raise your niece? What happened to your sister's husband?"

"They weren't married," said Rion. "They were together, but he wasn't ready to be a father, and she wasn't going to have an abortion, so he split, and I stepped up."

"How noble of you," she said with a smile.

Before she could ask another question, Gary asked, "Lots of gays in San Francisco, yeah?"

Rion turned to him. "Lots of gays everywhere, Gary. But yes, there is a huge community there."

"Hm," he grunted. "You don't look gay." Both his children snickered.

"Gary!" Emma scolded.

"Don't be a dick, Gary," Nick said nastily.

"It's okay, Emma. I should have brought my sequined pink feathery boa so I could be more presentable," Rion said with a straight face. Robby and Blair snickered again.

Gary let out a loud laugh. "Yeah? Maybe you should have. That would have been a riot."

Rion shook his head and smiled. He wasn't sure if he liked Gary just yet. He was loud and abrasive, the complete opposite of his reserved and put-together wife. From Nick, Rion learned that they met when Gary's father, Raymond Dorado of Dorado Oil and Gas, was in litigation with one of Nick's father's investments in San Antonio. Even though Emma was still in law school, she had joined the hearings, and thanks to her input and smart thinking, the suit was resolved amicably. But she had been accompanied almost daily by Mr. Dorado's son, who was quickly smitten by her beauty and brains, during the couple of months she had spent down in Texas. Both their fathers, who had begun other business ventures together, encouraged the match, so by the following year, when Gary asked for her hand in marriage, she did not feel like she could say no.

Emma continued to ask Rion questions about his life and his work. Rion talked about his sisters, nieces, nephews, and, very vaguely, about his mother. When asked about his father, he told them the same thing he told Nick when they first met, "He never met me." Emma smiled at that.

"So, what do you know about your lineage?" she asked.

"Ugh, Emma, don't," Nick groaned.

"It's just a question, Nicholas."

"It's a dumb ass question, Em," he said to her. "The majority of normal Americans do not trace their lineage back to a Rockefeller or a Kennedy. Only us rich snobs do that."

"Hey, you're a rich snob, too, Uncle Nick," Robby said with a smile. "Just because you're slumming it doesn't change that you're you one of us." Nick looked at him sharply.

"Slumming it?" Rion said and looked over at the sixteen-year-old. "Wow. And here I thought we were going to be good friends."

"Hey, no offense, man. I think you're cool," Robby said, leaning back. "But Grandmother is gonna shit bricks when she finds out about you. But your secret is safe with me, Uncle Nick."

"Thanks," Nick said sarcastically.

Blair giggled as Emma said sternly, "Robert! Leave this table at once!"

He stood up. "I'm full, anyway. Gotta meet Debbie tonight, so I'm taking the Benz. Nice to meet you, Rion."

"No, the Benz is in the shop. Take the BMW," his father said.

Robby began to protest, "But what if I wanted to pick up—"

"You're not picking up anyone tonight," said his mother. "You still need to bring your grades up in Advanced Science, so you're not staying out. Home by midnight."

He scoffed and said, "This place is a fucking prison!" Robby stormed out of the dining room.

"Wow," Rion said again with a shake of his head.

"He's not typically that rude," said Emma. "I think he's showing off for his uncle."

"Robby is a spoiled brat," Nick said. "Whether I'm here or not, he's still a spoiled brat."

"Hey, at least we have kids. Guess that's not an option for you anymore, huh?" Gary said smugly.

Rion looked at Gary in disbelief. Nick turned to glare at him. "Are you really this ignorant, or are you, too, showing off in front of company?"

Gary laughed and said, "I'm just talking about the natural way, that's all."

"How about you stop talking in general?" Nick responded angrily.

"Fuck you, this is my—"

"Boys!" Emma yelled, then touched her face. She said calmly, "Can you please be in the same room for once without the bickering and nasty insults?"

"Sure, sweetheart," Gary said and turned back to her brother. "How's the dirty mag, Nick?"

"It's doing well. How's my sister's money, Gary?" Nick said without looking at him.

Blair snickered until Emma gave her a stern look. But Gary laughed out loud. "Touché. But maybe I should be asking your new boy-toy here the same thing." Rion rolled his eyes.

"Nick, do not respond. Gary!" Emma yelled at her husband like he was her other son. "If you can't behave, you can leave this table, too."

Gary looked at her but stayed quiet. Emma turned to Rion. "I apologize on behalf of my husband. His issue is with Nicholas and not with you."

"Damn right!" Gary said again in a booming voice. "Because your little brother is a narcissistic fuck up. Always seems to purposely want to fuck it up for the rest of us." He turned to Nick. "Do you know that your mother is considering canceling the Masquerade Gala indefinitely? That's where twenty percent of my business comes from, those events she throws, and I'm going to lose money. All because you wanted to snake into some cheap whore's pants. And now you're flaunting a new kick-with-a-dick like that's not gonna send Madeline off the deep end. When are you gonna grow up and get your shit together, Nick!?"

"Fuck you," Nick murmured.

"No, fuck you!" Gary yelled.

"No, fuck YOU!" Nick yelled back.

"No, FUCK YOU!"

"NO, FUCK—"

"JESUS CHRIST!" Emma yelled at them.

Rion busted out laughing. They all turned to look at him. "I'm sorry. But this is … so *familiar*," he said, still chuckling. "I don't know why I thought it was going to be different than my own dysfunctional family. But I feel like I'm at Thanksgiving dinner with my family all over again."

Blair started laughing, too. "Don't let the Manolo Blahniks fool you. We're messed up, too. Especially when Uncle Nick is here." Rion looked at her and they laughed together. Nick smiled.

Emma rubbed her temples and said, "Blair, go to your room."

"I didn't do anything, Mother!" she protested.

"Now, Blair!" her mother yelled.

She pushed back her chair and stormed out of the room too. Emma clasped her perfectly manicured fingernails together in front of her face before she spoke.

"Gary is being an ass. But we do have questions," she said to Nick. "And Rion," she turned to him, "I want you to know that I loved getting to know you tonight. I think you are a very well-mannered, well-spoken, honest, and admirable individual. And I do believe you care about Nick. So please do not think this is about you. It could have been anyone, and Gary would have reacted the same way. And I would have the same concerns."

She turned back to her brother. "Nicholas. I need you to explain to us, to me, how you got here. And where you see this going."

She put her hands on the table and waited. Gary leaned back and put one leg over his knee. Rion looked at him, too. Nick let air out of his nose before he began.

"I'm in love with Rion," Nick said plainly. "I've been in love with Rion since last June. You both know I was never in love with Penny. I broke up with her in August because I wanted more for myself than just a marriage of convenience. I wanted love, a real partner, and happiness. I have that now. And no amount of Mother's interference is going to change that. Not this time around."

Gary scoffed. "That all sounds great, but I was here and saw that last train wreck happen when you gave us the 'I'm in love and nothing is going to get in my way' speech. At least this one is stronger than ol' Trixie; I'll say that for you. He was smart enough to agree to be your secret."

Rion spoke before Nick could retort. "For the record, I was the one that wanted to keep us private, not Nick. I needed us to ease into this relationship and figure ourselves out as a couple before the world tries to pick us apart. And I'm in love with him, too. This is as real to him, to us, as it's ever been. I understand that Madeline will not be happy with our relationship, so I just want to make sure we are solidified before I am introduced to everyone else. At least until we have a well-established foundation where I know for sure that nothing could get between us. We're still so new, and I would rather not have his family torn apart by our relationship just yet."

"That's very mature of you, Rion. Thank you," said Emma. "You seem to have a better head on your shoulders of the situation than my brother does." She turned back to Nick. "I agree with Rion. I think you need to continue to keep this quiet for a while. Repair your relationship with Mother. It is still on rocky terms since last fall. Talk to Father and get his approval first. Get him on your side. And solidify your foundation with Rion. If it's real, then he's right; not even Mother's antics can tear you apart. But you have to handle this correctly, or it will all blow up in your face."

Nick was exasperated. "I don't want to hide Rion anymore. But I hear you. Both of you. We'll continue to take things at the steady pace we are, and yes, I will try to rectify things with Mother. But make no mistake, Rion is in my life now. I know that nothing will break us apart. But since you all need me to prove it to you, I will. I will do as you say." He looked at Rion lovingly. Rion took his hand and kissed it.

"Why don't you stay the night? Go see Mother in the morning?" Emma suggested.

"I think that's a terrible idea," he said bitterly.

"No, it's a good one," Rion said, squeezing his hand. "You haven't seen her since the incident with Kierra. It's time. But if she's cruel, you walk away and don't look back."

Nicholas rolled his eyes as Emma said, "It's settled. The room is already made up for you both tonight. Gary will show you to the room, Rion. Nick, a word?"

Emma rose from the table, and Seppani came out of nowhere to begin to clear the plates. Nick kissed Rion on the cheek as they stood up. "Thanks for being you."

Rion responded with a touch on Nick's arm as they went in different directions, Nick following Emma to the back of the house while Rion followed Gary out of the dining room.

Gary began to explain the artwork in the expansive hallway as Rion trailed behind him on the way upstairs to the rooms. Rion stayed quiet and let him talk. When they arrived, Rion was not surprised to see that it looked like a hotel suite, complete with fresh towels on the edge of the bed.

"This is your boyfriend's room. It's full of his things," said Gary. "It's where he stays when he's in Rochester. He never stays at the Highton Estate. You're not that much smaller than him, so you can pick a new set of clothes from the closet in the morning."

"Thank you," Rion said. As Gary began to walk away, Rion asked him, "Hey, Gary? What's your problem with Nick? For real?"

Gary turned around and chuckled. "So you want to know what you're getting yourself into?" He came closer to Rion and leaned on the dresser, crossing his feet at the ankles.

"The Hightons are old money. I'm talking ten generations of wealth that they've just passed down and kept in the family. I'm not; I'm from new money. My grandfather made it rich in the Texas oil fields and built up his business from scratch. I don't know if you know, but even among the rich, there is a class divide. And Madeline made it clear that the Dorados' new money was not good enough for her daughter.

It was Niles who made Emma and I happen, despite his wife. And over the years, even Madeline had to respect the Dorados' hard work ethic and status, especially in the south. Once I had Madeline's acceptance, everyone else fell in line. Everyone except that asshole out there." He pointed toward the door. "When I met Nick, he was a thirteen-year-old dickhead kid, not unlike my own son. He did everything to make it clear that I would never be one of them. That my new money would never match up to the Highton's generational wealth. You heard that dig out there about Emma's money? That's the real Nick. He's a spoiled rotten, selfish, trust-fund baby who will constantly find a way to fuck up his own life because he knows as much as his mother despises him, she'll always be there to set him right back on his feet. She's the only one who can whip him into shape. How he managed to convince you that he has depth to him, I'll never know."

Gary raised his head triumphantly. "I'm more of a son to Madeline than he will ever be. And every time he fucks up, I'll be right there to remind him. He made my life hell. Now it's my turn. But I can tell you're a good kid. So I'll try to keep you out of the crossfire." Gary turned around and said, "Sleep tight," before he closed the door.

Rion sighed and plopped on the bed with his clothes still on.

Emma brought Nick into the garden. Seppani already had a glass of Courvoisier XO waiting for him. "Sit," his sister commanded. He did, right next to her on the long couch. "We haven't really talked either, you know. Since your interview," she started.

"I know. I'm sorry about that. I've just kept myself away from the family altogether."

"Because of Rion Daniel Matthews? A twenty-six-year-old almost college dropout turned erotic romance writer under the pen name Ryan D. Ryder, whose mother, Roslyn Elaine Matthews, has been in and out of jails and rehabs since she was fourteen years old when she had her first daughter, Muriel Hollingsworth, at the same age?"

Nicholas laughed, although it was anything but funny. "If you ran a check on him, what was with asking him all the questions that you knew the answers to?"

"I just wanted to see if he was going to be honest with me about his history. Which he was, for the most part. He barely mentioned Roslyn, but I wouldn't either if she was my mother."

"Hmm." Nick took a sip. "In all that digging, did you find out who his father is? I'm sure that information would be priceless to him."

"No," she said. "There is no record of his father. Rion was born in Springfield Medical Center at thirty-three weeks with cocaine in his system. Roslyn was twenty years old, high when she gave birth at seven months and had no idea who his father was, nor where her three other children were. He was in the NICU for six and a half weeks before Maurese Hollingsworth came to get the baby from the hospital, saying he was related. But we found no connection other than his only daughter, Muriel."

Nick shook his head. "Anything else you want to tell me about my boyfriend?"

Emma sipped her glass of red wine. "I have to be honest; I don't see this boding well for you."

Nick began to stand up. "Yup, thanks for the talk."

"Sit. And listen," Emma said sternly. He sat back down. "It's not because he's not handsome enough, smart enough, resilient, or loyal enough for you. Rion is all of those things. He obviously loves you enough to move clear across the country to be with you. But all I needed was his name and city of birth to find out all of this. Madeline is going to dig deeper. And I just told you his beginnings. His upbringing was … colorful, to say the least. He comes from a family of prostitutes and addicts riddled with mental health issues. Did you know this?"

"Emma, Rion has been completely straightforward with me about his upbringing and all the issues in his family from our very first conversation," Nick said in a bored manner.

"And you went through with this whole thing anyway?" she asked in disbelief.

He stared back at her in disbelief as well. "Went through with what? This whole *falling in love thing*? Because last I checked, you can't help who you love. But you and Brian didn't marry for love. You married for duty, so you wouldn't understand."

"Oh, Nicholas…" She sighed. "It's like you attract the worst kind of people around you, but then it becomes our fault when it all falls apart. We know Mother and Father are suffocating, so we've tried to guide you, but all you do is scoff at the decisions we've made, even when you know it's what makes it easier to deal with them. We make better choices. You make shitty ones."

Nick was about to protest angrily, but she held up her hand. "Again, I am not saying that Rion is a bad person or a shitty choice. I'm saying I don't trust this thing to work out well for you, even without Mother's influence. Even if Rion himself isn't after your money or status, that doesn't mean his family won't be. And even if his family doesn't want anything from you, I'm afraid you're going to be pulled into his world, a world so unfamiliar to you that you are wholly unprepared for it. I'm just saying, protect yourself. Protect your investments. And protect your heart."

"This is as enlightening as my Friday conversations with Mother. Thanks for it," Nick said dryly.

He began to rise again. She reached out and touched his arm. "The difference is that Mother always comes from a place of her own self-preservation. I am coming from a place of concern for your well-being. Make smarter choices, Nicholas."

Nick leaned over and said in her face, "Emma, the best decision I have ever made was to not sit in first class but to let American Airlines choose the seat 19C for me." He stood up and began to walk back inside the house. "I'll go see Mother in the morning."

Rion woke alone in the king-size bed with Egyptian cotton sheets, feathered pillows, and a comforter with gold embroidery. Nick had come into the bedroom the previous night, frustrated. He pulled Rion close to him and held him all night, then woke up early and left. Rion knew Nick had gone to see his mother that morning, and he was worried about him. After he took a long hot shower in a space that could fit four humans, he went through the walk-in closet, which was the size of a standard bedroom. It was mostly suits and dress shirts, with a few pairs of jeans here and there, but Rion was able to find a white t-shirt with A/X in big letters on it. He slid it on and went downstairs. The house was quiet, so he wandered around a little. He found the formal living room, the family room, and the game room. He walked toward the kitchen.

Emma was sitting at a breakfast nook near the picture window eating breakfast with Seppani, a cup of coffee and a plate of egg whites and avocados. Rion silently watched them, not wanting to intrude, but also wanting a mental picture of the two beautiful women sharing a meal. Seppani had soft brown hair, kind brown eyes, and olive skin, and Rion guessed she had Slavic roots. She was older than Emma, more than five years, but not quite ten. They were talking quietly, and their bare feet were touching under the table, toes caressing the other.

Rion waited a full minute, then he stepped intentionally into the kitchen. Emma looked up and gave him a smile, pulling her feet back. Seppani immediately rose from her seat with her plate and went to the island.

"Good morning, Rion. Come sit with me," said Emma.

Rion smiled at her and sat down in the seat that was previously occupied by the other woman. "Good morning. Where is everyone?" he asked.

"Blair has ballet every Sunday morning. She was picked up already. And Robby didn't come home, but that's not expected. I'll call the Benningtons later; he most likely stayed at Isaac's house. Or maybe he spent the night at Debbie Wright's house like he said. I don't know."

Seppani came over to place a mug in front of him and returned shortly with a tray. "Cream, milk, sugar?" she asked softly.

"Cream and three sugars, thank you." She poured him some coffee and added his requests. Rion asked, "And where is Gary?"

"He left not too long ago, some business meeting with my father. At least that's what he said," Emma said in a bored manner.

Seppani asked Rion, "What would you like for breakfast, Mr. Matthews?"

"Oh, Rion is fine. And I'm not a breakfast kind of guy. But thank you," he said again politely.

"Of course." Seppani gave him a smile, then nodded at Emma before she disappeared from the room. Emma watched her with warm eyes.

"She is very lovely," said Rion.

Emma smiled and turned to Rion. "She is. Seppani is not just a housekeeper. She's my rock. Seppani has been in my life since I gave birth to Robert. She was my doula back then. Then she became my helper, getting me through those early years since I was determined to raise Robby myself; I didn't want to be like my mother. After Blair was born and I went back to work, she stayed on the payroll as a house manager. Since I work full time for the family business—Highton Optimum Holdings is my only client—she makes sure everything at home runs smoothly. Seppani is," she took a moment to sip her coffee, then said, "the greatest thing that has ever happened to me."

"So she lives here on the property? With you?"

"She does now, yes. She didn't always, but she moved in seven years ago after her son went to college. Seppani has her own wing, right above the kitchen facing the garden."

"Far away from the other bedrooms with her own entrance from the kitchen," said Rion.

"Yes. She wanted her privacy but still wanted to be close."

"You two *are* close," Rion deduced.

Emma smiled. "Yes, we are."

"Closer than me and Nick," Rion said with a straight face.

Emma's smile faded. "Always the investigator, aren't you?"

"I'm just a curious writer, that's all," Rion said simply. "I pick up things others may not have."

"Hmm." She took another sip and looked at him. "Why Nicholas, Rion? You are handsome and witty and very sweet. I'm sure you have several options, ones that don't have you finding a man across an ocean, then following him across the country. What was it about Nick that you just had to have?"

"Such a weird way to phrase that," said Rion curiously. "There is nothing that he has that I had to have. Except his open heart. The way he gives me his love, affection, and attention. The way he provides space when I need it, closeness when I crave it. The way he just gets me. The way he makes me laugh. The way he makes love to me. The way he lets me make love to him. The way he takes care of me. Once he started freely giving me those things, then yes, I had to have them. I'm sure you understand that since you have someone in your life who does the same for you."

Emma did not respond, but gave a simple sigh and looked out of the window again. "Nick said that your marriage was pretty much arranged," said Rion. "Gary kind of said it too; said your fathers put the two of you together."

"Well, that's not entirely accurate," said Emma. "I was just starting law school when I assisted my father on a case in San Antonio" A property he was trying to acquire was getting blocked by Dorado Oil and Gas because it was on their gas line. I sat in on all the meetings during the day, and Gary and I got acquainted at night in my hotel room. I liked him, but yes, it was supposed to be a temporary fling. But Gary's father and my father also became acquainted and business partners after the settlement. It wasn't a bad choice, and I did have a say. I decided it was good for business for the two families to merge, especially since I am poised to take over the company. So we came together, had two children, and all is well with the world."

"But he doesn't make you happy," said Rion. "Gary is handsome and all, but he's not your type. He's brash and loud. You need calm, sweet, and nurturing. He's a provider and a protector of the home, the family, and the assets. You need someone to protect your heart."

"Very perceptive, Mr. Matthews," Emma said.

"I'm glad you found it," he said softly. "That thing that makes you happy. She really is lovely."

"Well, I think that we all find happiness where we can," Emma simply said, ignoring his comment. "And don't get me wrong, I see how happy you make Nicholas. And I see how happy you are with him. But like I told my brother last night, I don't see this boding well for him, for either of you. Your worlds are completely different. And when they start to merge, you'll have some decisions to make: either you put him through hell in your world, he puts you through hell in his world, or you let this go altogether."

Rion remembered Parker, Nick's best friend, telling him something similar in London. "What if we just create our own world?" he said.

Emma reached over and patted his hand. "Good luck with that."

Rion laughed. He put his hand on hers and said, "You know what, Em? Something tells me deep down you're rooting for this. You aren't able to love who you want to love openly, and you're a little proud of your baby brother for taking his life into his own hands. I know you're worried about how it's all going to turn out. I don't doubt that. But admit it: You're kind of loving the idea of Nick and me together."

Emma gave him a sly smile. Rion chuckled again.

Madeline Highton was in the sunroom, where she spent her mornings. She put a small pill of valium between her lips and drank it down with her cup of coffee. It was quiet there, and she had a full view of her purple azaleas, which made her happy. She sighed in contentment.

"Good morning, Mother," a voice took her out of her tranquil moment.

She turned her head and looked at her youngest son. Madeline gave him a once-over. "Consider a shave, Nicholas."

Nick touched his beard and smiled. He usually shaved off his beard by the first warm days of spring, but Rion liked it, especially when they made love because of the scratchiness against his most sensitive parts, so he kept it. But to his mother, he said, "I'll consider it."

He sat down in the seat next to her. Marika, one of the housekeepers, came over, placed a cup of coffee on the table in front of Nick, then exited the room.

They sat quietly until she said, "I assume you're at Emma's. When are you heading back?"

"This morning," he confirmed. "I just wanted to make sure I saw you before I head back to the city."

"For what purpose?" she said as she sipped.

Nick took a deep breath. "I want to apologize for my behavior at the masquerade ball last fall. It was inappropriate."

"And childish, and repulsive," she said. "You deliberately pushed yourself onto that girl just to embarrass Penelope, and that was the real travesty of the night. She didn't deserve that."

"I know you set up that faux engagement announcement together, Mother," Nick said.

"Penny only knew that I was going to put the two of you back together and set you back on the right path, like I've always done."

Nick was thoughtful. "So, it was your idea, not hers?"

"Oh, Nicholas." She paused to sip her coffee. "You and Penelope were a great match. You are never going to find someone who will put up with you the way she was willing to. You need someone to keep you in line. You are a lot to take care of, especially emotionally."

"But she wasn't what I wanted," Nick said. "What if I said to you that I already have someone in my life who is taking care of me? Taking care of me physically, mentally, and emotionally in the way in which I want and need?"

"I would say that without knowing anything about her, this new project you have given your time and attention to is temporary and will not sustain you wholly. But," Madeline threw up one hand, "what is my opinion but the words of a woman who has been where you are and learned from my mistakes?"

Nick scoffed. "Mother, your short stint as a cabaret girl in your twenties hardly constitutes you understanding how much I despise this world I have grown up in."

Madeline put down her cup and faced him. "I was a contemporary dancer," she said sharply. "And a damn good one."

"Fine, Mother," Nick conceded. "I apologize—"

But she cut him off. "You despise this world?" she said angrily. "This life that your father and I have given you? One of luxury and all the advances that people only dream of? A world where money is absolutely no object, and status and significance flow through your veins alongside the blood you bleed? You despise the life that has shaped the very core of your being?"

"Mother—"

"Is that what you have been trying to do all this time, Nicholas? All your rebellious behavior, getting involved with one lowlife after the next, writing about sex and debauchery, all of this is simply because you no longer want to be a Highton? After all we've done for you?"

"I'm not trying to *do* anything, Mother. That's the problem. You think by me simply living my life that I'm doing it somehow to spite you. This is who I am. But let's be clear: You've given me all of that except the one thing I've always needed from you."

"And what is that, Nicholas?"

"Love!" Nick said, raising his voice. "I just wanted you to see me, to know who I am, to give a shit about my existence, to ... fucking love me!" She stared at him blankly as tears formed in his eyes. "Why couldn't you just hug me and tell me that you love me no matter who I became, or who I loved, or what I did for a living? Even now, you can't say it, can you?"

Madeline looked at her son in contempt. "You have such a trivial notion of what love is. Love is not warm hugs and meaningless little words. Love is action. I had you when I didn't want to. That was love. Your father and I stayed together because I didn't want the Highton children to grow up in a negative spotlight with the stigma of a broken home and rich divorced parents, as his brother had done. That was love. I gave my last good years to raising a son I never asked to have. That was love. I gave you everything you could ever want, despite how many times you spat in my face. That was love. The fact that I am sitting here with you right now, even after the umpteenth time you have tried to tarnish the Highton name with your philandering with women *and* men, and your crude magazine, and your uncouth mannerisms—That is love, Nicholas. All these years, you've been so focused on waiting for a hug from your mummy and an attaboy from your daddy that you have completely missed all we have sacrificed for you. You, Nicholas. The one who wasn't meant to be. The one I should have never had. You."

Nick wiped the tears out of his eyes, horrified at her words to him. Madeline picked up her coffee. "But nothing will ever be enough for the selfish little boy who ruined my short cabaret stint and figure, then mocks me as a grownup." She took a sip and said, "I should have let you go be a farmer with that girl and told everyone that you died. It would have saved me the heartache."

Nick sniffed. "Her name was Beatrice." He sniffed again. "And yeah, you should have. In fact, you're right. You should have never had me."

Nicholas stood up and began to walk out of the sunroom. "Nicholas," she called his name. He stopped but did not turn around. "You have your inheritance money. Seven hundred million dollars that you despise. If you don't want it, give it all back. And then just... leave. Prince Harry has done it for love. You can do the same with your new ... *project*."

Nick turned back to her with tears on his face and gave her a smile. "And make your life easier? Not a fucking chance." He went through the sunroom door, saying, "Goodbye, Mother. Don't bother calling next Friday. I won't pick up."

"Jesus H. Christ, Nicholas! You were supposed to be smoothing things over, not starting a war," his sister said to him when he returned. He found Emma and Rion in the family room talking and told them about the conversation with Madeline.

"Did you not hear what she said to me?" Nick said angrily. "She basically admitted that she regrets my existence!"

"Mother says dramatic things when she is hurt," Emma said dismissively. "She will calm down—"

"But I won't," Nicholas yelled at Emma. "I am dead to that woman, and she is dead to me."

Emma's mouth dropped. "You don't mean that."

"The hell I do!"

"Nicholas!"

"Hey," Rion said. Everything Nick said angered him tremendously, but he kept his cool. He stood up and gave Nick a tap kiss. "Let's go home."

"No," Emma said, grabbing Nick's arm before he could turn around. "You have to go back over there—"

"No, he doesn't, Emma," Rion said firmly, standing between them and forcing her to let go. "I don't know Madeline, but I know what it feels like to have your mother say cruel things to you, whether she meant them or not. I know what it feels like to be at the mercy of wanting your mother to just act like a mother for once. I know what he's feeling, and he does not have to subject himself to it anymore. At some point, you have to cut your losses. Even when it's family."

He turned back to Nicholas. "Let's. Go."

Nick nodded, loving the way that Rion was taking control of the situation. If Rion were not there, Emma might have convinced him to go back to his mother sheepishly, and Nick was so grateful that he was.

"I'll call you later, Emma," he said to her.

"Wait!" Emma walked up to her brother and hugged him. "I'm so sorry she said those cruel things, Nicholas. I know she didn't mean them."

Nick hugged her back, surprised because Emma rarely gave actual hugs. "She did mean it, Em. But it's going to be okay." He gave her one last squeeze and followed Rion out of the home.

Nick drove in silence for over an hour, angry and hurt, before Rion made him pull over in Syracuse for gas and said, "Let me drive."

Rion took the wheel and drove for a while until he found a secluded park. He drove down the gravel until he came to the end and parked. He turned off the ignition.

"What are you doing?" Nick asked, his first words since he left his sister's house.

"I want to ride."

"What?" Nick was confused. "You are driving."

"No, Nick. I want," Rion got out of the car and opened the backseat door, "to *ride*." He slid in and closed the door behind him. "And you need to let go. So get back here with me."

Nick smiled at him. "It's broad daylight."

"Yup." Rion started taking off his shoes and unzipping his zipper.

"There could be children playing right over that hill." He pointed to an area that had a nearby playground.

"Could be." Rion slid off his sneakers, then his jeans.

Nick shook his head. "This is stupid. Let's go home."

"We will, right after we..." Rion slid off his underwear and grabbed his cock, stroking it upward. He stared at Nick.

Nick could never deny Rion any sexual attention. Especially since his cock started straining the moment Rion took his out. But then he thought about it. "We don't have lube in the car."

Rion licked his palm and continued stroking. "Nothing a little spit can't take care of."

"Ree, no. I'm not trying to hurt you in here." Because Nick knew the way he was feeling once Rion got on top, it was going to be an intense, hardcore fucking. That thought made his cock grow even more.

Then he remembered. "Wait, I have some cocoa

butter lotion." Nick began digging around his glove compartment until he found it. "Ah ha!" he announced proudly.

"Awesome. Now get back here before I finish without you," Rion said playfully, still tugging on himself.

"You will do no such thing," Nick growled.

He stepped out of the passenger seat and opened the back door. Once the door was closed, Nick moved Rion's hand away and engulfed Rion's genitals. Rion let out a deep moan and ran his fingers through Nick's hair.

"Fuck, don't ever shave," Rion said as Nick's beard tickled Rion's skin every time he deep-throated.

Nick popped off. "Fuck, I love you," he said seriously and kissed his boyfriend. "Now, let's do this."

After a few awkward tries in the backseat, roomy but still cramped to fit two people over six feet, Rion managed to get on top and began to ride with his t-shirt still on, slowly at first until he got comfortable, or the uncomfortable feeling was replaced by the euphoria of having Nick inside of him. His body was close to Nick's, with one knee stuck between the seat and Nick's thigh. Nick closed his eyes and held onto Rion's hips, and allowed his lover to take him away from all the hurt, pain, and sadness that his family gave to him. The car steamed up quickly.

Rion needed to move faster. He reached up, held onto the handle above the window, placed his other hand on the headrest, and started to bounce. They both lost inhibitions and began to moan loudly as the Tesla shook with Rion's movements.

"God, you feel so good, Nicky...I'm so close...I'm so—"

But suddenly, Nick roared and held onto Rion

tightly, involuntarily thrusting upward as semen spilled into his boyfriend. Rion kept moving, the feeling of Nick's warm milk bringing him even closer to the edge. As Nicholas was coming down from his high, he reached in and began to stroke Rion at the same momentous pace that Rion was sliding Nick in and out of him. It was too much, and Rion's mind went blank. He groaned, and his body reacted, pushing out cum on Nick's hairy chest and the leather back seat in long pearly strands, trapping Nick's cock in a death grip in his bottom. Rion slammed his hand against the window again as he fell forward.

Nick watched Rion try to catch his breath and eventually open his eyes. Nick smiled. Rion smiled back. "Feel better?" Rion said with a smile.

Nick chuckled and said, "Much," as Rion slid Nick out. But Rion did not move entirely. Instead, he put his face in Nick's neck.

Nick reached into Rion's shirt and rubbed his back. "Madeline's right about one thing," Rion said. Nick tensed, but he let Rion continue to speak.

"Love is an action word. And I love you, Nicholas. Not because you let me ride your dick in random parks and cum on your Italian leather seat in your expensive ass car. But I love you because you make me feel good. I feel good when I'm with you. I feel loved. I feel understood. I feel your love for me. And that's all I need. I don't need anything from you but to feel your love for me, too."

"Oh, Ree," he said, still rubbing his back. A single tear escaped from his eye. "You make me feel ... everything. Every fucking thing. When I'm with you, I'm not a Highton. I'm just your Nicky, and you're my Ree."

"It's not that I ignored him," Brian implored with a sip of his gin. "It's that by the time he was walking and talking, I was a teenage boy who had no use for a toddler."

Brian had called Nick and demanded he bring Rion out with him to the Brandy Library that evening, so the couple stepped out on a Thursday night. Brian had completed a successful surgery earlier in the day and was off for the next couple of days. Rion was happy to get to know Nick's older brother like he had gotten to know Emma and her family.

Rion sipped his whisky and glanced at Nick with a smile. "The way Nicky tells it, you didn't know he existed."

"He didn't," Nick confirmed.

"Hell no, I didn't," Brian agreed. "If it wasn't girls, cars, or video games, it didn't exist to me. But when he became a teenager, I showed him the ropes."

Nick laughed. "Yeah, getting me my first lap dance at eighteen. That was how he showed interest."

"It was something!" Brian said with a smile.

"I would have rather had someone to talk to," Nick said seriously. "You knew how overbearing they were, and you left me with them with no support and no refuge."

Brian shook his head. "Nicholas, you've always been sensitive and emotional. Yes, our parents are overbearing, but Emma and I survived it, and we knew you would, too. And anyway, I was a phone call away if you wanted to talk or needed advice. You could have just called."

"You were knee-deep in surgical work by the time I was sixteen," argued Nick.

Brian shrugged and turned to Rion. "See? He assumed I wasn't available, so now he has this false narrative that I wasn't there for him."

Rion said to Nick, "He has a point."

"Plus, as the oldest Highton male and heir to the throne, there was a tremendous amount of pressure for me to succeed," said Brian. "Don't tell me about them being overbearing. You think you had it bad as the youngest? Niles practically shit bricks when I told him I wasn't going into the family business. At the end of my sophomore year at Dartmouth, I told him I was entering the Geisel School of Medicine instead of the Tuck School of Business, and he literally cut me off, verbally and financially, until I agreed to go to Tuck. It was so bad that I overdosed on Ritalin and ended up in rehab for the last month of the semester and missed all my finals. Bet you didn't know that, did you?"

Nick was surprised. "No. No, I did not."

"Wow, Brian," Rion said, equally shocked. "I'm so sorry."

"Yeah, well..." Brian took another sip of gin and looked away. "Like I said, it was a lot of pressure. Honestly, they were more pissed off at me for actually getting the police involved in my *minor* suicide attempt, as they saw it, than the reason I actually did it. Mother kept it quiet, telling the school I needed a month of relaxation and would complete my finals over the summer. She convinced Father that if he stopped the checks for my tuition, it would look like we were having money issues, and you know she wasn't going to allow that rumor to even start. I was already accepted into the program, so they let me go. But he didn't really talk to me the whole time I was in med school. Not until two things happened: One, Emma stepped up, saying she would take over the family business when my father stepped down, and two, I had my first successful solo surgery."

"And Idalia," Nick chimed in.

"Yes," said Brian with a sigh. "And Idalia."

"Idalia?" Rion asked.

"My wife," Brian confirmed. "Idalia Mercurio was how my father forgave me. He acquired Mercurio Properties in Italy when the old man secured a husband for his spinster oldest daughter."

"Spinster!? How much older is she than you?" Rion asked, surprised.

"Oh, in Italy, you're a spinster if you aren't married by the time you're twenty-five. I had just turned twenty-four, and Idalia was twenty-seven, so not that much older. We were married two months after meeting across a conference table."

"Jesus, Brian," Rion said, shaking his head.

"And she had a set of twins by Brian's twenty-fifth birthday," Nick said, raising his glass to him. Brian raised his glass back.

"But to be married off like a business deal… that had to be rough," said Rion.

"Not really," said Brian with a shrug. "She was beautiful and satisfied me sexually. Not really my type, she was a little statuesque, but Madeline took care of that right away. She went from a size ten to a size four by the time the boys were two years old."

"Wow. That's … extreme," said Rion, his eyebrows furrowed together.

"No, extreme would have been chaining me to a desk looking at numbers for ten hours a day, six days a week. Whatever I needed to do, including marrying someone I barely knew, to have this one thing for myself, I did it. I had no desire to be a businessman. I knew that for a fact."

"No, your desire was to play God," said Nick cheekily.

Brian smiled. "And I've been doing a pretty fucking great job at it. Ninety-eight percent surgery success rate. Can God beat that?" Nick laughed.

"What kind of surgery do you do again?" Rion asked.

"Orthopedic," he said. "I focus on spinal injuries and deformities."

Brian delved into his surgery that morning at New York-Presbyterian and other cases. Rion was fascinated by Brian Highton. He was Nick—self-assured, confident, strong work ethic, and had a laid-back way about him. But he wasn't Nick. Brian had an air of superiority to him, a hint of arrogance bordering on narcissism that Nicholas didn't have. Brian was definitely part of the One Percent, and he relished it. Rion was grateful that Brian was absolutely accepting of Rion in Nick's life, just like Emma was. Rion was also sure that if he didn't have any connection to his brother, Brian would not have even noticed if he entered a room.

"...and I don't take cases unless I know there is some chance of mobility," said Brian. "Then I beat the odds. Like I did today, with a full spinal reconstruction surgery on a stuntman for Matt Damon's new movie." He sat back and smiled to himself.

"Wow. Nick also said you're world-renowned," Rion brought up.

"I had a couple of cases in Europe: a Chinese diplomat, and the son of a Japanese parliament member. And I was part of the team that operated on the Bolivian boy that fell down the well; we saved his life. So yeah, there have been a couple of journals written about my work," he said smugly and raised his glass to sip.

"Are you happy, Brian?" Rion asked unexpectedly.

Brian's glass froze on his lips. "Yeah, I'm happy. I have a wife and three boys, two fifteen-year-olds and a twelve-year-old. They're all happy. My father has his successor in Emma and has taken the boys under his wing in the business, so he's happy that at least one of them will follow in his footsteps, too, so his legacy continues. My mother and Lia are frenemies like a mother-in-law-daughter-in-law relationship should be. I have money, prestige, family, friends, status, and everything I want comes to me. Why wouldn't I be happy?"

But Rion was curious. "There has to be something else. You named everything you do for other people.

Even your line of work, which you obviously enjoy for the God factor, is about helping other people. What do you do for your own happiness?"

Brian looked at Nick. "Who is this kid, Barbara Walters?" Brian said with a laugh. Nick grinned.

Rion smiled too. "I'm just a curious writer."

"Hmm." He turned to his brother. "Did you tell him?"

Nick looked at him curiously. "Tell him what?" They stared. "Oooh." Nick's eyes lit up in recognition. "No! Never. No. I swear."

"Tell me what?" Rion looked back and forth from Brian to Nicholas.

They ignored him. "Rion has a way of getting to your core. Looks like he's gotten to yours, too," Nick said, winking at his boyfriend.

"Tell me what?" Rion asked again, this time looking at Nick.

But it was Brian who spoke. "I can show you better than I can tell you."

"Oh no," Nick said, shaking his head. "We're not going there."

"Going where?" Rion was intrigued and excited about all the secrecy.

"Nowhere, Ree," said Nick. "It's—"

Brian cut him off. "Do you have your gold card on you?"

"No!" Nick said, looking at his brother. "I haven't been there in years. In fact, I've never gone without you, so the last time we went together was the last time."

Brian let out a sly smile. "Then it's time."

"Time for what?" Rion breathed out, his eyes wide with anticipation.

"Brian—" Nick started.

"Hey Rion, you write erotica, right?" Brian asked, turning to him.

"Yes...?"

"What do you know about sex clubs?"

"Erm..." Rion looked at Nick, who shook his head. "Not much. I've read about them but never been to one. Why?" He lowered his voice. "Are you a member of one?" Rion whispered, eager to know.

"Not just a member," said Brian. "I'm a BDSM dungeon master. And I'm not talking about the D&D game."

"Ooooooh," said Rion excitedly, flicking his fingers back and forth. "Holy, holy shiiiiit! I knew there was something. There had to be something. You just seem like someone who would not be satisfied with the ordinary."

"My life is anything but ordinary. Well ... my other life," said Brian slyly.

"How often do you go?" Rion asked.

"At least once a month. I'm not due to work the dungeon until the end of the month. But we can stop by—"

"Wait." Nick put his hand out between them. "Can we take a step back?" He turned to his boyfriend. "Rion, do you really want to go to a sex club?"

"Just to observe," Rion said innocently. "For research purposes."

Nick couldn't help but laugh. He grabbed Rion's drink and sniffed. "Are you drunk?"

Rion laughed. "No, but I will be by the time we get to this club." Rion took the glass from Nick and swallowed the rest. Nick shook his head in faux disappointment.

"It's not your average club," said Brian. "It's a playpen for the rich. Any kind of depravity you can think of is bought and sold there. The lower the level, the higher the stakes. It's my job to make sure consents are signed, rules are followed, and people don't get hurt."

"Consent is so sexy," said Rion dreamily. Brian chuckled.

"How do you still have time for this, Brian?" Nick asked. "I thought you were reducing your playtime. Not doubling down and becoming a master there."

"I make time," Brian said simply. "Like Rion said, it's what makes me happy."

"I want to go," said Rion. "Take me into your world, Brian. Show me what makes you happy."

Brian let out a sly smile. "You're going to need a suit."

"I have a suit—"

"No." He turned to Nick. "Give him one of your suits. And a mask for anonymity. Get him ready."

Nick sighed. He couldn't believe they were actually going there. "What time?"

Brian looked at his watch. "Meet me there at eleven. I have to call Kara and let her know I won't be coming home." Brian picked up his phone and began to dial.

Rion was confused. "Kara? I thought your wife's name was Lia."

Brian raised an eyebrow. "It is." Then he spoke into the phone. "Sweetheart, change of plans. I'm going to the club tonight, and I'll see you next week." Brian opened his wallet and threw a couple hundreds on the table. "No, sweetheart, not tonight. You stay home." He held the phone to his side and said, "11 p.m.

Three hours." He began to walk away, talking to the mysterious Kara.

Rion turned to him with a question in his eyes. Nick shook his head. "Don't bother asking the obvious question. But Ree, are you serious about this?"

"Are you worried I'm going to get caught up in the lifestyle?" he asked with an amusing tone.

"No. I just…" Nick was thoughtful. "A lot of things happen there, and most of it is not pleasant. It's not my world."

"I figured that. You don't seem like the type into bondage and inflicting pain for pleasure." Rion touched his hand and said, "If you don't want to go, we won't go."

Nick squeezed his fingers. "We'll go. Just for an hour. But we better get moving. The location of the Gold Club is across the George Washington Bridge. And I have to dress you for the night."

By 10:30 p.m., Nicholas and Rion were in a car getting driven to the northern part of New Jersey. Rion couldn't help looking at the size of the homes. He felt like he was in a private, wealthy neighborhood in L.A. Nick had dressed Rion in all black: Black Versace suit with a black shirt underneath and shiny black Brunello Cucinelli shoes. Rion was sure his entire outfit was more expensive than his last book advance. He lifted his woven eye mask with the silk lining off to get a better look and to take pictures on his phone.

"No cameras and no phones," Nick reminded him. "You'll have to turn it in at the bar along with any car keys. They monitor your alcohol and substance abuse intake. Oh, and you'll get a finger prick. They test your blood on-site. That's how you're identified."

"Wow." Rion turned to him. "So, when was the last time you were there?"

"Six years ago, when I found out Trixie gave birth to her first son. I sent a gift. She sent it back. I needed something, anything, to take away the hurt I was feeling. That's when Brian suggested we go to the club to heal my broken heart."

"And did it?" Rion asked with a smile.

"Aaaah… it did something," Nick said slyly.

Rion laughed. "Must be some place."

Nick turned to him. "Listen, they take it very seriously in there, especially discretion. Don't speak to anyone unless directly asked a question, and limit it to one-word answers. Don't give anyone your real name. Ryan D. Ryder is fine. I would rather they think you're someone's sub and be afraid to talk to you than someone starts a conversation with you about why you're there. And you know you can't resist talking to people." Rion smiled. "I'm serious, Ree. This is not my world, and this is definitely not yours. Stay quiet and stay by either my or Brian's side."

"Aye, aye, Captain." Rion slid his black eye mask over his face.

They stopped at an elaborate, large white mansion where the closest neighbor, another stately mansion, was about three hundred yards away. "No talking," Nicholas said quietly as their driver opened the door.

Rion followed Nick out of the car and up the stairs. There was no doorknob. Just a double wooden door with a key card holder and a large camera facing the front entrance. Nick looked up first, directly into the camera.

"Keep your face forward," he commanded. "You don't need to look into the camera; I do, for facial recognition."

Rion kept his head straight. After a few moments, the red light on the camera turned green. Nick pulled a gold keycard out of his wallet and dipped it into the cardholder. A small *beep* happened, and the door clicked. Nick pushed it open. They entered a small foyer. "Close the front door," said Nick. "The second door won't open if the front door is open."

"Wow," Rion whispered and closed the door. Nick entered his key card in the second entrance, and the next wooden door opened. Nick walked through with Rion on his tail.

Rion was surprised. It looked ... normal. It was a large open space of tables, chairs, and couches, with people dressed up and talking. Some had masks like he did, and some had collars on, but other than that, it resembled a fancy dinner party. Nick walked over to the island that could seat ten people and was set up like a bar.

Brian was already there. He had also changed into a suit, charcoal gray, crisp white shirt with no tie. He handed his brother a glass of cognac. "What are you drinking, Rion?"

"Whisky is fine since I was drinking it earlier."

Brian tapped the counter. "Pappy on the rocks. A double."

"Pappy?" Rion asked Nick quietly.

"Pappy Van Winkle's Family Reserve," Nick said back quietly as he sat at the bar. Rion followed him. "A twenty-three-year reserve."

"Wow."

The bartender placed a glass of brown liquor in front of Rion. But he smiled at Rion's boyfriend. "Hello, Nicholas," he said. His voice was deep and dripped in seduction.

Nick nodded and said back politely, "Hello, Axel."

Nick placed a hundred-dollar bill on the counter. Axel slid it to himself, never taking his eyes off Nicholas. Nick turned away first. Rion looked at him as Axel the bartender moved on.

"This drink costs a hundred dollars?" Rion asked in astonishment while looking at his glass.

Brian smiled as Nick said, "No. The drinks are free. That was a tip."

"Shiiiiit..." Rion said, shaking his head. "Tip from doing *what*?"

Nick chuckled, but his face flushed. Brian chuckled, too. "Nicky has secrets—" he began to tease, but Nick swung his fist out and punched Brian on the side. "Ooooh," Brian said in pain, as his face scrunched up. "I'm going to get you back for that, you fucker."

Rion giggled and went to put the glass to his lips. But Nick said, "Wait." Rion's hand hung in the air. "Pick it up gently. Sniff it first. Take in the aroma. Then a very small sip. Hold it in your hand and wait a few moments before taking a real sip."

Brian grinned. But Rion did as Nick commanded, slowly taking the crystal glass in his hand and sniffing the drink. He smelled vanilla, maple, and oak; it appealed to all his senses. He took a small sip, and it went down smoothly.

"That's good shit," Rion breathed. Nick smiled, and Brian chuckled. Rion took a bigger sip.

"The Highton boys," an older woman walked up to them and announced. She was average height with silver glasses, and her hair was so blond it was practically white and came to her shoulders. She walked up to them in a long sequined evening gown and smiled as she set her eyes on the younger one.

"It's been a long time, Nicholas Highton." She held out her hand.

"Velane," Nick responded and lifted her hand for a kiss. "You're still aging like fine wine."

Brian stood, and they gave each other an air kiss. "Velane, this is Ryan D. Ryder. The one I told you we were bringing tonight."

If she thought his name was weird, she made no mention of it. Rion stood up and said, "It's nice to meet you."

She eyed him with a guarded smile. "And which Highton do you belong to?"

Brian shook his head, "No, he doesn't belong—"

"Me," Nick spoke up. "He belongs to me." Rion smiled.

"Aaaaah, yes," Velane drawled. "Your proclivity for the male anatomy is out in the open now. I guess you've officially chosen a side." She tsked. "Too bad. With all that length between your legs." Velane gave Nick a seductive once over. "But Axel has been wanting to worship you again for ages, so if you want to indulge tonight..."

All three men looked over at the bartender, who was watching them intently; his eyes were focused on Nick. Rion turned to Nick and looked at him amusingly. Nick looked back at him apologetically.

Brian chuckled and turned back to the host. "Get on with it, V."

She took out a small leather pouch from her purse and opened it. She pulled out a finger prick monitor and said, "Hold your index finger out, Mr. Ryder."

Rion did. She took the small pearl of blood and then typed some information into the machine. "You'll have your results within the hour, then you'll have full range of the playrooms."

"He's not playing," Nick said. "He's only here to observe."

Velane smiled at him. "That's what they all say."

Brian chuckled again. "In the meantime, give us the full tour. I want Mr. Ryder to know all the ins and outs of the club." She stared at him. "Yes, all of it," he answered her question. "Nicholas and I trust him completely."

Velane shrugged. "Okay." She took Rion's arm and said, "Welcome to the Gold Club. Where all your fantasies, and sometimes your nightmares, come true. I am Viper. The Mistress of the club." She began walking around with him; Brian and Nick followed.

"This is the parlor." She gestured around. "Everyone is to stop at the bar for a drink and to submit their cell phones and car keys, and we obtain their blood analysis."

"We didn't submit either," Rion reminded her, looking back at the bar. Axel was still watching them. "And I was the only one that submitted blood."

"That's because the Highton brothers can do what they want. They're Hightons," she said, as if he should have known that. "Also, they have vouched for you, namely Brian, who is a high-ranking member of the club. And if you reveal any of our secrets, then you will meet an untimely death. And so would they," she said with a straight face.

Rion almost laughed, but he wasn't sure if she was kidding or not. They walked farther into the room. She pointed to a white wooden door. "That is the women's lounge. You are not allowed in there under any circumstances. Even the staff are women."

"What about trans women?" Rion asked.

Velane raised her eyebrow. "The Caitlyn Jenners of the world are welcome here. We do not discriminate, Mr. Ryder. Anyone can join the Gold Club if they have the right … aptitude."

"Money," Rion confirmed.

She raised her palm. "Money alone cannot grant you entrance into this very exclusive atmosphere. We vet to the highest degree."

Velane walked to another wooden door, this time cherrywood. "This is the men's lounge. I am not allowed to go in, but the Hightons will take you in."

"Thank you, Velane," said Brian. He opened the door and motioned for Rion to follow him.

It indeed resembled a den for men. It was rustic, all wood everywhere, even on the ceilings. There were bookshelves with hundreds of books, leather armchairs, and leather seating. A large fireplace was at one end, and a small spiral staircase was at the other end, going to the next level of more bookshelves and seating. Another small bar was in the corner, but drinks were being served, rather than men going up to the bar. About twelve or so men lolled around, talking in small groups, one or two sitting quietly by themselves reading, one stretched out on a couch and snoring away.

Brian said, "It's usually quiet on a Thursday night. But this room can have up to sixty men at any given point. Business deals and legislation are made here. The Gold Club is not just about sex; it's about power." He paused as a man younger than Rion walked up to them with glasses.

"Gin, cognac, and whisky," he said.

Rion was surprised as he took the glass off the tray. "How did you know?"

"They know everything," said Nick. "Everyone is being watched. And it's being noted. So the next time you come here, no matter how many years later, you'll have a glass of Pappy waiting for you." He also took his glass and sipped.

"Wow," said Rion.

Before he could say anything else, a middle-aged man stepped up to them. "The Highton boys, together again," he said jovially. He stuck his hand out to shake Brian's first, then Nicholas's.

"Good to see you, Russell," said Brian. "It's been a while since you've graced the club."

"Yes, well. My nephew, Todd Porter, is stepping up in the gaming industry, and I thought he could use a night to relax." He waved another man over.

Todd Porter was tall and lanky, and not attractive. But he, too, had an air of arrogance that Rion could sense right away. That, and a desperation to be accepted. He came over smiling and shook hands with

Brian and Nick. Rion took note that neither Russell nor Todd acknowledged him.

"Nick Highton," Todd said as he shook Nick's hand. "We went to Arcadia Academy together."

"I remember," said Nick impassively. "You played lacrosse."

"And Rowing," Todd said smugly. "Brought Arcadia four championships in the years I was there."

"And Todd's competitive spirit is why he's so successful," his uncle said, patting his shoulder.

Nick gave him a polite smile in response. "Excuse us, I see John Herring, and I need to have a word with him." He gave Rion a head nod for him to follow, and Rion dutifully did.

When they were out of earshot, Rion chuckled softly. "You don't like him."

"Todd Porter is an arrogant shithead," Nick said nastily as they walked toward another group of men. "Everything that Gary thinks I am, Todd actually is. A spoiled rotten, trust fund baby that will always fall back on his generational wealth and his family's clout to get him out of trouble. He's never worked for anything a day in his life. All he does is get into trouble, and his family, full of attorneys and judges, gets him out of it. Last I heard, he was accused of sexually assaulting a woman, but the charges were dropped. I'm sure Russell bringing him into the Gold Club was so that he could sexually assault women with consent."

Before words could utter out of Rion's open lips, Nick put on a genuine smile and tapped an older man on the shoulder. "I thought that was you."

The man turned around and smiled. "Nicholas!" The two embraced. "What are you doing here? This isn't your scene. Or is it...?" He looked at Rion over his spectacles, making Nick laugh.

"No. Not quite my scene."

"Your little stunt made international news. I'm still upset with you that you didn't give us exclusive rights for the interview."

"Well, you taught me how to turn a shitshow into a profit, so I did," said Nick. Nick turned to his boyfriend. "Ryan D. Ryder, meet John Herring, the CEO of NovaTel Print Media. He owns The City Chronicle. And he was my mentor in the business."

Rion shook his hand. "Which City Chronicle? The one in New York?"

John smiled. "All of them."

"Oh, like ... *all*? In every major city in the U.S.?"

"Every single one. Are you in print media?" he asked.

"I write, yes," Rion said sheepishly.

"Ryan writes erotic fiction," Nick boosted him. "Very well, I might add. He's a successful published author."

"Ah," he said. "It all makes sense, this pairing. Nicholas obviously enjoys a good sex story." John winked. "Speaking of sex stories, when are you going to give me the real story about your London tryst? Just give me a name; I have friends all over Europe who will have his full C.V. by morning."

Nick and Rion both smiled. "You'll find out when the rest of the world does," said Nick mysteriously.

Brian walked over to them. "That guy Todd is a pain in the ass. I could tell he just wants to be one of the big boys. I told him to call me Mr. Highton and sent him away." Nick and Rion laughed.

"So," Brian said to Rion, "You're ready to see the real club?"

8

rian had Velane take them upstairs first. It was a long white painted hallway that curved around the bend. "There are twelve rooms on this level and the one above," she said. "If a door is closed, that means it is a private affair. You cannot go in, but you can listen."

They stopped at a closed door and heard moaning. "Sometimes, being vocal is done on purpose. A low-level exhibition act."

She looked at five people standing at another closed door, three men and two women. The three of them walked over to it. It was obvious someone was getting drilled by someone else right up against the door. A woman was hollering, and a man was grunting loudly in time with the banging against the wood. One of the men listening had his hand on a woman's shoulder and was massaging it gently. Her eyes were closed, enjoying the sensational touch and erotic sounds.

Velane walked them over to an open room. They stepped inside. To Rion, it looked like an expensive hotel room that had a small couch, a big bed, and a minibar. Rion walked over to the dresser and looked at the assortment of condoms and lubricants, along with items such as handcuffs, colorful ropes, soft feathers, and small paddles.

"If you have a request for an item, or are in distress, just press the intercom," she said, pointing to the one near the bed. "There is also an intercom in the bathroom."

"Are there cameras in the rooms?" Rion asked, looking up at the tray ceiling.

"No," Brian spoke for her. "We value privacy and discretion. But there are cameras in the hallway. So we know who went into a bedroom together. And it is expected that if you go in together, you leave together."

"And when you are done," she said, "you keep the door closed so we know to go in there and clean for the next guest."

"How long are the rooms available for?" Rion asked.

"I don't understand the question," said Velane blankly.

"I mean, is it by the hour? Can you stay here all night? Three nights? A week? A month?"

"It depends. If you prearrange it, then yes," said Brian.

"At an additional cost, of course," Velane chimed in. "We had an unnamed president hide his mistress here for six months."

Rion's mouth dropped again. "Who?" he breathed out.

Everyone ignored his question. "If the door is open, even slightly, it is an invitation to come in," Velane continued. "Those are the rules. If you don't want company, you keep your door firmly closed. If you want to be seen but not have another join you, you do this."

She went to the main door, pulled out a white cotton divider from inside the doorjamb, and spread it to the other side, then hooked it in. "This creates a barrier. You can see, but you cannot enter."

"So, do people leave the room door open slightly on purpose?" Rion asked.

Velane smiled, but it was Brian that answered. "Correct. It's all a game. Maybe a woman had a stressful day at work and wants to get sexual attention but not seem desperate for it. So she'll come in here and leave the door slightly open and pretend to get undressed or try on lingerie in full view of the door. Another person comes in. And what they do in this room together, whether it's a love-making scene or rape fantasy, is their business. And as long as the door remains open without a barrier, more than one person can come in."

Nicholas spoke up. "It's what I did the last time I was here."

Rion turned to him in surprise. "Really?"

Nick nodded. "I just ... left the door open."

"For how long?" Rion asked.

Nick hesitated, looking at his brother's amused face. Then he looked back at Rion. "All night."

"Holy, holy shit, Nick!" Rion exclaimed. Brian grinned at him.

A man was walking by the room they were in, then he stopped. He looked into the room at the two men, then at Velane. He smiled and stood there, expecting a scene to begin to play out.

Velane smiled sweetly and walked over to him. She touched his face and said, "Not now, Mr. McCarthy. I'm just doing a tour."

"Pity," he said. "This looked like the beginning of a good time. No matter, Mistress, I requested you later."

"And your wishes shall come true. Later," she said sweetly but firmly. He smiled again and moved on. "Come," she said to the other men. "There is more to see."

Velane led them through the hallway to the other side. The doors that were open were mostly of women cuffed to a bed and having sex with one or two men. Most doors were closed. Velane walked them to a stairwell with stairs leading up or down. The stairs up were blocked off with a sign that said, "Elite Members Only." Velane started walking down. At the bottom, she pushed the door open. Rion was shocked at the contrast. The walls were stony and painted black, and the lightning was a dim yellow.

"Welcome to the dungeon," she announced.

They walked down the same curved hallway as upstairs, but there wasn't any privacy. The space was more open, like the first floor. There were a few more people in the area, and most of them were naked. Men and women were tied against walls, hung on posts, or crawling on the floor, being led around by chains or ropes attached to their collars. The ones tied up were either getting whipped or penetrated. The smell of sex in the air was palpable. Rion found himself moving closer to Nick.

"It's depravity at its finest," Nick said softly, averting his eyes.

"Yes. And yet they are all here. Willingly. It's … fascinating," Rion whispered back as a man dragged a woman by her hair across their path.

"Nicholas doesn't come down here," Brian said to Rion. "My brother has always been more sensitive. But you seem intrigued. So ask any questions, and I will answer them honestly."

"The rooms don't have doors," Rion noticed. "Scenes are playing out from room to room and right in the hallway."

"Yes," said Brian. "Most of this is open; for anyone to see. But you must get permission from the member to participate in a scene that is already in play."

Brian walked ahead of Velane, leading the tour, as this was his area of expertise. He pointed out the room specifically for oral sex: Floor pads for kneeling, ottomans for sitting, a wall of holes for fellatio, and a wall where someone could slip their bottom half into it and allow another person to lick them, vaginally or anally. Rion stopped to watch a couple sharing a very large cock coming out of a glory hole.

"This room gets a lot of visitors: those looking to give or receive. Or to watch," said Brian, looking at Rion with amusement.

"I bet it does," Nick said and nudged Rion along.

Rion turned to him and giggled. "Sorry." Nick smiled and took his hand.

Brian led them to another door. "One more level."

They followed him down a shorter staircase and through a smaller hallway. They heard the sound of spanking, and Brian led them to a room with no door. A heavily obese woman was on a bed no bigger than a gurney. Her ankles and wrists were tied to the metal ends below, so only her torso remained on the surface. A naked man had a heavy paddle. He turned to look at the four curious faces, then went back to his job. He held the paddle up high and brought it down hard on the woman's already bruised ass.

She yelled as the skin of her enormous bottom jiggled around. When she stopped yelling, he raised his arm and did it again. It was methodical. Controlled. Rion was in awe.

Nick turned away first. "I would rather not see a man beating on a woman for his own pleasure."

"She's the client," Rion said, watching the whole scene as she yelled again.

Brian turned to him with a smile. "That's right. She is."

Nick looked at him. "How can you tell?"

"She's the one getting the most pleasure out of this. His arms are tired. He wants to stop. Look." Rion pointed, and they all watched the man roll his right shoulder twice before he paddled her again.

"Want to take his place?" A deep voice behind them spoke. They turned around. A handsome, medium build African American man was standing there. "Just can't stay away, can you, Highton?"

"Just taking someone on a tour." Brian reached out and patted the man's shoulder. "This is Elijah. He's the dungeon master tonight. We call him The Prophet." He pointed. "You know my brother Nicholas. This is our friend Ryan D. Ryder."

"Mr. Deep Strokez himself." Elijah gave a smile to Nick. "I owe you. Bisexual men like me are 'In' now because of you."

Nick laughed out loud. "You're welcome."

"However, I don't know you," he said, looking at Rion curiously. He reached one finger out to the bridge of Rion's nose and slid Rion's mask up onto his forehead. "I want to, though," Elijah said seductively. "Ryan D. Ryder. Right?"

"I'm a nobody," Rion said and adjusted his mask back onto his face.

Elijah squinted and shook his head. "You're definitely not a nobody. Your name has a double meaning."

"Yes, it does," Rion admitted. "But not for you."

Elijah narrowed his eyes slightly again. "You belong to Nicholas?" he asked him directly, not looking at Nick.

Rion raised his chin up a little higher. "Yes. I belong to Mr. Highton. The younger one." Nick smirked.

"Unfortunate. The things we would do together..." Elijah gave him a sly smile. "Very well. Excuse me."

Elijah stepped into the room, and the man stopped mid-swing. He stepped back and immediately got on his knees with his head down. Elijah did not glance at him once.

"What are you—" the woman began. But she was silenced by Elijah standing before her.

"Mrs. Dunlap, it's been forty minutes. Take a break. Or switch out to someone else. Hmmm?" he said gently.

"Go get Axel," she drawled out.

Only then did Elijah glance at the man at his feet. "Go."

The naked man sighed in relief. He practically ran to the backroom to get dressed. Elijah spoke into his walkie quietly as he walked back over to the Hightons and company. "A man's work is never done," he said as he left them.

The trio continued walking through the hallway. There were only two other rooms occupied, one with a man tied to a bed with a couple putting objects in all of his various entrances. Rion could tell they were high by the way they moved around the room and laughed uncontrollably. The other room was with two women, one much older than the other. The younger woman was suspended from the ceiling wearing nipple clamps, her body already bleeding and wounded from her latest brutal flogging. She was crying. Her arms were high above her head, her toes barely touching the floor, while the older woman was beneath her, petting, licking, pleasing her. Rion watched them longer than the others, not because of the sex but the sensuality of it all.

The last room had a door with a Nine on it, but it was open. It was dark, and the bulbs were red. Something caught Rion's attention, and he stepped in. There was a tall wooden cross in the center of the room. Rion walked right up to it and touched it. "Wow," he murmured to himself. He looked over at the other piece of furniture: a large bed with long steel bars for the headboard and bars going across the top for suspension. He went over to it, and the sheets were black silk. "Wow," Rion said again. He turned around and walked to the armoire, and opened it. He expected to see the ropes, chains, and cuffs. He did not expect the number of paddles, from small and cotton to large and heavy leather; metal poles with balls of spikes at the end that could do serious harm; heavy leather whips of all sizes for flogging; collars made for choking.

"Holy, holy shit," he breathed out.

"You found my room," he heard Brian say.

"You're shitting me," Rion said in astonishment.

Brian chuckled and stood next to him. "Well, not my personal room. But I do use it often." He looked into the cabinet with Rion. "I don't engage in blood play. I draw the line there. But sometimes—" Brian picked up a leather whip and touched it affectionately, "I go right up against it."

Rion turned to him. "What do they call you here?"

Brian smiled. "The Doctor."

Rion chuckled. "Obviously. You know how to cause pain without making someone actually bleed or causing serious harm, don't you?" said Rion.

Brian smiled again but didn't answer. Instead, he tapped Rion's shoulder. "Come. Let's head to the main foyer."

Velane was waiting for them at the door at the other end of the hall. She pushed open the door, and it was bright as their eyes readjusted to the white walls. The four of them began walking up the stairs.

"So people come here to play, as you call it, or just hang out and talk business deals?" Rion asked.

"Exactly. It's not all sex and sadism all the time," Brian explained. "When V said everything you can think of is bought and sold here, she wasn't kidding. And sex is a huge part of deal-making."

"Who owns this place?" Rion asked.

"You'll never know," Nick said to him.

Velane laughed. "Some of the employees don't even know. I am one of many faces that manage the entire facility. They come to me if something has gone wrong. Brian and Elijah are other trusted faces."

"But you know who is doing what," said Rion. "You record movements, you take blood samples, you watch everything from what people are eating to their choice of drink. There is anonymity, but not from those behind the curtain of this Emerald City." Rion noticed they came up from a stairway at the front entrance near the bar.

Brian began talking. "It's how we operate. But we—"

But Brian stopped cold. Rion and Nick turned to see what he was staring at. A young woman was slowly, gingerly walking toward them from the bar. She was about 5'7", thin but curvy. And extremely beautiful. Her raven-colored hair was parted in the middle and hung halfway down her back. Her skin was smooth, and even though she had a full face of makeup, Rion could tell her beauty was natural. The woman wore a sparkling silver dress that had chains for straps on her shoulders, and it stopped mid-thigh. Her shoes were the exact same shade of silver. Her only accessory was a white collar around her neck with big, shiny diamonds dotting the length, coming together with a silver hook at her throat. Somehow, Rion knew the diamonds were real.

"Well," Velane said, sensing danger. "I have some other business to attend to, so I will leave you gentlemen to it." She walked away from them.

Brian folded his hands in front of him. The woman walked right up to Brian, ignoring the other two. But that did not stop Nick from greeting her. "Hello, Kara."

She did not turn her head when she said back, "Hello, Nicholas." Her voice was soft and sweet.

Brian and his mistress stared at each other. He waited. She lowered her light brown eyes and concentrated on his mouth instead. "I'm sorry, sir," she practically whispered.

Brian raised his left hand up, leveling with his shoulder. Both men watched to see what he was going to do. Rion was sure he was going to strike her. But Brian surprised everyone by putting his thumb and middle finger together in a firm snap.

Kara flinched; she also expected Brian to slap her. But then she immediately got on her knees and sat on the floor at Brian's feet, her hands in her lap, her head slightly bowed. Rion's mouth dropped. Nick looked at the woman and frowned.

"You will be," Brian said to her in a hauntingly low voice. Then he looked up and picked up where he left off, ignoring the beautiful woman on the ground.

"As I was saying," he said in a normal voice, "yes, we monitor everything that goes on, but for safety purposes. The people that come here know they can trust us with their lives. If a secret ever got exposed, you would go after them publicly, but we would go after them privately and destroy their livelihood and their reputation. The risk of coming here, even for the Doms, is submission to the house rules. You sign a contract, and you abide by it. And we never, ever, lift the curtain in Oz."

But Rion was barely listening. He was watching Kara sitting still as a stone on the floor in the middle of a large room, and not one person seemed to be bothered by it. Axel kept on serving and wiping down the bar, party-goers continued to mingle around them, and no one said a word about Kara.

Nick was also not listening and continued to frown. "Brian? Get her up."

"Why?" Brian asked.

Nick narrowed his eyes at his older brother. "Because it's demeaning and embarrassing."

"Embarrassing for who? You? I'm sure you had plenty of people on their knees in front of you before. This one just happens to be fully clothed."

Nick's face flushed pink, but he was not amused. "I don't want her sitting there all night like your plaything."

"Does she look like she's in distress?" Brian asked without looking at her.

Rion looked down at her. She did appear to be comfortable, as if she had been in that same position many times for long periods of time. He knew Kara heard every word, but the only thing that moved on her was her long eyelashes as she blinked every so often.

But Nick didn't care. "Brian—" Nick said his name with annoyance.

"Up," Brian said calmly. Kara immediately rose to her feet. "Look at me." She lifted her eyes once more to meet his. "Go downstairs to room nine and wait for me." She hesitated, and a hint of fear washed over her face. Her eyes welled with tears.

Brian lifted one eyebrow. "Don't you dare cry. Don't. You. Dare." Kara blinked them away. Instead, she gave him a slight nod.

Kara began to walk away. But Brian gently took her arm, and she turned back. He kissed her lips and said softly, "Undress, Petit. And wait."

"Yes, sir," she whispered and went in the direction of the basement steps.

"What just happened?" Rion asked in fascination.

"She disobeyed me," Brian said, watching her walk away. "So she will be punished for it."

"How?" Rion asked.

"Rion," Nick said warningly.

But the other two ignored him. "How?" Brian repeated.

"Yes. How will she be punished?"

Brian turned all the way around to face Rion. "I'm going to put her on that cross you just saw, spin it upside down, and beat her eighteen times with the whip I was holding."

"Why eighteen?"

"It's our agreed upon number."

"But why that particular number?" Rion pressed. "What's the significance?"

"It's the age she was when I first took her," said Brian.

To Rion, Kara barely looked older than eighteen. "How old is she now?"

"Same age as you," said Brian.

"Oh." He asked another question. "Why upside down?"

"I did not give her permission to come to the club tonight. So her punishment is upside down on the cross to symbolize what I will unleash on her. The sign of hell," Brian said seriously. Nick scoffed.

But Rion continued to be fascinated. "Oh. Wow. Then what?"

Brian hesitated, not sure how much he should tell him. "Then I'm going to restrain her with her knees up and spread eagle, put my hands around her throat, fuck her hard, and choke her at the same time until she has an orgasm," Brian said. "I will let her neck go for about fifteen seconds so she can catch her breath, then fuck and choke her again. Then again. And maybe one more time after that. When I'm ready, I'll cum inside of her as a thank you for disobeying me. Because that's why she came. She's possessive and a Brat. But she loves me and can't go three days without me. It's been like this for eight years."

"And that makes you happy? She makes you happy, even when she's disobedient?"

Brian smiled. "Yes. She does."

Rion smiled back. "Will you ask her for consent first?"

"I've had her consent for years. But also, she knew exactly what she was doing and the outcome. She could have said her safe-word at any point, including when I told her to go downstairs. She didn't."

"But if she did, then what?"

"Then we would stop. The scene would immediately be over, and I would send her back home in a car, and she would see me tomorrow. I would never penalize her for using her safe-word. She just wouldn't get me tonight."

"But she didn't want that," said Rion. "She needed you tonight. No matter what the consequences."

Brian smiled again. "Correct."

"Will it hurt?" Rion asked.

"Yes."

"Will she bruise?"

"Yes."

"But no blood play?"

"Never," Brian said seriously.

"Will she cry?"

"Yes."

"So why does she do it if she knows the tremendous amount of pain she will be in?"

"You would have to ask her that," Brian said in amusement.

"Can I?" Rion asked, wide-eyed.

"Can you... *What*?"

"Can I ask her? What it feels like to physically, mentally, and emotionally submit herself to you like that."

Brian raised an eyebrow, the same one he did to Kara. "You want to watch?"

It was Rion's turn to hesitate. "Not the whole thing. Maybe just the whipping. And ask questions."

"What!?" Nick said in astonishment.

But Brian said, "Yes." He turned to Nick. "Want to watch, too?"

"Fuck no," Nick said and grimaced. "I do not want to watch you beat then plow into Kara. Not my idea of a good time."

"Sounds like it might be Rion's, though," Brian said and chuckled.

"Whoa," said Rion, getting wide-eyed again. "This is strictly for research purposes. I'm not into S&M. I've been getting an idea for a new story the whole time I've been here, but I need to understand the why for it to be authentic."

Brian shrugged. "Sure." He looked at his watch. "Meet me at the entrance of room nine in thirty minutes. I need to get ready. And she needs to wait." Brian walked away.

Nick turned to Rion. "So you've officially lost it, huh?" Nick asked. "If you're trying to get closer to my brother, there are easier ways than watching him become a naked sadist."

Rion grinned. "I'll turn my head. Don't worry. I'm not interested in Brian's dick. Just his Dom skills."

Nick shook his head. "Have fun researching. I'll be right there in the men's lounge waiting for you."

An hour and a half later, Rion plopped down next to his boyfriend on the leather couch and slouched in the seat. The room was even quieter than before; only a handful of men were there. Nick looked up from a book he had borrowed from the bookshelf.

"Got what you wanted?" he asked, amused.

Rion said, "I'm gay."

Nick smiled. "Yes. I know."

"I'm very, very gay. Nongay things do not turn me on."

Nick tried not to laugh. "Buuuut?"

"I'm so pent up right now; it's fucking crazy," Rion said.

"What happened? Wait—" Nick held his hand up. "The abbreviated version."

"I didn't see much. Because your brother Brian is a fucking master. He was in full control of everything, including me. When we came in, she was kneeling on the floor naked except for her collar in front of the cross; her back turned to us. She must have been like that for at least forty minutes. Brian got her consent for me, asked her if I could stay, observe, and ask her questions, and she agreed. Then he commanded that she answer me honestly, no matter what I asked. He put a white blindfold on her and cuffed her to the cross backward, like some sacrilege shit. Then he put me in a chair in the corner, in full view, but he cuffed one of my hands and one leg to it, so I couldn't get up either.

Before he got started, I asked her how she felt. She said, 'Excited and terrified.' I asked her what was the scariest part. She didn't know if she was going to get punished with a flogger, a whip, a cane, or a swatter. It was the whip, a long leather piece like a belt with a metal tip. I saw Brian take it from the armoire, but she didn't know that. I asked her if she wanted me to tell her. She said 'no,' it would ruin it for both of them. Brian slowly turned the cross upside down and started talking to her about being a bad little patient and disobeying the Doctor's orders. It wasn't angry, but it was cold. And at the same time, he was touching her sensually, all her body parts. He stepped back, stopped talking, grabbed the whip, and just stood there. For a full minute, nothing but silence. I could sense her trepidation. Then out of nowhere: wham! She wasn't expecting it, and neither was I. Even I flinched."

"Did that excite you?" Nick asked.

"No," Rion said, shaking his head. "She screamed. Oh my God, Nick, the way she screamed. It wasn't a long, drawn-out moan like Mrs. Dunlap. It was an honest-to-God, blood-curdling scream. I was ready to beat the shit out of him for her. And I think that's why he cuffed me, because he knew I was either going to stop it or walk away. But then she yelled out, 'Eighteen!' He did it again. She screamed, then yelled, 'Seventeen.' Each one she counted down. It made me even more curious about her. She started crying at eleven, her blindfold getting wet. That's when I asked her, 'How does it feel?' She screamed at me, 'It hurts.' So I asked her, 'Then why?' And she said, 'Because the pain makes me feel alive.' I was stunned. By the time he finished, she was shaking and had red welts everywhere from her shoulders down to her thighs. But she didn't bleed. He knew not to hit the same place more than twice. Then he started touching her sensually again, talking to her softly as he turned her right side up. I couldn't hear what he said, but it soothed her.

"I asked her, 'What made you disobey him, knowing this was going to be the outcome, the blinding pain before the soothing pleasure?' Kara said, 'I was already in pain. My heart was hurting. I was at home crying and shaking because he refused to come to me tonight. I needed The Doctor.' Stunned, Nick. I was stunned. But I got it. I understood her. Then he comes over to me with a black blindfold and says, all commandingly, 'That's enough. You will lose your sight now. And you will stay quiet for a while.' Brian didn't ask; he told me what was going to happen. And you know what? I fucking submitted, too," Rion said with a grin. Nick laughed.

"I didn't see anything after that. But I heard them. Heard him bring her down and cuff her metal links to the metal bedposts. Heard and smelled their sex, her choking, heaving, gasping for air, her moaning, every time she had an orgasm. I heard him, too, grunting, thrusting. Even his growl when he came." Rion turned to Nick and said, "I'm still gay. But he sounds like you."

Nick smiled. "Did that turn you on?"

Rion groaned. "I couldn't help it. I kept visualizing it was you and me, even though we've never done anything like that before. She came hard five times before he came. Five. He told her so sweetly that she's the best thing in his life, the one thing that makes him happy, a couple of other things while he was choking her. At the end, she was sobbing. I asked her again, 'How do you feel now?' She said, 'Loved. Protected. Wanted. I die when he's not around. The Doctor brings me back to life. I am alive again when we're together like this.' I'm going to use that line somewhere."

Rion sighed. "The soft touch, hard pain, hard pain, soft touch, it all makes her feel alive. The needing, the yearning, the pain, the pleasure, I understood it. I'm definitely not a masochist like she is. Because of the shit I've been through growing up, I don't confuse pain and pleasure. But I empathize with needing someone that deeply to take all of you, make you a complete puddle of mud on the floor, and then mold you back together for their own will. It was how I felt about you in London. Especially when you came back for me. That's why I dropped to my knees so fast, why I literally spread my cheeks for you. That wanting, needing, yearning for you after being apart for seven days. You could have split me in two, and I would have died happy."

Nick felt his own cock stiffen at Rion's words, remembering that day just as vividly. Rion continued.

"Brian never took the blindfold off me. He simply walked over to me, uncuffed me, and said, 'You're done now,' opened the door, and pushed me out, leaving me in the hallway. I took it off myself. I peeked into a few other rooms, but I knew I needed to get back to you, and fast."

Nick's hand moved to Rion's stiff cock in a room of other men. If others noticed, they made no mention of it. It was painfully unyieldingly hard. "Let's go upstairs," said Nick. Before Rion could protest, Nick stood up and grabbed his arm, making him stand, too.

"Wait, Nick," Rion said, allowing himself to be dragged through the wooden doors. "I am many things, but I am not an exhibitionist."

"We'll keep the door closed," Nick reassured him. "But just like we were listening, others will be listening to us. You okay with that?"

Rion smiled. "Yeah."

Nick took Rion up the stairs and went to the first door they saw that it was slightly open. Nick pushed the door open, and there was a couple already there.

"Hey, Nicholas," Todd said, getting off the bed in his underwear. He looked at Rion and said, "I respect your preference, but I'm sorry, this isn't that type of room."

"I don't want to fuck you, Todd," Nick said in disgust. "Get out."

The man paused. "We're just getting started."

"Go sexually assault her somewhere else," Nick said seriously. "I need the room."

"I had the room first," Todd whined.

"You left the door open," Nick countered. "Next time, follow the rules and close the door all the way."

"C'mon, man—" Todd began.

Nick stepped up to the man's face and said, "Need I remind you who I am?" Nicholas said coldly.

Todd looked up in fear. He answered, "No, Mr. Highton."

"Good. Now get out." Nick turned to the woman. "You too, sweetheart. I'm not fucking you, either."

She immediately got out of the bed in her lingerie. Todd picked up his clothes from the couch and followed her right out the door. Nick slammed the door shut. Then he turned around and began to unbuckle his trousers.

Rion's mouth was slightly open. He had never heard Nick talk to another person like that. "That was sexy as fuck, Nick. I mean Mr. Highton." He bowed playfully.

"Less talking, more sucking," Nick said as he kicked off his pants.

Rion obliged and dropped to his knees like Kara did, albeit nowhere near as graceful, putting his hands in his lap and waiting for Nick's command, grinning. Nick walked up to him, still in his shirt, tie, and suit jacket, and Rion took him down his throat.

Nick moaned incredibly and unusually loudly. "You're so fucking good at this, Mr. Ryder. Keep sucking that cock."

Rion came off and laughed. "Really?" he whispered.

"Why not?" Nick said with a shrug. "Let's give them a show."

Rion resumed sucking on Nick. Nick continued to moan and talk loudly. But then he stepped back and moved over to the couch. "Take off your fucking clothes," he said in a commanding tone. "Just the clothes."

Rion giggled, but he began to strip, leaving the mask on. Nick took off his suit jacket and tie but left his white Christian Dior shirt on, unbuttoned. He sat on the couch and waited for Rion to finish taking off all his clothes.

Nick was watching him. He said quietly, "You do look really sexy in that mask, Ree."

Rion got on top of Nick, kissing his neck and torso. "I'm Ryan D. Ryder tonight." He reached behind him, putting Nick's cock between his cheeks, moving back and forth. They kissed hungrily, moaning loudly.

Then Nick stood up with Rion, turned around and flopped him back onto the couch. He turned Rion around on all fours, prepared him, and entered him. Rion moaned loudly. "Yes, Mr. Highton," he called out. "Fuck me hard."

"Jesus, Ree," Nick whispered in his ear. "You're really getting into this, too."

He began to thrust hard into Rion, his thighs hitting Rion's bottom with a loud slapping sound. He kept going, hard and fast, making the slap sound echo in the room. Rion found himself moaning loudly. Nick paused to catch his breath, but Rion kept moving, pushing backward, impaling himself. So Nick held his position and let Rion do all the work.

"I'm cumming," Nicky groaned eventually.

"Breed me, Mr. Highton," Rion yelled. Nick growled, held onto his waist, and came deep inside Rion. "I feel it! I feel you cumming!" Rion screamed out.

Nick groaned again as he emptied out. But he was still hard, and the fantasy was not over. He pushed Rion flat down and began to pump into him again. Rion hollered as his cock was pressed into the couch, as Nick called Rion obscene things, yanked his hair, and drilled into him.

"I'm cumming! I'm cumming! I'm cumming!" Rion hollered.

Rion squeezed his cheeks as he came, feeling the wetness between his abs and the softness of the couch.

"Fuuuck," Nick roared as he came a second time. He collapsed on Rion's back.

They both were breathing erratically. Rion started laughing first. "That was some hot shit."

"And I didn't even have to choke you for it," Nick teased. Rion laughed again.

They slowly found their clothes and got dressed. As Nick predicted, once he opened the door, there were a few people in the hallway. They clapped as Nick and Rion stepped out. Rion was thankful for the mask and shyly took Nick's hand. Nick smiled and led him down the stairs and back to the main parlor. There was no one there; everyone in attendance had found a playroom or was in one of the sitting rooms for the night.

Nick walked over to the bartender. "Tell my brother I went home."

"Will do, Mr. Highton," Axel said, his eyes still smoldering for Nick.

They stepped out, and their car was waiting for them, parked right where they left it in the circular driveway. Nick tapped on the glass, waking up his driver, who immediately hopped out and opened the door for them both. As they began to drive back to the city, Rion stretched over and put his head in Nick's lap.

Rion sighed with his eyes closed. "This was fun. Let's never go back there again," he said sleepily.

Nick responded with a smile. He ran his hand through Rion's hair all the way home, knowing that his boyfriend would be asleep within moments.

*R*ion thought he was dreaming, the sound of the buzzing so far away. Then it stopped. He was about to fall weightlessly back into sleep when he felt Nicholas tap his leg.

"Rion, wake up," he said with urgency. "Gabby is on the phone, and she's hysterical."

Rion snapped his eyes open and sat up, reaching out into the darkness to grab it. Nick put Rion's cell in his hand. "What's wrong?" Rion said.

"Oh, Ree!" she wailed. "I can't do this on my own. I need help!"

"Help with what? What's wrong!?"

"Ava's gone, and now Mama's gone missing too, and—"

"What do you mean Ava's gone!?" Rion yelled. Nick gently touched his shoulder.

"Oh, Ree," Gabby said again. "Remember Sunday when you said Ava hasn't been in group chat in a few days? That got me thinking. I hadn't heard from her either. When I asked Muriel, she said that Ava was with her boyfriend, that new guy. Remember, she mentioned a Cedrick? But even if she's with some guy, she always checks in with me. She hadn't checked in with me in three days. So I started blowing up her phone, no answer. I went to Muriel first, and she brushed me off, saying Ava was fine and will come back. Mama was the only one that seemed concerned. She said to me not to worry, she'll find her. But that was two days ago, and I can't find Mama either! So now Ava's been missing for almost a week, and Mama's been missing for two days, and either something really, really bad happened to both of them or…"

"Or they're both using," Rion finished for her. He had already gotten out of bed and begun putting clothes on as Gabby was explaining. "Why did you go to Roslyn? You know she can't handle these kinds of things. She folds under pressure, Gabby!"

"Because Muriel wouldn't listen to me!"

"Why didn't you tell me!?" Rion yelled back. "I would have listened. I would have been there already."

"Rion, I didn't want to get you involved unless I absolutely needed to. But there is only so much I can do, so many places I can go with a seven-year-old in my backseat." She paused and said, "I want to go see the 781, but I can't take Morgan with me."

He scoffed. "You better not go anywhere near there!"

"They won't harm me. They—"

"I don't give a shit!" Rion yelled. "You don't go anywhere near there!" Rion put the phone to his ear and walked to the closet. "I'm coming, Gabbs. Don't do anything stupid. I'm coming."

"I'm so sorry," Gabby cried. "I didn't want to pull you back into our shit, but I didn't know who else to turn to. I left a message for Maurese, too."

"I'm coming," Rion said again. "I'll call you back with the flight information. Stay put." He hung up before she could speak.

Rion started pulling clothes out of the drawer and off the rack. "Rion," Nick called his name gently. "Rion, what are you—"

"FUCK!" Rion screamed. He reached for his orange bag at the top of the closet, and other items fell on top of him. "Fuck, fuck, fuuuuck!"

Nick stood in the doorway of the closet. "What can I do? How can I help?"

"Nothing," Rion mumbled. "I gotta go. I'll come back for my stuff in a few months when everything is settled."

"Wait... *what*!?"

Nick walked over to Rion and grabbed his arm to whirl him around. "Talk to me, Ree. I heard some of the conversation. Your sister and your mother are missing, right?"

Rion looked at him. "Yes. And I need to go find them."

"Did she file a missing person's report?"

"No. That would be pointless."

"How would that be pointless? The manpower alone is—"

"We live in different worlds, Nick," Rion said, cutting him off. "The San Francisco police department is going to take one look at both of their records and ignore the shit out of Gabby. Roslyn's a prostitute and an addict, and Ava's record consists of everything from arson to assault and battery of a police officer. They aren't going to help."

"You don't know that for sure—"

"Are you fucking deaf!?" Rion snapped at his boyfriend. "I do know that because I've tried that. I've been here before. And it's been me finding Ava high and squatting in some abandoned house, me finding Roslyn coked up and turning tricks on the street, me cleaning them up and putting them back together. Me!"

Rion pulled his arm from Nick's grasp. "I told you last year, you don't want to get involved with someone like me. And now you see why." Rion started stuffing underwear and t-shirts into his bag.

Nick had to admit, he was a little stunned. And frightened. "Okay, you have to go. I get it. But why does this mean that you'll get your stuff later? Like you're never coming back?"

Rion didn't look at him as he continued to pack, walking to the bathroom and grabbing toiletries. "I have to be there, Nick," he said. "Once I find Ava, she's going to cling to me. I have to be there for however long she needs me until she can stand on her own again. She's going to need rehab. Counseling. A place to stay. It may take a few months. It may take a year. I don't know. I just know I need to find my sister and bring her back to us."

Nick decided right on the spot. "Then I'm going with you."

"What? No," Rion said abruptly. "Besides the fact that it's a stupid idea, you just launched the new site three months ago, and you have to be in the office to troubleshoot issues. You have to be here for your team."

Rion tried to walk past Nick, but Nick stood in front of him. "I need to be there for you. Let me be there for you the way you are there for everyone else, including me."

"I can take care of myself, Nicholas," Rion said with an attitude.

"I know you can." Nick touched his shoulder. "But it's okay to reach out for help, too, just like Gabby did tonight. Listen, I'm going to book the flights right now, and we're on it together. And we'll find your sister. And your mother. And then see what the next steps are. But we don't have to end our entire relationship because you're in crisis. I'm here to help you through it. Okay?"

Rion wanted to run away from this, run from Nick. He didn't want to introduce Nick to the dark side of his world. But fear gripped his chest again, knowing his sister had been out there for days. He knew he had to go, and he knew Nick would follow him, so he let it happen.

"You don't know what you're getting yourself into, Nick." He sighed. "But okay. Book the tickets. One way."

Nick understood. He went to his phone and called Zoey while he started pulling clothes out of the closet, too.

She answered on the second ring, groggily. "What do you need, Boss?"

"I need two one-way tickets to San Francisco, the next flight out, and a car waiting to take us to the airport in the next hour. Rion has a family crisis."

"On it," Zoey said more clearly than she had spoken before and hung up.

Nick grabbed a duffle bag and began to add in clothes. He left a voicemail for Mrs. Anne and Marcel, letting them both know he was out of the office for a few days due to a family emergency and that he'd call when he got to California.

Zoey called him back seventeen minutes later. "Alaska Air, flight 1328 non-stop from JFK to San Francisco. There will be a car service waiting on the ground for you there. Total flight time is six hours and seven minutes. It leaves at 7:30 a.m., so if you don't have any checked luggage, you'll make it. I've already checked you both in. The car will be at the building in nine minutes. I've sent everything to your email."

"Thank you, Zoey. Check your account later on today."

"You don't have to do that, Nick. Just let me know that everything is alright with Rion and his family, okay?"

Nick realized Zoey sounded worried. "Gabby and Morgan are fine, by the way."

"Oh, thank God!" Zoey let out a sigh of relief.

"I'll message you when we land. Thanks again."

Nick left the room and went to go find Rion. Rion was standing in front of the glass window, looking out into the early morning darkness. He was fully dressed with his orange bookbag on his back, his computer strap stretched across his chest, and his hands in the center pocket of his hoodie.

"Ree?"

Rion didn't turn around as he started talking. "I should have never gotten on a plane last December. This would have never happened if I didn't leave," he said softly, more to himself than Nick. Rion was kicking himself for not checking in with Ava earlier, or finding out more about this boyfriend of hers.

But Nick heard Rion's comment differently, and it stung. "It's all arranged. Car service will be here in eight minutes."

Nick grabbed his duffle bag and his own laptop and headed to the front door.

It was raining on the way to JFK, but they made it there a little after 5 a.m. and to their terminal by 5:45 a.m. Zoey had booked first class seats, the only ones that were available, so they could get off the plane quicker than everyone else.

The flight attendant came by and offered them soft blankets and actual headphones. Rion wanted to be impressed; it was his first time in first class. But his mind was clouded, and a pit formed in his stomach. He knew his sister was out there in a dangerous and helpless situation, and he couldn't help blaming himself for it.

As the plan began to move, Rion said, "It's the first time I've been on a plane since I came to New York. I was nervous for so many reasons back then. And now I'm going back, nervous for different reasons. But at least it wasn't a fucking storm outside."

"Well, you got me here with you this time," said Nicholas.

Rion did not respond. He counted backward from fifty, taking slow deep breaths. Nick silently reached over and took his hand. The takeoff went into the air bumpier than both of them would have liked. Rion squeezed his eyes and Nick's hand until the plane was leveled in the air. But the aircraft did not stop being bumpy, which did not help Rion's anxiety. He kept reaching for the armrest, the window, and the headrest in front of him to stabilize himself. His heart was beating faster, and he felt a panic attack coming on.

"I hate this shit, I hate this, I hate this shit..." he repeated.

"Relax, Rion," said Nick, squeezing his hand.

"I forgot to take a gummy this morning. I'm so fucking stupid."

"Rion, it's going to be okay."

"It's just my luck that we're flying in the middle of a storm," Rion bemoaned.

"It's just a little—" Nick started, but the plane jerked with enough turbulence that it made his body jolt too. Rion yelped and threw his arms out sideways. Nick caught one and squeezed it again. "It's just a little rain and clouds," Nick said, trying to be confident for Rion.

"Well, it doesn't feel like it," Rion grumbled.

"Talk to me," Nick demanded. "Tell me about your new story."

"I don't wanna," he whined as the plane dipped again. He was near tears with how badly he wanted to get off the plane, and they were only ten minutes into their six-hour ride.

"C'mon. It's fresh in your mind," Nick said. "And you've been writing it non-stop for months. It has to be near completion now."

"I'm done," said Rion, opening his eyes. "Just proofreading now."

"When is it due?" Nick asked as the plane shook again.

"Ah!" Rion yelped.

"When is it due?" Nick asked again.

"It's... it's not. I haven't pitched it to my publishers yet." Rion looked around and noticed he was getting the attention of other passengers, which made him even more nervous.

Nick turned Rion's chin back to him. "What's it about?" Nick asked, still trying to occupy Rion's mind. "Erotic romance or fun eroticism like your last story?"

"It's not a love story," said Rion. "It's actually kind of tragic and beautiful. It's about two men, best friends who love each other and secretly slept together since they were roommates in college. But one is a narcissist and continues to drag the other along. He's rich and arrogant, and keeps their relationship a secret while he—" The plane jerked and Rion flinched.

"Go on," Nick encouraged him.

"While he dates women publicly," Rion continued. "And any relationship that the other is in, he immediately sabotages because he wants his lover all to himself. But he also wants to continue to date who he wants. He'll never commit to anyone, especially not his best friend. The one he really loves."

"That doesn't sound like love," Nick said, shaking his head. "It sounds like possession."

"Exactly," Rion said, getting into the story, not noticing the small shaking of the plane. "It's not love. And Travis realizes that. He's spent the last ten years of his life pining for something that will never really be. So he decides to take a job in Europe, and Dean freaks out. Dean does everything in his power to make him stay: he manipulates, he threatens, he tries to sabotage his career, and eventually, he cries and begs. But all it does is show Travis that this is not love. And he walks away."

"Wow. It sounds ... intense."

"It is." Rion nodded. "It's heart-rending, and it's going to hurt. Like I said, it's not a love story. It's about self-preservation and walking away from toxicity."

"Then it is about love," said Nick. Rion looked at him curiously. "Self-love. Learning to love yourself and want better for yourself than to be someone's plaything. Valuing yourself to know you deserve more than the scraps you're given." Nick thought about him walking away from his mother earlier in the year, knowing he deserved better for his life than to be an object she could move around. "It is a love story."

"Wow," Rion said. "I didn't think about it like that, but you're right. You're absolutely right."

A soft chime went off, and they both looked up. The seatbelt light had turned off, and they realized the turbulence had stopped. Nick squeezed Rion's thigh. Rion looked back at him, noticing they were now smoothly traveling above the gray clouds.

"I love you, Nicholas," Rion said. "Thank you for that."

"Anytime, Ree," Nick said back. "And I love you, too."

They looked at each other and Rion smiled at him, his first smile of the day. Then they both looked up as the flight attendant offered mimosas.

As soon as they crossed the last exit, Gabby ran up to Rion and fell into his arms, sobbing. Rion patted her back. "We'll find her, okay?" he said soothingly.

"Both of them?" Gabby bemoaned.

Rion swallowed. "I'm more concerned about Ava. What's Rel saying?"

"Rel went to work," Gabby said as she let her brother go and wiped her eyes. She hugged Nick hello and said, "She said she can't do it this time. I don't even know what that means!" She sniffed angrily. "But Maurese called me back, and he's on his way here from Stockton. He's driving."

"Okay. Let's go. We're going to the diner first to get Muriel and find out what she knows. Where did you park?"

Nick interrupted, feeling like an outsider. "Zoey ordered car service. It should be right... ah..." He looked around for the woman holding up the sign with his name on it. "There."

Both Rion and Gabby stared at him. "I'm not getting in a fancy car, Nick. Gabby's Honda will do just fine. I'm sure she drove to the airport."

"Oh, right, I wasn't thinking... I'll cancel it." Nick walked over to the chauffeur.

When Nick was a good distance away, Gabby slapped his arm. "Why are you pushing him away?"

"I'm not pushing him away—"

"Yes, you are. Stop it!" she yelled in a whisper. "He got you here in record time, and he's here to help. Let him help."

"Other than that awful flight, I don't need his help," Rion said dismissively. "I want to park him at Muriel's house and find my sister. He has no idea what he's getting himself into."

"We need all the help we can get," said Gabby. "Nick's money and influence can go a long way. We might need a car not connected to any of us if we go into 781 territory. So stop being a dick to your boy-friend and let him help." She touched her brother's shoulders. "Do not push him away, Rion. Don't do it."

Rion didn't respond as Nick came back to them. "Okay, I canceled the car service. But if we need another one, or if we just need a rental, we can call them back. I have his card and it's attached to my credit card. So where to? Muriel's job, you said? Because we need to talk to her first, since she was the last person to see Ava."

Rion stared at him. "Yeah. Muriel's job." He turned to his sister and said again, "Let's go."

"God *dammit*, Ree!" Muriel said loudly.

Rion had not seen his sister in person since last Christmas. He wanted her to be happy he was there, but she frowned upon seeing him walk into her diner as she was servicing a customer at the counter.

She walked over to her brother and said, "You are not supposed to be here!" She wrapped her arms around him, and he hugged her back tightly. "You were free from all of this. You were enjoying your life with—" She glanced over at Nick. "This fucking gorgeous specimen of a man."

Muriel let Rion go and hit Nick's chest hard. "Why the fuck did you bring him here!?"

Nick looked at the beautiful, tall, brown-skinned woman in astonishment. "Bring him? Have you met your brother!?" he said sarcastically. "I had to grab the bottom of his shirt to hold on as he ran out the door!"

Muriel wrapped her arms around Nick in response. He hugged her back. "It's good to meet you, too, Muriel. In the flesh."

Muriel stepped back and looked at her brother. "I can't do it." She began to walk away.

"Can we just talk?" Rion called out to her.

"You want a table?" she said instead. "I know you haven't eaten a thing since Gabby called you last night."

"I'll eat if you sit down and talk to us," Rion bargained.

"Table five in the corner," she replied, waving her hand in the direction. The three of them sat down and Muriel went to the back.

Gabby was tapping her fingers on the table. "I took a couple of days off, but I have to get Morgan in two hours."

"I can pick her up," said Nick. "And take her back to your home. Just give me the address and let the school know my info." They both looked at him. "I need you both to stop looking at me like I'm some foreign alien," Nick said with an attitude. "Let me help." Then he relented. "Please."

Gabby reached out for his hand. "Thank you, Nick. You've been awesome so far and we're so grateful for you."

Rion leaned over and kissed Nick's lips. "I know I'm not acting like it, but I am glad you're here with me. Thank you."

Before Nick could respond, Muriel came over and put three egg and sausage bagels on the table and glasses of water and slid into the booth next to Gabby.

"Eat. All of you," she commanded. None of them touched the food.

"Rel," Rion started.

"I can't, Ree," Muriel said, shaking her head. "Not this time. I have a lot going on, and I need to focus on my children. The school year just started, and I don't like the company Reese hangs out with. He's already been suspended once. They raised the rent on the house, so I'm working more hours and can't watch him all the time. I want to ask my dad to take him back to Stockton for a while; that's how worried I am. And Jeffery is getting bullied in school, so I'm in talks with the principal. And Kate is shutting down, doing the non-talking thing she does when I'm yelling too much. So I'm back in therapy too, so I don't fall apart."

"Why didn't you tell me any of this, Muriel?" Rion said angrily.

"Because, like I said, Rion, you're not supposed to be here. You're not supposed to get sucked back into all this drama. Not mine, not Gabby's, and absolutely not Ava's. You don't belong here anymore."

"What do you mean by that?" said Rion, hurt by her words. "This is my family. I could never just walk away. If I had been here, I could have helped! I could have sent you extra money for the rent. I could have watched Reese after school for you. I could have—"

"Baby bro, you've been taking care of us for too long." His oldest sister reached out and touched his hand. "I don't need your help. I told you I'm in therapy, I'm at the schools, and my dad is supporting me financially. I'm getting by just fine. And so is Gabby. We don't need you to step in when things get rough anymore. We're all managing our shit without you."

"Well, Ava needs me," said Rion stubbornly. "And if you won't help—"

"Ava is fine," Muriel said dismissively. "She's going to turn up after her binge like she always does."

"And what if she doesn't, Rel?" Gabby said it with fresh tears. "We don't know anything about this Cedrick. What if this time she doesn't?"

Muriel's face displayed a brief moment of concern. Then she said, "I know someone that does know him. I'll tell you what I know."

She looked at Rion. "Cedrick works at Sunrise Trust. That's where she met him. I don't know which branch, though. You'll have to go to Jay and ask questions."

Fuck, he thought. But to her, he said, "Okay."

She turned to Gabby. "Ava has been using again for a while. Nothing hard, but popping pills, yes. And she's been hanging out in Fresno. She said she's not hanging with the 781, but why else would she be there?"

"I knew it. I have to go see Felipe," said Gabby.

"Not by yourself, you're not," Rion said sternly. "Wait for Maurese. Or me. Or both of us."

"Excuse me?" Nick interjected. They looked at him. "Sunrise Trust as in Sunrise Trust Loan and Savings? If this Cedrick guy worked there, I can use Zoey to get a full name and address. I will need to know the branch, though. I'm not sure how many Cedricks there are working for them in the entire state of California."

"That would be amazing," Gabby said happily.

"Okay," Rion said. "We can get that info today."

"And 781? What is that, a meeting house of some sort?" Nick asked. "Because I can—"

"It's a gang," Muriel said. "And a dangerous one."

"Oh." Nick was worried, but tried not to let it show on his face.

"They'll never harm us," Rion said to him. "We're family. Roslyn is like royalty to them, and Gabby is untouchable. Her father, Gabriel Hernandez, was one of the founding members and ran it for many years before he died."

Nick stared at him. "I'm assuming not of old age."

"He was shot and killed by police, holding them off so his crew could escape capture," explained Rion. "He's a martyr to them, and Gabby is his only daughter."

"Got it. So when do we go see them?" Nick said confidently.

Muriel raised an eyebrow. "Rion said they'll never harm *us*. They are going to smell you coming a mile away, Richy-Rich."

"I can dress down. I can fit in." Nick turned to his boyfriend. "You aren't going there without me."

Rion gave him a once over. "We'll see." He turned back to Gabby. "I'll head to the bank before it closes. You go get Morgan. Then—"

Gabby's phone rang, startling all four. She quickly grabbed it and answered. "Maurese? Yes, we're at the diner with Muriel... Okay... Okay, we'll meet you at the apartment... No, we haven't heard from her either... Okay... Okay, thanks."

She hung up. "He's here. He's at Mama's apartment. He said don't do anything without him."

And Nick realized. "Hey, all this time, you've been talking about Ava being missing. What about Roslyn?"

Rion rolled his eyes. Muriel said, "Roslyn is probably using Ava's disappearance as an excuse to get high right now."

"That's not true," Gabby implored. "She was really worried."

Rion stood up. "I'm here to find my sister. If we find Roslyn smoked out and tricked up along the way, that's a bonus." He turned to Nick. "Let's go."

Muriel pushed the plate to him. "Sit down and eat first."

Rion shook his head. "Rel, we gotta—"

She pulled out a car key from her pocket. "I had a feeling you would hop on a plane. So just in case you did, I have BlueBird. You want your baby back? Eat."

Rion stared at her, then plopped back down. He lifted one bagel and took a bite. Muriel turned to Nick. "You too, Mr. Deep Strokez. Eat." Nick gave her a small smile and grabbed the other one. Gabby grabbed the last one.

Satisfied that her siblings were eating, she went to go check on her tables. Rion ate fast and drank half the water, so by the time she came back, his plate was empty. He held his hand out. "She's good?"

Muriel handed him the key. "Still purring, waiting for you."

He stood up again and they hugged tightly. "I'll come see the kids and have a talk with Reese."

"Let his grandfather do that," Muriel said. "You do what you came to do and get back to your life in New York City."

Nick came out of the booth and also gave her a hug. "Again, I'm so glad to finally meet you, albeit under terrible circumstances."

"Me too. But get him out of here, Nick," she said out loud for her brother to hear. "He doesn't belong here anymore. He belongs with you."

Rion rolled his eyes and pulled Nick's arm. "Come on." He turned to his other sister. "Gabby, meet me at Mama's after you pick up Morgan."

"And bring Morgan to my house," Muriel said. "I'm not running the streets looking for either of them, but I can keep Morgan safe and occupied while you four do."

Gabby hugged her sister tightly. "Thank you."

Rion and Nick walked into the parking lot together. Rion beeped the car, and they followed the noise to a cerulean blue Jeep Wrangler Rubicon. The back of the jeep was covered in stickers with words like "Saving the Planet" to "Being Gay Sucks Dick," the marriage equality "equal" sign, lots of rainbow stickers, and one long sticker that said, "If you're going to ride my ass, at least buy me dinner first." Nick was about to chuckle at his labels when he noticed the car was missing some very important items.

"There're no doors," Nick said as Rion hopped in and started the ignition. "And no windows. And no top. It's just a shell."

Rion smiled. He had driven Nick's cars here and there, but he missed his BlueBird. "Get in or go babysit for Gabby," said Rion, pulling the seatbelt across himself. Nick reluctantly slid into the bucket seat and strapped his seatbelt. Then pulled it twice to make sure it was secure.

"Hold on," Rion told him but didn't give him enough warning before he stepped on the gas and streaked out of the parking lot. Nick's body jerked back, then forward, as Rion turned onto the highway heading west.

Rion weaved in and out of traffic, his curls and Nick's blond hair blowing in the wind, making his BlueBird fly. Nick held onto the skeletal car and didn't look over to his right at all. Rion tapped the glove compartment in front of Nick and it slowly opened. He grabbed a pair of sunglasses and put them on, then grabbed another pair and handed them to Nick without looking at him. Nick put on the shades and sat back.

"I hate why we're here," Rion said loudly above the sounds of the road, "But I sure did miss my BlueBird and this California sun."

Nick smiled at him. "Once we find Ava, maybe we could soak up a west coast tan."

Rion's smile faded. Nick reached out and patted Rion's thigh. "We're going to find her, Ree. We will." Rion's only response was a sigh.

Rion pulled into a bank parking lot and backed into a spot near the front. He sat there for a moment. Nick was about to ask what was up when he turned to him and said, "My ex is in there."

"Who? Jason?"

"Yeah. That's Jay. Jay is Jason," Rion confirmed. "He works there as a branch manager, but he rotates through three other branches. I haven't seen him since..."

"Oh." Nick let a moment pass, then said, "So are all your feelings rushing back—"

"Fuck no," Rion said with a grimace. He leaned over and put his tongue in Nick's mouth. Nick slowly reached his hand up and into Rion's hair, kissing him back.

Rion pulled back first. "I'm just letting you know. It's going to be awkward as fuck." Rion unhooked his seatbelt and stepped out, saying, "You don't have to come in."

"I'm definitely coming in. I'll just hang in the background." Nick stepped out of the car.

It was a standard bank with tellers on one side and desks in small cubicles lined up on the other side. Rion went to the sign-in desk and asked, "Is Jason Williams available?"

"I'll send a message and see if he is. What is this pertaining to?"

"A bank matter," Rion simply said.

"Please sign in." The woman picked up the phone and spoke into it as Rion did what she asked. She relayed the message and told them that he would be right out.

Nick took a couple of steps away from him. Rion looked at him curiously. "Just pretend I'm not here," he said, amused. "I want to see this reunion from the outside."

"Jesus, Nicky," Rion murmured as a man stepped out from the glass doors in the rear and began to walk over to him.

Jason was not as tall as Nick, not a centimeter over 5'10", but his presence was commanding in his charcoal gray suit and crisp white shirt. Nick was aware of how handsome he was with golden-brown skin, a faded haircut, and a surprised smile on his full lips.

Rion tried not to smile, but Jay's smile was infectious. Jason walked right up to him and gave him a professional handshake, but squeezed his hand tightly.

"Rion. It's been a whole year since I last laid eyes on you. I heard you moved."

"I did," Rion confirmed. "I live in New York now. It's good to see you, Jay."

"You look really great, Rion. Not as much color, but a lot of light in your eyes, like you aren't stoned at all."

Rion's smile faded. "I'm not." Nick frowned, too.

"Finally left that holistic shit alone and took my advice, huh? Got you some good ol' fashion therapy? Real medication for your trauma?"

"No," Rion said stonily. "I've just been happier since I left."

"Good," Jay said. "Whatever you're doing, it's working for you. You look amazing."

"And you look ... the same."

"I'm going to take that as a compliment," Jay said with another smile.

Rion sighed, then said, "Is there somewhere we can talk?"

"I was going to head out for a smoke break if you're okay talking outside."

"Yeah, that works. That might be better for the conversation I need to have."

"That sounds serious," said Jay as he began walking toward the front doors. "What's going on?"

But Rion didn't respond. He followed Jason out, and Nick walked out behind them. Jason politely opened the door for both of them but was startled when Nick stood there on the sidewalk. He looked at Nicholas curiously, then at Rion.

He pointed at Nick and asked, "Who's this?"

Nick began to respond, "I'm—"

But Rion cut him off. "That's not important right now. Ava is missing."

That immediately got Jason's attention. "What!? When!? I saw her last week."

"She was with one of your tellers? Cedrick?"

"Yeah," Jason confirmed. "She's been hanging around at the end of his shift, and they leave together. Not this location, though."

"What's his full name?" Nick interjected.

Jason looked at Nick. "Cedrick West. Why?"

"What location is he stationed at?" Rion asked.

Jason turned back to Rion. "The one on Fifth and Locust," he said. "I'm there on Tuesdays and Thursdays now. I just saw her last Thursday over there."

"Well, she's been missing since last Thursday, according to Gabby. That's the last time anyone heard from her. It's been six days. Was he at work yesterday?"

Jason was thoughtful. "No, he wasn't. I think he was one of the call-outs, but I would have to check with Lynne, the scheduler for that location."

"Okay, find out the last time anyone saw him for me. And if you can get an address for me, that would be great."

Jason opened his mouth, then closed it and frowned. "Why do you want his address?"

"Because I need to find him. He's the last person to have seen her. If he's missing, too, then they're together, but if not..."

Jason's frown deepened. "I'm not going to give you his address so you can kick the shit out of him for information, Ree."

Rion stepped closer in anger. "I'm going to find him anyway, Jay. And if he corrupted my sister and left her in a ditch somewhere—"

"He's a good kid," said Jason. "He's a good kid and comes from a good home. If anyone corrupted the other, we know it's her."

"Lemme guess," Rion said with his hand on his chin in a faux manner. "He's a clean-cut, rich white boy from the good side of town that occasionally smokes weed and has a fetish for Asian girls. Did I get that right?"

"That's not fair," Jay defended. "I'm just saying if something went down, it's not on him. You know how your sister can get. She's not unlike Roslyn in a lot of ways."

Rion nodded. "Good to know how you feel about my sister and my mother, who is also missing, by the way."

"I haven't said anything that you haven't said about Ros and Ava yourself," said Jay defensively.

"They're my family, Jay!" Rion yelled. "I can say the things I say because they're *my* family. You say the things you say because you're a judgmental asshole."

"Oh, here we go," Jay said, rolling his eyes. "I'm the bad guy because I'm speaking the truth. I heard all this before."

"Well, you don't have to hear it again," Rion said simply. "Thanks for the info."

He began to turn around when Jason reached out for his arm. "Wait. Talk to me a bit. I haven't seen you since I left your house that day. Are you good?"

Rion slowly slid his arm from Jason's grasp. "I'm good. In fact, before I got the news that Ava was missing, everything in my life was going great. So it's really important to me that I find her and make sure she is okay. I need to get back to my life there," Rion said without looking at Nick.

"Yeah, yeah, I get that. I just want to know ... are you really happy? Happier now than with me?"

Rion could see the pain in Jason's eyes, and it immediately made him regret coming to see him. "Yeah," he said softly. "I'm happy."

Jason nodded. "Okay. Then I'm happy for you," he said unconvincingly.

"I gotta go," Rion responded.

He walked away from Jay and stood before Nick. He stared at his boyfriend apologetically. Nick gave him a small smile. He glanced at Jason, who figured out that Nick was more than just a friend helping out, before looking at Rion again.

"Let's go, Ree," he said, pulling him closer with one arm around his waist.

Rion grabbed Nicholas's hand and walked toward his car. Neither of them glanced back at Rion's ex-boyfriend.

y the time they made it to a small four-story apartment building in Golden Gate Heights, Zoey had already called back with all the information for Cedrick Damien West: a thirty-year-old full-time teller at Sunrise Trust Savings and Loan, part-time DJ and MC host, who lived in a house with four other young adults. Rion immediately turned the car around and went to the address.

As Rion rang the doorbell, Nick asked, "So, what's the play here? Are we going to ask him nicely, or are you really planning to kick the shit out of him for answers?"

"We'll see," Rion said. He rang the bell again, then knocked loudly.

The door opened, and a college-aged-looking guy stood before them, eyes bloodshot. "Sup?" he said casually.

"Is Cedrick here?" Rion asked.

"Yeah." He began to turn inside and yell, "Yo, Ced, there's—" But Rion pushed the young man out of the way. "Yo, what the fuck?" the man drawled out again.

Rion walked through the living room as another man was coming down the stairs. He looked at Rion curiously. "Who are you?"

"I'm Ava's brother," Rion said.

Cedrick's eyes went wide, and he began to run up the stairs. Rion immediately gave chase.

"Rion!" Nick yelled, and ran after them.

Rion caught Cedrick on the second-floor landing and pushed him to the ground. He grabbed Cedrick by his shirt and lifted his fist. "You got one chance to tell me what happened to my sister, or I'm going to beat the shit out of you right here and right now."

Cedrick held up his hands. "I'm sorry! I'm sorry, I didn't mean to leave her! But he told me he was going to do stuff to me too, and I—"

"Leave her where?" Rion screamed in his face.

"Fresno!" Cedrick cried. "She convinced me to take the drive to Fresno for the real stuff last weekend. I didn't know what that meant, but then she took me to this hotel, and she knew all the dealers there. We got a room and did a couple of patches—"

"Fentanyl patches!?" Rion yelled again.

"Yeah, man. She said it was cool, that she trusted those guys. So we hung out in the room that Thursday night to Saturday."

"So, why did you leave her?" Nick asked, standing over them. He gently pulled Rion off the man who was still on the floor. Two other guys came out of their room because of the commotion.

"This dude, she called him Frank-T, the one that was supplying us for free; he came into the room and told her that she needed to pay up. I didn't know what that meant at first."

"You knew what it meant," Rion said angrily. "Nothing is free."

"Right, but I thought he just meant her... not me, too."

Rion's eyes narrowed at him. "So you left her there to turn tricks for the drugs that you both used?"

"I—" Cedrick looked around at all the faces, then sighed. "I allowed some things to happen, but I got scared, so I jetted."

"Some things like what?" Rion asked.

"Rion," Nick called his name quietly. In Nick's mind, no one needed to know what Cedrick did.

"Some things like what?" Rion said again, ignoring Nick.

Cedrick didn't answer. Rion swung his foot out and kicked Cedrick in the groin. Cedrick howled and grabbed himself. "Some things like what!?" Rion screamed.

"He made me suck his dick!" Cedrick yelled as tears came out of his eyes. "He made me suck his dick, but when he told me he was going to put it in me, I knew I had to run. So I pretended to be a part of it while he was doing her, but then I ran out of there, jumped in my car, and came home." He looked up at Rion. "Is Ava alright?"

"You left my sister at a crack motel in the middle of the night, high off fentanyl, getting raped by a drug dealer?" Rion asked. "And you're going to ask me if she's alright?"

"There was no crack," said Cedrick. "Just pills, H, and patches—"

Rion grabbed the man and began to punch him repeatedly. Nick grabbed Rion by the shoulders and pulled him back. Rion came out of his boyfriend's grasp and kicked Cedrick in the face one more time, leaving Cedrick bloodied and bruised.

"We gotta go, Ree," Nick said, dragging him back down the stairs.

But Rion yelled, "If something happened to my sister, I'm coming back to give you the same fate, Dickhead."

Nick drove them back to Golden Gate Heights in silence. His mind was spinning, and he couldn't help but remember his sister's words about being brought into a world that was so unfamiliar to him and how he would not be prepared for it. Nick was not prepared for Rion's reaction, and it frightened him, he had to admit. But he also understood him. Rion was scared and worried out of his mind for his sister. And Nick knew that it wasn't the first time Rion had to go to this length to find and pull his sister out of a dark place. If Emma went missing, Nick realized he would be scorching the earth to find her, too. That thought alone made him want to continue to support Rion, no matter how dark the path they went down, as long as they were together.

Rion pointed. "Park over there, near the back entrance," he said. "Her apartment is right above us."

Nick did. Rion sat there for a moment, closing his eyes and flexing his knuckles. "I lost it in there. Sorry."

Nick chuckled. "I literally just had the thought: If Emma went missing, I would probably be scorching the earth to find her. So you know, if you gotta kick the shit out of a few people to find your sister, I'm right here with you."

Rion opened his eyes and looked at Nick. Nick smiled first. Rion smiled back. Then he opened up the car door, and they entered the building together. They took the elevator to the fourth floor and rang the doorbell. A tall African American man opened it up and stood before them.

Rion looked up at him. "Hey, Maurese."

"Hey, Ree," Maurese said back. He opened his arms, and Rion went into them for a full-on hug. "Don't worry," he said, "We'll find them. Both of them."

Rion nodded and let him go. Maurese stepped back and let them both into the apartment. "This is Nick," Rion said, introducing the two. "He's with me."

"Of course he is," Maurese said with a smile. He reached out for a handshake. "Nicholas Highton. I'd know that face anywhere."

Nick knew he was referring to the sex tape, but neither mentioned it. "It's nice to meet you, Maurese," he said.

Gabby was already on the couch and stood up when they came in. Rion told them both what happened and what he found out. Neither was surprised at Rion's violent outburst toward Cedrick.

"Okay," said Maurese. "Which means Ros went there, too, looking for her."

"Or Roslyn is right here in San Fran getting high," Rion countered.

"She's not," Gabby implored. "She went to find Ava. I know it."

Rion was not convinced. Maurese also looked skeptical. "How would she get there? It's a three-hour drive and she doesn't have a car."

"We could see if she took public transportation," Nick chimed in.

"How?" asked Gabby.

Nick picked up his phone instead and called Zoey. "What do you need, Boss?" she asked right away.

"Check Amtrak, Greyhound, flights, and other modes of transportation to see if Roslyn Matthews bought a ticket to Fresno or any surrounding areas," he said.

"On it." Zoey hung up.

They all looked at him. "What?" he asked. "Don't you want to know if she did go to find Ava or not?"

No one responded. After a few minutes, the phone rang again. He answered it on speakerphone. "Yes?"

"Greyhound bus, 8:42 a.m. on Monday morning to Fresno, California, 2660 Tulare Street. It arrived at 2:58 p.m. Roslyn Elaine Matthews was on it."

"Thank you, Zoey."

"Of course," she said.

Nick hung up. Gabby walked up to him and wrapped her arms around him. "Thank you for doing that." He patted her back.

"So we're headed into 781 territory," Maurese said with a sigh. "Unless Fox needs me, I stay out of there at all costs. But for Ava and Ros, we gotta do it."

He looked at Rion, who nodded. "We gotta do it," Rion said.

Then Maurese looked at Nicholas. "He can't go," he said to Rion. "He'll immediately be recognized."

Nick spoke before Rion could. "I'm going," he said plainly. "I'll dress down, I'll cover my face, I'll dye my hair, I'll do whatever you need me to do. But Rion's not going anywhere without me."

Maurese looked at Rion. "If he goes, he stays in the car."

Nick spoke again. "Do not speak around me like I'm a child," he said angrily. "I care about Rion, which means I care about this family, too. So we'll all do what we have to do to make sure we find Ava and Roslyn and bring them home safely." He turned to Rion. "What do you need me to do?"

Rion stared at Nick, his boyfriend, his partner, his lover. He could see Nick's worry for him, his determination not to leave his side, and the love in his eyes. Rion walked over and kissed his lips. He turned to Maurese.

"He's going. I'll take care of it." He turned back to Nicholas. "Come with me. It's my turn to get you ready."

Rion drove another thirty minutes over to a small apartment building and parked on the street. As he stepped out, a woman standing in front of the bar across the street yelled, "Rion!"

He turned around and grinned. She crossed the street, and they hugged. "Hey, Shereen."

"We missed you around here. You look goooood, baby," she drawled out. "Real good. What's your secret?"

"High protein, less carbs," he joked.

She laughed. "Well, I know what kind of protein you're getting," she said with a wink.

Rion laughed out loud. He turned to Nick and said to her, "This is my boyfriend, Nick. Nick, Shereen. She's the best thing to ever happen to this neighborhood."

"Well, somebody has to keep all the boys in line," she cooed. Then she looked at Nick closely. "Do you know who you look like? What's that guy's name? The one with the singer on the sex tape?"

"Not him," Rion said. "But he gets that a lot. Listen, is Manny in?" he asked, changing the subject. "I have to talk to him about selling the place."

Nick was surprised, since less than twenty-four hours ago, Rion was yelling at him about leaving New York and not coming back.

"He's at the bar. Where else?" she said with a flick of her hand. "I'll tell him to stop by your apartment."

"Thanks, Shereen. And you look great, too," he told her. "Really, really great."

She grinned at him. "You were always the sweetest. I should have had you when I had the chance." She pinched his cheek, making Rion blush.

"Later, Shereen." Rion grabbed Nick's hand and led him inside the apartment building.

They started climbing the stairs when Nick asked, "No elevator?"

Rion rolled his eyes. "I apologize for the inconvenience, Mr. Highton, but our escalator is down for maintenance. Would you like a glass of cognac while I carry you up four flights?"

Nick reached over and pinched Rion's butt, making him yelp. They laughed up the stairs until Rion got to his door and opened it. Nick glanced around the small one-bedroom apartment.

"How long have you been here?" he asked as he walked to the window. It faced the bar across the street.

"A little over four years," Rion said as he used another key to open the hallway closet. He started pulling out clothes as he spoke. "It's how Jason and I met. It was his apartment, and he sold it to me." He held clothes out. "Here."

Rion gave him a loose pair of gray sweatpants and a pair of basketball shorts. "Both you wear low, the sweatpants at your thighs, the shorts halfway across your ass, your underwear showing."

"My briefs are Armani Exchange," Nick said seriously.

Rion let out a smile. "Of course they are." He handed him an oversized t-shirt and a black hoodie. "This should hide any gold lettering."

Nick began to get dressed. Rion watched him turn himself into a regular guy from the streets as he gave instructions. "Remember what you told me about Brian's world? Where we're about to go isn't my world, Nicky, so it definitely isn't your world. You stay close to me. Anybody asks, you say you're with me. You don't look anyone directly in the eye unless they're threatening you in some way, even verbally. Then you look them in the eye and let them know you mean business."

After Nick put on the hoodie, he asked, "How do I look?"

Instead of responding, Rion placed an old 49ers cap on his head and put the black hood on top so it shielded his eyes. "You keep your hands in the center pocket at all times so nobody knows if you're packing or not. It's a fifty-fifty chance that no one even looks at you. If you have to talk, you make sure they know you aren't fucking around. I got your back, but you have to watch your surroundings, too. Don't crack a smile, even if something is funny. None of that Highton charm I love so much." Nick grinned. Rion shook his head. "See? You already failed." Nick giggled. "You're staying home."

Rion turned around, but Nick grabbed his arm and put a kiss on his lips. "I can do this. I can blend in or fade into the background. Trust me."

Rion looked him up and down and met his eyes again. "Doesn't matter if you're in a suit or sweatpants; you're so fucking hot it's criminal." He returned Nick's kiss. "Let's go. It's a three-hour drive."

Muriel brought Morgan over to Roslyn's house to see her mother before they headed out. Morgan was excited to see Uncle Ree and Uncle Nicky, then became extremely agitated when she realized that she wasn't going with them.

"But why can't I gooooooo, Mommy?" she whined.

Rion promised to come back and spend a full day with her, and Nick promised to take her to Disneyworld for the birthday if she was a good girl for Aunt Muriel. Not surprisingly, the Disneyworld trip was what calmed her down.

At Gabby's suggestion, Nicholas called the car service to rent a car. A six-passenger black Acura MDX arrived by nightfall. Maurese drove with Gabby in the front seat, and Rion sat in the back with Nicholas. It was mostly quiet as they drove the three hours to Fresno. Nick ended up falling asleep, exhausted from all that had transpired so far, leaning his head on Rion's shoulder. And Rion kept his hand on Nick's thigh most of the way.

As they turned a corner, Rion tapped Nicholas awake. "We're here."

Nick sat up straighter. He watched Maurese open the glove compartment and put a loaded gun into the front part of his jeans, then pull his shirt over it. He pulled his window all the way down, and so did Gabby, despite the wind chill in the air. Nick was about to do the same when Rion touched his arm and said, "Only them." So Nick pulled his hand back.

Maurese slow-crawled through the neighborhood. He nodded at a few people, and a couple of times, someone approached the vehicle, greeting him, "Grease! Whaddup!"

When they did, Maurese would stop the car and talk for a moment, then casually ask, "You seen Rosebud around here?"

And the response was always something similar to, "Nah, I haven't seen her in years."

Maurese drove around a little more, then turned onto a dead-end block and parked. He turned around to Rion, looked at Nick, then back at Rion. "You ready?"

Rion nodded confidently. Maurese turned to Gabby and said, "Let's go, *Princesa*." They both exited the vehicle.

Rion touched the doorknob, then said to Nick, "Remember what I told you. Don't speak unless spoken to."

"Okay," Nick said. His heart was racing in anticipation and fear.

Rion could sense it. He leaned over and kissed Nick's lips. "You're fine. You're with me."

"Okay," Nick said again. He opened his door and stepped out first, then put his hands in the center pocket of his hoodie.

The four of them approach a Victorian-style home in the middle of the cul-de-sac. There was one man out front with a large gun strapped around him. "Oh shit, Reese the Grease," he said as he threw away his cigarette and stood up. "Haven't seen you around here in years."

"Yeah, Bones, you know I stay busy," Maurese said, dropping his vernacular completely. They connected palms and did a three-move handshake, then touched pinkies. "I'm looking for someone. Fox round 'ere?"

"He's in the back. Yo, is this little Ree?" The man called Bones looked at Rion with a wide grin.

Rion gave him a genuine smile. "Yeah. Not so little anymore."

"Yoooo," Bones said excitedly. He reached his hand out for a dap, and Rion gave him one. "'Member when I took care of you and Gabby for like two months? Rosebud was in the wind? You remember that?"

"Yup," he said. "Thank you for taking care of me. Taking care of both of us, Bones. If it wasn't for you..."

"That Yorkie dude would have sliced you up, I remember. I took care of him for you, tho'," he said knowingly and touched an unconcealed weapon on his side. "Of course, I would. You one of us." Then Bones turned to Gabby. "*La princesa es aqui*," the man said happily.

Gabby gave him a genuine smile too, and hugged him. "Hi, Uncle Tone."

Bones adjusted his AK-47 to hug her fully. "You look beautiful, Gabby. You're all grown up and so beautiful. He-Man would have been so proud to see you today." Bones crossed himself, kissed his fingers, and pointed to the sky. "Él *nos está vigilando*."

She smiled at him and touched his arm. "*Sí*, Uncle Tone. *Sí*."

Reese said, "Hey Bones, we're looking for the other one of Rosebud's. Ava."

"Rosebud's Asian girl? Yeah, she was around last week with some loser-ass white boy. Tell ol' girl she could do much better than that." He laughed out loud.

"When did she leave?" Rion asked, stepping up.

Bones shrugged. "I don't know. She was with Mus for a while cuz that asshole left her here. I think he put her up in one of our spots."

All three spoke at the same time:

"Was she high?" Rion asked.

"Which one?" Maurese asked.

"Did she seem okay?" Gabby asked.

"Woah, calm down y'all," Bones said, raising his hands. "Let me make sure Fox is free. He'll answer all your questions."

Bones picked up his walkie and spoke into it in Spanish, ending with, "*Bueno*." He said to them, "Come inside and have a seat. He'll be ready to talk in ten minutes." As they began to walk in, Bones reached out and touched Nick's chest. "Woah. Who dis?"

Nick looked at the man's hand, then back up in his face. "Get your fucking hands off me," he said menacingly in a strong New York accent.

Before Bones could respond, Rion stepped between them, physically removing Bones's hand. "He's with me," said Rion.

Bones looked at Rion. "You trust him?"

"With my life," Rion said seriously.

"I do, too," Gabby said, vouching for Nick. "He's good. He's with us."

Bones looked at Nick. Nick's mean glare did not change. "Aight. Relax, homie."

Bones turned around and led the way into the living room. Rion sat on the couch first as Maurice and Gabby greeted everyone. Nick slouched down on the couch with his hands in his hoodie pocket.

"Was that good?" Nick said softly, not looking at him.

"Nick..." Rion was trying really hard not to smile. "Remind me to let you fuck me really hard at some point. Because that was perfect and sexy as fuck."

Nick gave a brief smirk, then his face went back to hard and stoic.

Maurese walked around with Gabby, saying hello to others, giving the same mysterious handshake. Gabby smiled politely and reciprocated hugs willingly. Nick asked softly, "So, Reese the Grease?"

"That's what they call him," Rion spoke softly back. "He was known for getting himself out of slippery situations. Thirty years in a gang and he's never been arrested, not once. Fox used to say that Maurese would slide right out of shit and not look back."

Nick watched Maurese navigate extremely comfortably around the house. "Like getting himself out of the gang?" Nick whispered.

Rion looked at him. "There are only two ways out of a gang. I'm sure you know this." Rion stared at Nick until he nodded. "But Maurese has managed to live his life outside of the 781, and they let him. Mostly Fox lets him because they came in together as fourteen-year-olds. Now that Fox is running it, he doesn't pull Maurese in unless he absolutely has to. At least that's my understanding." Nick nodded again.

After more than twenty minutes, the door to the back room opened, and a few men stepped out. Everyone in the room stopped and looked at it. Rion stood up and Nick followed his lead. An obese Hispanic man came out last and looked around. His eyes landed on Reese the Grease.

"C'mere, brother," he said.

Reese grinned and walked up to him. They did the same handshake, then hugged. Gabby also hugged him, saying, "Uncle Felipe."

"Wow, look at you, *Princesa*. So happy to see you doing well. How's your mom? She was just here a few days ago."

Gabby tried to smile. "She's..." Her voice caught in her throat.

Maurese rubbed her shoulders. "That's why we're here. Can we talk?"

Felipe "Fox" Valencia motioned with his head back to his office. Gabby led the way while the others followed. When they all entered the room, Nick closed the door behind him and stood in the back, his hands still in his center pocket.

Fox turned around and leaned on his desk. He held his hand out. Gabby took his hand, and he said to her, "What's wrong, sweetheart?"

They all stayed quiet and let Gabby explain that she couldn't find her sister, and after she told her mother, Roslyn went missing, too. "I was told that she was here a few days ago, so I came to see you to ask for your help."

"I saw Rosebud, yea, but not Ava. Was she here at the house? Or here on the streets?" he asked.

"We don't know," Rion chimed in. "Her loser ass boyfriend just said he drove her down here, and they got patches from someone she knew, and they were up in some hotel. The only people Ava would trade with is 781, so we came to see you."

He turned to Rion and said, "You're a grown-ass man now, aren't you? Deep voice and everything."

"Yeah," Rion said back and gave a small smile. "It's been a while, Fox, I know."

"Doesn't matter how long. Even though you're not official 781, you're still family, you know. All of you. And we take care of our own." He hugged Gabby. "Don't worry, *Princesa*, I'll find Ava for you. I'ma tell you the same thing I told ya mom: if anyone on the streets seen her, it would be Mus."

He took out his phone and put it on the table, pressing a call button.

"Yo," a voice said.

"Mus," Fox said back. "Rosebud's Asian girl, Ava. The one that used to run with you. You seen 'er?"

"Yeah, she was here. Why, wussup?"

"Where is she?" Fox asked.

"I 'ono," Mus mumbled. "She paid for patches on 221 from Frank-T and was at Pocket Motel with some *gringo*. Frank-T said he didn't like his energy, so he stomped him out real quick, then made him suck his dick. After that, he scrammed, and she left. She came back like a day later without him and got the whole spread: patches, crack, molly, dust, all of it."

Rion put his hands on his head and muttered, "Fuck."

"So she was out of it," Fox said, looking at Maurese's face. His eyebrows were scrunched up in concern.

"Gone," Mus confirmed. "For two days. I had to move her. She was taking up one of my rooms. That was Monday."

Rion looked up sharply. "Move her where? Where did you put Ava?"

"At Riverside Valley, but she ain't there no more."

"Where did she go!?" Rion yelled.

"Yo, who dat?"

"It's Rion. Rosebud's boy," Fox said. "Grease is here, too."

"Oh shit! Lil Ree's a grown-ass man now, ain't he?" Mus said, similar to what Fox said.

"Yeah, I am, and I need to find my sister," said Rion with an attitude. "Now, where is she, Mus?"

"I don't know. Rosebud came and pulled her out. Screamed on me and everyone there that we had her daughter up in there and dragged her to a car."

"... What?" Rion said in shock. "Roslyn actually got her out of there?"

"Oh my God..." said Gabby, equally as shocked. She turned to her brother, and they grabbed hands. "What does this mean?"

"I don't know Gabbs," said Rion. The siblings continued to murmur.

"Is that *la Princesa*?" Maximus said from the phone. "Must be a family reunion in that bitch! All we need is Junior to claim his son and get the whole crew back together."

Nick watched Maurese's eyes widen. "Shut the fuck up, Mus," he said and reached over and pressed the end button on the phone. "Thanks, Fox. Now we gotta find Ros."

Gabby turned to him. "Why'd you do that? We don't even know if she was clean." She said to Fox, "Call Mus back. We have questions."

"No," Maurese said sternly. "He doesn't know anything. We'll find Ros together. There's only so many places she could have gone in 781 territory." He reached his hand out to the drug kingpin and slapped palms, doing the handshake again. "Thanks, Fox." He turned to the others. "Let's go. Now." He turned around with the expectation that they would all follow. Nick stared at the older man suspiciously.

Gabby sighed. "Thanks again, Uncle Felipe."

"Come see us before you head back, *Princesa*," he said, standing up to give her a hug. He gave Rion a half hug and finally looked over at Nick. Bones had already told him they had a fourth person with them that they trusted.

"That you?" he asked Rion with a head nod toward Nick.

Rion turned around to look at Nicholas too. "Yeah. That's me."

"Cool," Fox said casually. He patted Rion's back and said to Nick, "Take care of him. Rion isn't like us. He's one of the good ones."

"With my life," Nick replied seriously. Fox nodded, and he nodded back.

Maurese drove them around, stopping on corners and asking questions to Fox's men, then stopping at various motels, apartments, or homes. Gabby had curled up in the front seat and fallen asleep at one point. A few hours in, he stopped at a house that was dark. He rubbed his eyes tiredly.

"I'll be right back," he said. He got out of the car, took a deep breath, and walked with purpose toward the house.

Rion sighed. "I lived there," he said quietly so that he wouldn't wake his sister. "In that house with Roslyn and Gabby, but Roslyn was never there. I was about eight. I used to sleep in the downstairs closet curled up on the floor under a coat and hope they forgot I existed. Most of the time, they did. Sometimes they didn't."

"And if they didn't?" Nick asked.

Rion stared at the house that brought back horrible memories of physical and sexual abuse and didn't answer his question. "Bones got me out of there one night when he saw what they were doing to me. He took me and Gabby to his studio apartment instead, one of his safe houses. He made sure we had three meals a day and a bed to sleep in. He actually enrolled us in school and walked us there every morning, and picked us up every afternoon. He even took us clothes shopping, bought me my first pair of Jordans. He killed at least three people in front of me in those two months, but at least he took care of me and didn't abuse me."

"Jesus, Rion," Nick said sadly and touched his hand.

"It's all good," Rion said with a shrug. "I've had a lot of therapy over the years, especially in college. I can acknowledge what I've been through, see how far I've come, and move forward with my life. Leaving Fresno helped put some distance between me and my past traumas tremendously. Getting into community college saved my life. San Francisco was like a breath of fresh air."

"I'm sorry, Rion."

Rion turned to him. "For what?"

"For... I don't know. Meeting you. Making you fall in love with me. Making you move across the country to be with me. Maybe you shouldn't have left San Francisco. I know you have regrets, and I never wanted you to feel like you were choosing me over your family."

Rion shook his head. "I don't feel like that, Nick. I made a choice to be with you. I made the choice to get on a plane last Christmas because I needed to be with you. And no, I don't regret that choice."

"But you regret not being here for your family," Nick countered. "It's the same thing."

"It's not the same thing," Rion said, shaking his head again. "I regret that I wasn't here for Ava. I don't regret being with you. I would make the same choice over and over again as long as it led me to this moment right here, you sitting in a cramped Acura in gang territory with me, driving around trying to find my mentally ill and drugged-up sister, holding my hand. I'm scared, I'm worried, my anxiety is through the roof, and the only reason I'm not freaking out right now and going off the deep end is because of you. I need you, Nicky. Being with you is like a breath of fresh air, too."

Nick pulled Rion close, and they hugged tightly. Rion's phone went off in his pocket. Rion quickly pulled away and looked at it.

[Roslyn: The Pearl. Room 17.]

"Oh my God!" he exclaimed.

"What!?" Gabby jumped up, wiping the drool off her face.

"It's Roslyn. Let's go."

He jumped out of the backseat and slid into the front seat, then started the ignition and beeped the horn.

"Where is she?" Gabby asked.

"At the Pearl. Room 17."

"We went there hours ago," said Gabby. "Nobody saw her."

"Then she must be lying low."

"Is Ava with her?"

"I don't know, Gabby," Rion said, exasperated. He honked the horn again.

Maurese came out of the house. Rion flashed the lights. Maurese came to the car. Before he could speak, Rion said, "Get in. We're going back to The Pearl."

The Pearl was a rundown open-air motel that was used for one thing. A prostitute walked right up to their car and tried to proposition Rion, but he stepped out of her way and ignored her, walking toward the building. The four of them approached Room 17 cautiously. Rion knocked on the door. Roslyn opened it a crack and looked at all the faces staring back at her. Her eyes landed on Maurese, but it was Rion who spoke first.

"Avalon?"

Roslyn nodded but stepped out and closed the door behind her. "She's sleeping. She's only on day three from detox, but today was a good da—"

Gabby cut her off and hugged her tightly. "I was worried about you, too."

Roslyn hugged her back. "Oh, Gabby sweetie, I'm fine. Look at me." She pulled back and held her daughter's face. "No slip-ups. I'm fine, I promise." She kissed Gabby's head, and Gabby hugged her again.

Nicholas got a good look at Rion's mother. They resembled each other, but not by much. Roslyn was no bigger than 5'6". Her wavy brown hair was pulled back into a ponytail and Nick could see the stress lines all across her face and forehead. Her cheeks were sunken in from years of substance abuse and not taking care of herself. But she was alert, and her eyes were clear. Roslyn was not using drugs.

Roslyn stared at her son. "Hey, baby boy. What are you doing here?"

Rion was at a loss for words for a moment, then asked, "Why didn't you ask for help? We could have helped, Roslyn."

"She's my daughter, Rion," his mother said plainly. "I don't need your help to care for my own daughter."

Rion's mouth opened slightly. "Oh. Okay," he said softly.

"But you had us all worried," Gabby said. "You could have at least told us what you were going to do."

"I did tell you, Gabrielle," Roslyn said back. "I said, 'I'm going to find her and bring her back.' And that's all you needed to know." She looked at both her children. "Neither of you needed to come down here. I have it all under control. God knows I've done it enough times to myself to know what to look out for and what supplies to have on hand. I'm okay. And so is Avalon."

"Can we see her?" Rion asked, still in disbelief that his mother had actually handled the situation. Roslyn had not been known to handle much of anything.

"You can sit with her, but let her sleep," she instructed. "It's the longest stretch of sleep she's had since I got her."

"Okay, Mama," said Gabby. Her mother handed her a keycard.

Gabby opened the door and looked back at her brother. "You coming?"

"Yeah. Yeah, I... yeah."

But Rion first walked up to his mother and put his arms around her neck. Roslyn opened her mouth in surprise, then quickly wrapped her arms around her son's back. They held each other for a long moment.

Rion said softly, "Thank you, Mama."

"Oh," Roslyn said, and the tears that had been threatening to come out finally dropped. "You're so welcome, baby."

He pulled back, and she touched his face lovingly. Rion followed his sister into the motel room. They stepped in; the room was dark and smelled of vomit and urine. Rion went to one side of the bed, Gabby went to the other, and they both quietly slipped into the bed that Ava occupied.

Avalon opened her eyes and sat up, startled at the movement. Her mouth dropped as she looked at Gabby, then opened even wider at the sight of her brother. She hugged him first. He held her back tightly, even though she was skin and bones to him. Ava turned around and hugged Gabby, too. Then Rion hugged them both. All three siblings began to cry.

As soon as the door closed, Roslyn let out a big sigh. She turned to Maurese, but he was already by her side waiting for her. She grasped his arms and fell into them, sobbing. They embraced, and she cried on his shoulder. Nick stood by silently and awkwardly.

"It's okay, Ros," he said, comforting her. "You're doing great."

"Thank you," she said to him. "I'm trying so hard."

"And they see that. And I see it. You're doing so great, Ros."

Roslyn sniffed again and let him go. Finally, she noticed Nick. "Mr. Deep Strokez, in the flesh," she joked, with tears still in her eyes. She gave him a smile.

Nick chuckled. "I usually go by Nick."

Roslyn reached out and clasped his hand. "Thank you, Nick."

"Oh, I haven't done anything but stand around and look intimidating," Nick said with a smile.

"And he's doing a pretty fucking good job at it," Maurese said, also smiling. He turned to Roslyn. "Any vending machines around here? I could go for a soft drink."

"It's around the corner," she said. "I can go—"

"Nick," he said, cutting her off, "Do you mind going over there, grabbing me something? Get yourself something, too." Maurese handed Nick a couple of dollar bills.

Nick had the suspicion that he was being sent away, but he allowed it. "Sure." He turned the corner that was just one door down, but then stood there. And he listened.

"How did you know she was with them?" Nick heard Maurese say.

"Because this is where she goes. The 781 is where I used to take her to use safely. Ava's just following in her mother's footsteps," Roslyn said sadly. "But it's okay now—"

"You might have a bigger problem," Reese cut her off. "Mus made a comment. I don't know if Rion heard it or if he'll process it later—"

"What comment?"

"He said something about Junior being Ree's father. About Junior claiming his son."

"Fuck!" Roslyn said and turned around, looking at the closed door Rion had just gone through. She turned back to her ex-lover. "Does he know? Did he hear—"

"I don't think he caught it. But that doesn't mean when all the adrenaline has left his system, he won't figure out who Junior is. And Junior still doesn't want to have anything to do with him."

"That's because your brother is a schizophrenic piece of shit, even when he's clean," said Roslyn nastily.

Nick's mouth opened in shock. He had heard enough and began to walk farther down the hall to the vending machine. His head was still spinning as he walked back over to them. As soon as he turned the corner, they stopped talking.

Maurese gave him a smile and held out his hand. "Thanks, man."

"Sure," Nick said casually. "I'm going to go get a room for Rion and me. You two keep talking." He looked from one to the other.

Maurese's face was impassive, but Roslyn's face showed fear. Nick turned around and went downstairs to the main lobby.

Nick texted Rion.

[Room 12.]

He took a long, hot shower and got into bed. Since the day had already started on the East Coast, he checked in with Marcel to make sure things were going smoothly at the office the last couple of days. Then he called Zoey to let her know everything was fine now, but he would most likely still be in San Fran for the next couple of days, maybe a few weeks, and to take Izzy for a while. Then he began to check emails from his phone, waiting up for his lover.

As the sun began to rise, there was a knock on the door. Nick jumped out of bed to open it. Rion came in, looking exhausted. Nick closed the door and gathered him up in his arms. He felt Rion's entire body relax as Rion hugged him back. Wordlessly, Nick took Rion's hand and pulled him into the bathroom. He turned on the shower first, making it steaming hot, and started at Rion's feet, taking off his sneakers, then his socks. Rion stood there and allowed Nick to strip off his clothes, one article at a time. Nick slid off his basketball shorts and pulled Rion into the bathtub with him, closing the cloth curtain around them.

Rion stood under the showerhead and closed his eyes. The weight of everything over the last two days came crashing down on him, from the frantic phone call, the awful flight, seeing his sisters again after almost a year, seeing Jay again, beating up Cedrick, coming face to face with the 781 and the memories of his traumatic childhood, driving around for hours fearful that something bad had happened to both his mother and sister, seeing Ava small, sickly, and broken once again. It was all too much.

Maybe Muriel was right. Maybe I shouldn't have come at all, he thought sadly. Muriel had continued on with her life as usual, and Roslyn did tell Gabby that she was going to handle it. And more importantly, she actually did handle it. They didn't need him. Rion was conflicted in his feelings about that thought. It made him happy that his sisters, and even his mother, could stand on their own and didn't need his protection anymore. But it also made him incredibly sad.

He felt Nicholas place the soapy washcloth on his shoulders and begin to move in a circular motion. Rion allowed Nick to wash him, kiss his neck from time to time, and use his hands to knead away all the tension. Eventually, Rion broke down and began to sob. Nick gathered Rion up in his arms again and held him in the same manner that Maurese had held Roslyn. Rion held onto Nick tightly, never wanting to let go.

After the shower, they went to bed without their clothes on. Nick was willing to wait, but Rion made every indication that he wanted it, pushing his bottom into Nick as they lay on their sides, then turning around and stroking their cocks together. Using the conditioner they found in the bathroom as lube, Nick turned Rion onto his side and made love to him slowly, thrusting from the back and stroking him from the front until Rion came first, then Nick released inside of him. Nick was about to pull out when Rion grabbed his arm and held Nick's hand close to his chest.

"Hey, Ree," Nick whispered after a stretch of silence.
"Yeah?"
"This was fun. Let's never go back there again."

Rion began to giggle, and Nick smiled. Nick held onto Rion tightly until he heard Rion's breath become long and even. Only then did he fall asleep, too.

Nick and Rion sat in the front seat, with Nick driving back to San Francisco, while Maurese and Roslyn occupied the middle seat, both falling asleep pretty quickly into the ride, and Gabby sat in the back with Ava's head on her lap. They drove all the way to Roslyn's apartment and stretched upon leaving the vehicle. Rion let the others walk ahead and into the building and leaned on the car instead, putting his shades on. Nick noticed and stood beside him, also putting his shades on. They stood side by side for a while until Nick broke the silence.

"Good ol' California sun."

"Yeah," Rion said and sighed.

They were quietly watching the busyness of the street. "Honestly, I like the way this MDX drives," said Nick. "I just might get one when we get back."

Rion smiled, then he said, "I have to stay a while, Nick. At least a month."

"I know you do," Nick confirmed. "And I'm going to stay a while with you."

Rion shook his head. "You don't have to. I'm coming home. I need to make sure Ava is set up in a good rehab place, and then I'm coming home."

Nick smiled at Rion saying home. "We'll go home together. Maybe we'll rent a Toyota and drive the whole way. After we've made sure that everything on this side of the country is fine, we'll head home together."

Rion sighed again. "Muriel was right. I didn't need to come."

"You did need to come, Ree," said Nick. "They're your family, and you needed to be here to make sure everything was okay."

"But they didn't need me to handle it. They don't need me for that anymore."

"That doesn't mean they don't need you. That doesn't mean that Gabby didn't need you to step off that plane yesterday morning to hug and reassure her, or Muriel wasn't relieved that you were here to find them so she didn't have to, or that Ava didn't need to see your face last night. They may not need you to handle things for them in the same way you were doing, but they need you to be their brother. And you did that." Nick reached over and touched Rion's shoulder. "So we'll stay because Ava still needs you around, and you need to make sure your sister is okay before we go home."

"Yeah. I have to start looking for rehab places and the costs. The detox was the first step. But she has to go someplace and get continuous help."

"I can have Zoey—"

"No," Rion interjected right away. "Zoey is going to find the most amazing place with a ninety-eight percent success rate and the fee is going to be astronomical, and you already know I'm not taking a dollar from you. The last thing I ever want is for anyone in your family to think that you take care of mine. So let me find her a rehab that I can afford so it doesn't become an issue between us later. Because money will never be an issue between us."

Nick frowned. "I wasn't going to offer to pay," he lied.

Rion smiled. "Yes, you were." Nick smiled back slightly. "Come on. Let's go inside so I can do a sweep of Ava's room."

Once inside, Rion indeed went right to the second bedroom that Ava was occupying and wordlessly started going through her dressers and closet. Ava sat on the edge of her bed and shook her head.

"I'm fine, baby bro. I'm not going to relapse. At least not anytime soon." But then she pointed. "My Louis Vuitton shoebox."

He picked up the large shoebox on the floor. When he opened it, he saw knee-high, black, suede boots. He stuck his finger inside and pulled out a bag of little white pills. Rion shook his head.

"Ava—" he started.

"At least I told you," Ava said. "That's a sign that I'm okay now, right?"

Rion put the cover back on the box. "Right." He put the pills in his pocket with the intent to flush them down the toilet later. He walked over to the bed and sat next to her. "Do you need anything?"

"Other than getting the last six months of my life back? Nothing."

"You really liked him, didn't you?" asked Rion.

Ava sighed. "I did. I thought, 'This is it. He's the one.' He only smoked weed and popped Zanny's on the weekends; otherwise, he was straight and narrow. I thought we could be great together. But last Thursday, he said he wanted to try something stronger. And I don't do anything hard unless I know where it comes from. So I thought we'd have a fun weekend in Fresno, and that's it. If I had a clue that he was going to get ridiculously disrespectful with Frank-T, which was why Frank-T made us pay up and do all those things, I would have never brought him down there."

"Frank-T is gross, but Cedrick left you," said Rion. "He should have found a way to bring you both back home instead of leaving you there."

She shrugged. "I'm a big girl. I could have rented a ride, gotten on a bus, anything to get myself back home after Frank-T finally let me go that Sunday. I didn't want to. It's not on Cedrick. It's on me."

"Well, I kicked his ass for you, anyway."

She looked at her brother and smirked. "Of course you did, baby bro." She put her head on his shoulder. "I can always count on you."

That made Rion smile.

After protests and pushback from Rion, Nick ignored him and ordered a lot of food from a local Chinese restaurant for the whole family. Muriel came by with her three children and Morgan for dinner.

She walked up to Ava. "You're back?" Muriel asked simply.

Ava nodded. "Yeah. I'm back."

Muriel nodded, too. "Try not to die, okay? You got a lot of people worried about you."

Ava smiled at her sister. "I'll try."

And that was the extent of their conversation.

They sat in the small living room on the couch and floor with their white styrofoam cartons and ate together as a family. Rion opted for him and Nick to stay at his mother's house on the pull-out couch rather than drive him and Nick across town to his apartment. When Nick suggested that he spend one more night in his apartment before selling it, Rion simply said, "I don't want to leave Ava's side."

"Then you should go to work, Mama," said Muriel, pointing a chopstick at her. "Because I know you didn't call out. You just left, didn't you?"

"I actually did call out," their mother said. "I said I had a family emergency and I would let them know if or when I could return to the supermarket."

"Well, you're back now," she said. "And part of your sobriety is keeping you on a schedule and to your commitments. Work is a commitment."

Roslyn glared at her oldest daughter. "I've been there for two years, Rel. I know what my commitments are; I don't need you mothering me."

"I'm just getting you back on track," she said back.

"I haven't left the track," Roslyn said angrily. "I told you I'm fine."

"I'm just—"

Rion cut his sister off. "She's fine. Back off. Mama is fine." He looked at his mother. "You'll go to work tomorrow and I'll be here with Ava. I have to make a stop in the morning to my landlord, but Nick will be here at the house."

"So she's *'Mama'* now?" Rel said sarcastically to her brother.

Rion shrugged without looking at anyone. "You told me to try, so I'm trying."

It was quiet, but Roslyn was smiling, happier today in a room full of her family than she was at Thanksgiving the year before.

Rion knocked on Roslyn's bedroom door and didn't get a response. He knocked again with intention and slowly opened the door into the dark room. "Mama? I was headed in the direction of the supermarket and was going to offer you a ride to work."

He saw his mother's head come up from the comforter. "Mama, you okay?" he asked with concern. Then another head came up underneath her as his mother reached over to turn on the side table lamp. Rion took one look at Maurese's hairy torso and jumped back.

"Aaah!" he screamed.

"Rion!" Maurese called to him.

"Jesus!" Rion yelled again and left his mother's room, slamming the door behind him. He walked over to the kitchen area, his face scrunched up in disgust, putting his hands on the counter and facing the cabinets.

Nick, who was in the kitchen, was alarmed. "What? What happened?"

But he didn't have long to wait for an answer as both Rion's mother and her former boyfriend emerged from the same room. Maurese was putting on a shirt while Roslyn was wrapping her robe around her waist.

"Oh," he said in amusement, and took a sip of his coffee.

"Hey, Rion," Maurese began, "Sorry about that. You shouldn't have had to see us like that."

Rion did not turn around to face them, but he scoffed. "Please. I've seen my mother in worse positions. That was nothing."

"Well, you shouldn't be barging into my room anyway," Roslyn said haughtily.

"I was trying to offer you a ride to work. But I see you already got a *ride*," he said, emphasizing the last word for the double meaning.

"Don't talk to your mother that way," Maurese reprimanded.

"Shut up, Grease," Rion retorted. "Don't you have a girlfriend or fiancée or whatever waiting for you in Stockton?"

"Okay, enough!" Roslyn raised her voice. "We are two grown, consenting adults, and neither of us needs to be scolded by you. This is my house, and I do what I want in it, got it?"

"Got it," Rion said, still not turning around to look at either of them.

"Thank you." She ran her hands through her hair and said, "Now, if you're still offering that ride to work, I'll be ready in fifteen."

Nick raised an eyebrow at him. Rion sighed. "Sure, Mama."

"Thank you." She turned to Maurese and stood on her tippy toes to kiss his lips. "Drive safely." Roslyn walked back to her room to get ready.

Maurese was still standing there. "Rion, look at me."

Rion looked at Nick, who smiled, enjoying the family drama that was not his own. Rion did not smile back. He tapped his knuckles a few times on the counter before he turned around.

Maurese took a few steps closer. "I'm sorry that I've disappointed you with my actions."

Rion's face softened a little. He realized he did feel disappointed in his father figure. Maurese continued. "You have to understand that I've loved Roslyn since we were fourteen-year-olds. And I always will."

"Well, then maybe you should marry Roslyn instead of whats-her-face," Rion mumbled.

He was surprised by Maurese's smile. "Maybe I should." He touched Rion's shoulder and said, "I'm headed back home. You call me if you need anything, okay? You can call me anytime."

Rion nodded. "Yeah, okay."

Maurese pulled him close and gave him a hug, which Rion returned. He reached out and gave Nick a handshake. "I'm glad we got a chance to meet. You're a good man, Nick."

"Good to meet you, too," Nick said back as he shook Maurese's hand.

When the front door closed, Nick began to snicker, and Rion turned to him with a stern look. "What?" Nick said with amusement. "You're not the first kid to catch your parents having sex, and you won't be the last one."

Rion scoffed and snatched Nick's coffee out of his hands. "They aren't my parents. Maurese would have claimed me, just like he claimed Muriel, if he was my sperm donor. I know that for sure."

Nick was reminded of the huge secret that Maurese and Roslyn were keeping from Rion. He knew now would not be the right time, but Nick also knew he could not keep it from Rion for long.

"Maybe so, but..." Nick chose his words. "Do you think he would have told you if he knew who your father was?"

Before Rion could respond, his mother came out of her room, dressed for work. "I made pasta last week for myself, so you and Ava can eat that for lunch, Nick. Let her know I should be back around five o'clock." She walked up to Rion and linked her arm around his. "Now, if you're going to give me shit, then I'll take the bus," she said to her son.

Rion rolled his eyes. "Let's go, Mama." He touched Nick's face, and they kissed. "Take care of Ava today."

"Absolutely," Nick said. They kissed again, and Rion and Roslyn left the home.

Ava came out of her room a few hours later and Nick looked up from his laptop. "Morning, Mr. Deep Strokez."

He smiled at her. "Good afternoon."

She plopped down next to him on the couch and crossed her legs. "I guess you got the short end of the stick? They left you to babysit me?"

He smiled. "I volunteered."

She smiled back. "Yeah, right."

He told her, "Your mother went to work, Maurese headed back to Stockton, and Rion went to go see about selling his apartment, officially."

"Maurese was still here?" she questioned in confusion.

Nick shook his head. "I don't know if you want to know about that drama this morning."

"Nope, I don't." She shook her head. "Any food?"

"Roslyn said she left a pasta dish for you," said Nick, turning back to the email he was reading.

Ava turned up her nose. "No, thanks. Mama is a horrible cook. Can we order a pizza?"

"Sure. What do you want on it?"

"Sausage, jalapenos, green peppers, and extra cheese."

"Got it." Nick placed his laptop on the ottoman that his feet were on and grabbed his phone instead.

Ava looked at the computer. "Where's that? It's beautiful."

"That's the surroundings of a monastery in Thailand that I want to go to." He lifted his laptop back up, and Ava drew closer. He started at the Home page. "Wat Chai TiPat. They have a ten-day Buddhist retreat coming up. They do it every year around this time. I haven't gone yet, but I will one day."

"That's right, you're Buddhist. Or at least studying to be," she said. Nick looked up at her with a curious smile. She giggled. "Oh, I know everything about you. I watched your interview and sex tape like a million times."

Nick's face flushed red, and he turned away from her. "Not one of my finest moments."

"No, it was a pretty *fine* moment to me," said Ava teasingly. "But back to you being a Buddhist. I would love to sit in a monastery and learn. I had an escort client from Cambodia who tried to teach me to meditate. But all I was thinking of was the crystal bong he had on his dresser."

She started laughing and Nick shook his head with a smile. "We gotta get you thinking about something other than drugs."

"C'mon Richy-Rich. Don't act like you don't have a drug of choice. I've been to parties in the Hills and I know the good shit the One Percent got going on there."

"It was coke," Nick admitted. "But the last time I used was that infamous night that I unknowingly was recorded. And when I told Rion I used it, he looked at me like how he looked at his mother, somewhere between disgust and disappointment."

Ava nodded knowingly. "That's because he was a coke baby."

"What?"

"He was born premature with cocaine in his system."

"Oh right," said Nick. "I did know that."

"But you don't know how bad it was," Ava countered. "It did real damage to him. He had the most god-awful seizures when he was a baby until some doctor got him a medication that worked, and then he grew out of it around six. But the cocaine and the seizures gave him ADHD and social anxiety. Can you imagine having a childhood of seizures, hyperactivity, and also being afraid of your own skin? And on top of that, living with addicts, gang members, and drug dealers?" Ava shook her head in sadness. "Rion didn't like any kind of drugs, prescribed or not, but definitely not cocaine. But he started taking CBD when he was thirteen after going to a holistic doctor that Maurese brought him to, to treat his ADHD and anxiety. He went from using CBD oils to gummies to smoking joints, and that's the extent of his drug use. He really should be a basket case like me. But nope, he healed himself and channeled all his energy into fucking useless men and then writing about fucking useless men." She giggled.

"And is that what you're trying to do, too?" asked Nick. "Heal yourself with fentanyl?"

"Gotta do something to forget the abuse and abandonment," Ava said simply. "I was left to my own devices by the time I was seven, started getting passed around in the 781 when I started developing breasts at ten, and was turning tricks in hotels for the crew by twelve. We were all abused, but Muriel had Maurese to protect her, Gabby had Gabriel, and since she and Rion were so close in age, he tried to protect Baby Bro, too. I had no one."

Nick reached out and touched her hand. "Does talking about it help?"

Ava gave him a small smile. "I've been talking about it. At every rehab or mental institution they put me in since I was sixteen. And I'm going to do it again: go to rehab for a month or two, talk about it, take my meds, and get on track. Until something else happens, and then I'll use again." She shrugged.

"What do you think will help?" Nick asked.

"I don't know," Ava said helplessly. "I've tried everything. They told me to confront my demons, the thought that keeps me up at night. So I did. I confronted Danny Santos, and he pretended he didn't know me. But his wife did. Right before she slammed the door in my face, she told me that I would never be a part of his life or their family. She had no idea how much that triggered me. So yeah, I got drunk and high on Percocet, grabbed lighter fluid, and burned the front and back doors. Then I sat there in the street and watched it burn. I thought I was going to get three hots and a cot, but they put me in a straight jacket in a white room instead for eight months. I tried to forget and go straight again and join the police force. One of Fox's police contacts got me in, despite arson on my record. And I was great at it. Until one of the lead officers pulled my jacket, saw I had a prostitution history, brought me into his back office, and raped me. Then he told me I would be his good little chink as long as I gave him what he wanted when he wanted. The next time he pulled me into his office, this good little chink beat the shit out of that old man. And that's why they kicked me out. It had nothing to do with me being bipolar; I was on meds at the time. But I never told anyone about the rape. I just let them all believe it was just Ava being crazy again."

Nick touched her hand again. "I'm so sorry, Avalon."

"Don't be. It was a learned lesson," she said. "I realized how people saw me, so I tried it a little in your world, too. I started turning tricks for myself, no pimp, no abuse, just me being selective about who my clients were, and ended up becoming a high-powered escort from L.A. to Vegas. I was great at that, too. Me and a group of girls that were determined not to let men rule us. But I overdosed one night after a gang-bang, and the LAPD picked me up, so it was back to rehab for me. When I came out, the girls told me I was a liability to their clientele, and I was back to being abandoned.

"I've tried, Nick. I've tried to go straight, I've tried to walk the line, I've dug deeper into the underground world, I've tried to forget, I've spilled out my guts over and over again, I've tried NA, AA, Al-Anon, I've tried every single denomination of Christianity, I've tried every single medication for the allotted six to eight weeks before I stopped it, and I always ended up right back here."

"Have you tried to just start all over, like Rion did?" Nick asked. "Move away from everything and everyone that reminds you of your past? Maybe get a name change, drop the Santos, and just start over?"

Ava was thoughtful. "I guess I haven't tried everything."

"If you want to start all over, I think Rion would love to have you in New York with us," he said. "And I would, too."

She shook her head. "I couldn't do that to him. He has a full life out there with you. I wouldn't want to burden him or want him to feel responsible for me. Muriel keeps saying that Rion is free from all of this and she's right. Me being there with my shit would just pull him back in. Then, eventually, he'll abandon me too out there. And so will you."

"Ava, whether you are here or there or anywhere, your brother would never abandon you. Before Gabby finished telling him what was going on, he was already packing a bag and headed out the door, ready to abandon *me* to find you and take care of you for however long it took to get you back on your feet. There is at least one person on this earth who would never abandon you. Two, if you count Gabby, who never stopped screaming about your disappearance until people started listening. Three, if you add your mother in there, who dropped everything to find you. Four, if you include Muriel in her own way. Five, if you are gracious enough to let me be there for you, too."

Avalon blinked tears away. "So you're gonna teach me some chants or what?" she asked, changing the subject.

Nick closed his laptop and turned to her. He crossed his legs on the couch and put his hands in his lap. She mimicked his hands and his posture. "I haven't done this in over a year, you know. I've been so wrapped up in work and my romantic life that I haven't given a whole lot of thought to my spiritual one."

"And I've been so wrapped up in my drug habit that I haven't given one thought to my spiritual life," she said in amusement.

Nick smiled at her. "Repeat after me: *Oṃ maṇi padme hūṃ.*" Nick spoke slowly and enunciated each syllable of the mantra.

"Om Ma Ni Pad Me Hūm," Ava repeated. "What does it mean?"

"Praise to the jewel in the lotus. Or Praise to a lotus that is a jewel. There's a debate among scholars. But what they all agree on is that it's considered one of the most powerful mantras in the world. It is said to contain the essence of the entire teaching of Buddha. Om brings forth perfection of generosity, Ma, ethics, Ni, patience, Pad, perseverance, Me, concentration and Hūm, wisdom."

"Wow. Okay, let's do it," Ava said, getting comfortable.

Nicholas set up the meditation loop on his phone and placed it on the table. "Two minutes of silent meditation, twenty minutes of chanting, then another two minutes of meditation. When you hear the first chime, we begin."

Together, they took a few deep breaths. Nick closed his eyes first, and Ava followed him. He cleared his mind, pushing Rion's beautiful face out of his head so he could concentrate. When the soft chime went off on his phone, Nick began to chant, slowly. Ava's voice joined in for the second round and blended with his. They both found themselves drawing further inward, allowing the sound and feeling to bring them into a higher state of consciousness. The soft chime went off again. Nicholas stopped first, listening to Ava continue to chant. Eventually, she slowed down and stopped. They quietly meditated until the chime went off a third time.

The two slowly opened their eyes. "That was..." Nick began. Then they spoke at the same time.

"Enlightening," said Nick.

"Beautiful," said Ava.

Ava grinned and reached in to give Nick a hug. Nick patted her back. "You're welcome, Avalon."

"I want to do more of that," she said. "Will you teach me?"

Nick nodded. "We'll learn together."

When Rion turned up later on, he found his sister and his boyfriend cozy on the couch, binge-watching DMZ on HBO. He smiled at them.

Ava grinned. "I really like your boyfriend. Can I have him?" she asked.

Rion sat on the couch. "I don't think he wants what you got."

"I don't think you watched his sex tape," Ava said back.

Rion laughed out loud as Nick shook his head, continuing to be embarrassed by his faux pas. Ava stood up and kissed Nick's head. "Thanks, Nicky."

"You're welcome," he said back. She went back to her room.

Rion moved closer and put his head on Nick's shoulder. "Sounds like you had a good day, *Nicky*," he said, teasing him about his nickname.

"I did," said Nick, not at all bothered by it. "But I missed you, Ree."

Rion lifted his head up. Together, they moved closer and kissed sweetly. "I missed you, too."

"All good with the apartment?" Nick asked.

"Yup," said Rion. "I got it cleaned out and moved what little stuff I had to Muriel's house, then spent some time with my nephew before heading back here. I just needed to sign some paperwork and give Manny permission to put it on the market. He'll take care of everything, take twenty percent, and forward the balance to my bank account. I just might go buy that Toyota Camry. Is there room in the garage back home for me?" Rion smirked playfully.

Nick smirked back. "I want to run something by you," Nick started. He told him about the conversation earlier with Ava and their meditation.

Rion listened. "So, what are you saying? You want me to look at rehab places in New York so she can be with us when she gets out, and you can teach her Buddhism?"

"Actually…" Nick opened up his laptop and showed him the retreat. "I want us to take her here. To Thailand. Instead of another rehab place, she does this instead."

Rion looked at the screen, then back at Nick. "How is this going to help her?"

"How has rehab been helping her?" Nick countered. "She said she has tried everything and always ends up right back where she is today. And it's because she doesn't feel connected to anything, not even her family. Ava has felt abandoned her whole life and is desperate to feel a connection, and I know what that feels like. Ava needs to feel connected to something, to the ground under her feet and the air around her, to a community. This trip could start her on a path of feeling connected to herself again, so she won't need the drugs to forget."

"And after ten days?"

"Well, how do you feel about her coming back with us?" Nick asked gently.

"I would love that, to have my sister close to me," Rion said automatically. "Not just to keep an eye on her, but to have family nearby that I don't have to get on a plane to go see. But does she want that?"

"All she said is that she didn't want to be a burden on you. So you'll have to talk to her about that. But all I know for sure is that she can't come back to California.

All her demons are here. She needs a new environment to start over."

Rion looked down at the screen. "So you want to take my sister on a flight to Thailand with you for ten days?"

Nick chuckled. "You're going, too, Rion. You're going with me and Ava on this spiritual journey."

Rion grimaced. "I gotta get on a plane, though? Isn't it like a ten-hour plane ride?"

"Actually, two planes, most likely, but yes, about ten hours each. And either another small plane or a drive to the Song Phi Nong district."

"Twenty hours!? Holy, holy shit, I'm not going," Rion said, shaking his head.

Nick laughed out loud and kissed his face. "Scaredy cat. I'll be there to hold your hand, like always."

Rion knocked on the room door. "Come in," Ava called out.

Ava was folding her laundered clothes and listening to music. She glanced up. "Hey baby bro, what's up?"

He looked at his sister, who was thin and still looked sickly, but was starting to get some color back in her cheeks. She also looked happy. Like she was calm and balanced.

Rion took a deep breath and asked, "So we're going to Thailand in three days?"

She looked up sharply. "Nick told you about the ten-day retreat?"

"Yup."

"Wow." She nodded in approval. "I would have thought the plane ride alone would make you say no."

Rion gave her a frown. "Don't remind me."

"Oh, you'll be fine," she reassured him. "I'm glad you're going. You guys will have a great time. And don't worry about me, I'll be fine here. I'm back on track now. I just scheduled an appointment with my psychiatrist tomorrow. I can do outpatient rehab, take my meds, and practice Buddhism. Bring me back some books so I can study up, too." She went back to folding clothes.

"No, Ava," Rion said. "*We* are going to Thailand in three days. You, me, and Nicholas. Nick is going on a spiritual journey, you're going to start over and begin to feel connected to things again, and apparently I'm going to get over my fear of flying." He grimaced again.

Ava looked at him again. "Seriously?"

"Yup."

Ava jumped off the bed and threw her arms around her brother's neck. "I don't think I've ever been so happy in my entire life!"

Rion smiled and hugged her back. It was enough to realize that Nicholas was right. She needed this.

Nick threw on the black hoodie again and a pair of Rion's Jordans. He wanted to be as incognito in the airport as possible. They were getting ready to get on a nine-hour redeye flight to South Korea, then a six-hour layover before they traveled another nine hours to Bangkok. Zoey tried, but that was the best she could do, short of making it three very small flights.

Nick turned around to say something and watched Rion grab a handful of gummies and toss them in his mouth, then begin to chew.

Nick frowned. "I'm pretty sure that wasn't the right dosage."

"It's not," Rion said with his mouth full.

"Rion? Are you sure that's what you want to do?" Rion continued chewing. Nick shook his head and walked over to him. He kissed his lips. "Let's go."

They walked into the main area, where Avalon was waiting in the living room with her mother and sisters. They were hugging each other tightly.

Rion joined them, hugging Muriel and Gabby, then hugged Roslyn last. She held onto him the longest. "Call me every day," she said.

"I don't think I can, Mama," he said. "I'm pretty sure we have to put our phones away."

"We do," Nick confirmed. "No electronics for ten days. Although I think we have access to them if we really need them."

"Well, if you can," Roslyn said. She hugged Rion again. Then she hugged Nick, too. "Thank you so much for taking care of my baby. Both of them."

"They're in good hands, Roslyn," Nick said back. "And keep taking care of yourself."

"Thank you, Nicholas," she said sincerely. "I made a lot of mistakes with them. All I can do now is keep showing up when they need me to."

"As someone who is estranged from my mother, a woman who would never apologize for the mistakes she made with her own children, I can tell you that it means a lot." Roslyn gave him another strong hug.

Ava, Nick, and Rion left the apartment and took the car service over to the San Francisco International Airport. Because it was so late on a Monday evening, the TSA line was considerably shortened for such a busy airport. Nick left them to go through Pre-Check. Rion had been gradually feeling the effects of the amount of THC he took, but it didn't register to him until he had to take off his shoes. Then he started rambling.

"Why do we still take off our shoes? Is it because of the shoe-bomber all those years ago? Do they think someone would try that again? Or is it that they just want to see our feet? Or the size of our feet? Is there some secret government process that measures the size of our feet to determine if we're bad or not? I'm a size eleven. Am I bad? I haven't always been a size eleven. Maybe I'm a size twelve now. Maybe—"

"Rion!" Ava cut him off. He stopped talking abruptly and looked at her. Then he started giggling. "Holy shit, Rion. How much did you take?"

"A lot," he admitted and laughed again. "Don't worry, I'll fall asleep soon."

"Jesus," she said, shaking her head. "You think you can get through airport security without alerting the whole damn airport how high you are?" Ava whispered.

"I feel bad," he said sadly. "You can't get high anymore. How are you going to make it through ten hours on the plane?"

"I don't need to get high to get on a plane, baby bro. I'm not the one freaking out over flying. You are."

"So no one else is afraid of flying but me?" he said again with a frown.

"Hey, can you move it along!?" someone behind them yelled.

Ava realized they were standing in place. She pushed Rion toward the body scanner and said, "Don't talk. Don't laugh. Do what they say and get past them. Got it?"

"Roger dat," he said jokingly, then began to giggle.

"Jesus," Ava said again. "We're all getting arrested."

But Rion managed to stay still as he went through the body scan. He grabbed his new carry-on with old clothes from his old apartment and rolled it over to Nick as Nick was waiting for them on the other side.

Before Nick could speak, Rion said, "Do you know that they think I'm a shoe-bomber?" Then he began to giggle again.

Nick stared at him, then looked at Ava. She shrugged impassively. Nick looked back at Rion and touched his face lovingly. Rion closed his eyes and leaned into Nick's hand. "Don't worry, I'm okay," Rion mumbled. "I'll fall asleep."

"Okay, babe," Nick said gently. He put back on his hood, then took Rion's hand. They walked through the nearly empty airport to their terminal.

Rion laughed through take-off and, indeed, fell asleep soon afterward. Ava and Nick both smiled at him, then began to exchange notes and information on Buddhism before they settled on which movies they were going to watch. Rion woke up six hours later to pee and eat, then went back to sleep and did not wake up again until they had already landed at Incheon International Airport in South Korea.

"How do you feel?" Nick asked as they made their way through "Connecting Flights."

"Sluggish, but I'm okay," said Rion. "I'm not going to fall asleep again, but my body is too relaxed to have a panic attack."

"Just one more flight," Nick reassured him. "Then we're there."

"Yeah, but we gotta come home at some point," Rion whined.

"Don't think about that," said Nick. "Think about the here and now. Stay in the moment at the moment."

Rion smiled at him. "I think you're trying to turn me into a Buddhist."

"It wouldn't be a bad thing. Look at Ava just soaking it all up these last couple of days. She's going to love the retreat. And so will you."

On the next flight, both Nick and Ava fell asleep on Rion. He managed to get out his laptop and get some writing done. Then he was bored. He stood up and began to walk the length of the plane. The plane was filled with people from all over the world. He struck up a conversation with an older man from Georgia who was on his way to Thailand to meet a woman he had been talking to online for the last six months. If all went well, he would propose to her right away. They joked about him ending up on the TV show 90 Day Fiancé. Rion talked with one of the flight attendants, finding out about her life in the U.S. and met the co-pilot, Peter Giles, who let him take a peek into the cockpit. The pilot explained all the controls and systems they have in place so that the plane would not crash and that he was safer up there than he would be in a car. He also explained what turbulence was, a change in airflow, and most of the time they know when it is coming, so they give their passengers a warning. They talked for a while until Pete had to get back to work, but before he did, they took a picture together. Rion was thankful for the information and told the Caucasian pilot he was going to write a sexy, erotic story about him and his African American girl-friend, Jordanne. By the time Rion made it back to his seat, Ava was awake and reading one of Nick's books about Zen meditation.

As they were descending, Nick watched Rion closely, ready to hold his hand. But Rion appeared calm to him. Rion still closed his eyes and counted backward from fifty, but he could see the pilot at the controls, safely bringing them down. The plane made a soft bump and Rion opened his eyes, then smiled. He clapped with the rest of the passengers.

"Wow," Nick said. "You made it through that smoothly. I guess the gummies did their job."

"No," said Rion. "It was Pilot Pete. He did his job."

Nick looked at him in confusion but didn't say much as they made their way off the plane. He gave Rion another confused look as Rion hugged the pilot before he got off. "What was that about?"

"You'll read about it in another story," Rion said slyly.

There was a driver waiting for them with Nick's name when they came out of Suvarnabhumi Airport. They drove a little over an hour into the mountains, and Rion realized he had another fear: falling off a cliff on a bus. He did not like how close to the edge they were. But suddenly, they stopped at a clearing in front of a large stone building with a huge Buddha statue in front.

They stepped out in awe of it. "How beautiful," Ava said first.

They rolled their suitcases through the glass opening and stopped at the front. The woman at the desk bowed her head slightly and said, "I am Dao. Welcome to Wat Chai TiPat. Please give me your names."

Nick was first. He was given a key to his locker, a brown Zen meditation robe, shoes, a mat, a notebook and pencil, and a folder with the meditation times, including silent meditation times, workshops, and a map of the grounds. Rion was given the same, and so was Ava, except her meditation robe was light blue.

They followed two men down a corridor and stopped at a large room filled with lockers. "You must put away all your electronics," one of the monks said. "You are not allowed to use them anywhere in the temple. If you need to make a phone call, you would have to go past the labyrinth or go into the main office."

Rion sadly locked his laptop away. Nick sent Zoey a quick message letting her know he was starting and would not be in contact for the next ten days. Ava put her items away, knowing that she would be back every day to grab her cell phone at some point. They were brought to another corridor lined with doors that had keys in them. One of the monks took Ava away to the female quarters. The other one pointed at Nick, then to the row of doors. Nick took a key out of one of the doors and entered. The room was small. It had a twin-size bed with a mosquito net over it, one dresser, and one window. There was also a sink in the corner. Nick had expected it, but he couldn't help looking around and asking himself if he could do this.

As if Rion could read his mind, he stepped next to him. "This is fine. We're minimalist for ten days, remember?"

Nick walked over to the bed and touched it. It immediately squeaked. He turned to Rion with a grimace.

Rion laughed. "Listen, remember I slept at the bottom of a closet for months. This tiny cell is an upgrade for me." He turned around and left the room. Nick stood in his doorway and watched which room

Rion went into, across the hall and two doors down. He winked before he disappeared inside.

Nick sighed, then went back into his room. He began to unfold his clothes into the tiny dresser and put his books on the ground next to the bed. He threw water on his face and stared out the window for a moment. It was nothing but greenery around him. He changed into a pair of sweatpants and put his meditation robes on. Then he sat on the floor, closed his eyes, and began to meditate.

At the sound of the bell, he stepped out of his room and walked into a sea of people, all heading to dinner together. Rion caught up to him, wearing his robes as well. They walked side by side into the cafeteria. Rion searched the room for Ava with his eyes but realized that her peanut butter skin tone blended right in with the sea of Asian women. So instead, he followed Nick to the line and added Pad Thai Noodles and kept it safe with Thai dumplings and fried rice with sausage.

As they ate, Rion kept looking around. Nick noticed. "She's fine," he reassured Rion. "At some point, you're going to have to let her go, baby bro." Rion looked up at Nick sharply, who grinned. "Hey, if you can call me Nicky, I can call you baby bro."

Before Rion could think of a snappy comeback, he heard her voice. "There you are!" Ava called and walked over with a group of three other women. "You would think I could pick out my white-skinned brother in all these brown Asians."

She introduced her new friends: two were sisters from the United States and the third was a young Scottish woman who was as new to the experience as

Ava was. One of the sisters immediately said, "Hey, aren't you Mr. Deep Strokez?"

Nick smiled. "If you keep it quiet for the next ten days, I'll go live on your IG account with you after the retreat. Deal?"

The woman couldn't believe her luck. "Deal!" she practically screamed.

"I just came to check on you," said Ava. "But I'll be with them all week. That's okay, right?" She looked from Nick to Rion.

Rion put on a brave face. "Sure, of course. It's your journey."

Ava hugged Rion's neck and said, "I'll be around." Then she left with her new friends.

Rion watched her walk away. "I'm still here," Nick teased.

Rion looked at his boyfriend. He reached his hand across the table and caressed Nick. "And I'm so grateful that you are."

Rion walked into the room and there were about thirty people at that early morning workshop named "Why are you here?" It was a beginner's workshop for understanding the principles of Buddhism, mindfulness, and meditation, and it was every morning from 6 a.m. to 9 a.m. Nick, who considered himself an intermediate and a novice at meditation, had knocked on his door before the sun rose to tell him he was doing an early morning meditation then walking a labyrinth, and he would find him before the regular morning meditation at 10 a.m.

Rion spotted Ava, but she was with her new friends, so Rion plopped his mat down and sat on the other side of the room. The teacher came in, stood in front of them, clasped her hands, and bowed. Rion expected to see another Thai man or woman, but the woman in front of him was white, with blond hair in locks hanging down her back. And when she spoke, she had an English accent.

"Welcome, all of you, for taking a brave step and coming to your first workshop at Wat Chai TiPat. My name is Hagar. This is the first part of a very long journey in your life. So please, let us start with some light meditation. Two minutes to quiet down your mind, open your heart and be ready to receive."

Rion had not meditated a day in his life. His anxiety made it impossible to focus his mind on one thing. But he laid on his mat like the rest of the participants and closed his eyes.

As if she could read his mind, she said, "If you find it hard to concentrate on your own, focus on the sound of my voice. Let us begin."

Hagar rang a bell and began to hum in a low tone. Then she would take a breath and hum again. Rion found that focusing on the sound did help him concentrate. She did it on and off for two full minutes until the bell went off again.

"Do not open your eyes," she said quietly. "Feel how your back feels against the floor, the breeze through the open window, how your shoulders feel in the clothes you are wearing. Take notice of any twitch,

itch, or pain in your limbs. Stay in the moment, and feel every single moment."

Hagar walked them through a body scan for the next eight minutes. Then she said, "Congratulations. You have successfully completed your first ten-minute meditation of mindfulness."

She made them stand up and stretch, then sit down or lay on their mats any way they felt comfortable, as long as they kept their eyes closed. Rion chose to sit crossed-legged with his back against the wall. Before he closed his eyes, he saw that Ava chose to lie on her back.

"When I tap you," Hagar said, "I want you to tell me why you are here. The first thing that comes to mind. The honest truth. What you feel in your core."

She must have tapped someone because a voice said, "I just got divorced and I'm trying to find myself again."

"Did you lose yourself?" Hagar asked softly.

"Yes. I forgot who I was before him. He made me into a neurotic person, and I don't want to be that person anymore."

"So don't be," Hagar said simply. "Life will happen the way it happens, and there is nothing you can do about it, except hold on to the good that you have. Name one good thing to come out of your marriage?"

"My daughter," the woman said automatically.

"Then, when you feel yourself become neurotic, remind yourself of her. Her face, her laughter, something funny or kind that she has done. Combat the negative energy with a positive thought or feeling."

She touched someone else. "Why are you here?"

A man said, "It's my third year. I do this retreat annually on my birthday month."

"Happy birthday. And welcome back," she said softly.

She went around and touched each person and let them explain to the group why they were there. Rion was actively listening, waiting for his turn, when he heard his sister's voice.

"I'm here because I need to feel connected to something, anything, before I spiral again. I want my last binge to be my last binge."

"Substance abuse?" Hagar asked gently.

"Yes."

"So you want to come off one high for another high. The elevation of mind, body, and spirit."

"Yes," Ava said with a smile.

"But you cannot hide behind the Buddha. If you want to feel connected to people, places, and things, you have to stay in the moment long enough to actually feel. Feel pain. Feel joy. Feel heartache. Feel broken. Feel confident. Feel surprised. You have to want to feel it all, then move past it because nothing, not even feelings, is infinite."

"I've felt it all," Ava implored. "I've been broken. I've been alone. I have no connections with anyone. No one cares about me, whether I live or die."

"I care," Rion said softly. No one spoke, so Rion continued. "I got on a plane and flew three thousand miles to find you. I got on another plane, two in fact, just so you can heal. That's three terrifying plane rides, all for you. I care about you, Avalon. You're my sister. My family. I love you."

He heard Ava sniff a few times. Hagar said softly, "It seems you have at least one connection. But also, know that everything that has happened to you in your life has brought you here with us, to this very moment. You spiral because you fall into old habits. Leave the old behind. Stay in the present with us all week. Can you do that?"

"Yes," Ava said.

Rion felt a soft hand on his shoulder. "Why are you here? Other than for your sister."

Rion told the truth. "My boyfriend made me come." A few people laughed.

But Hagar did not. "So you have no desire to center yourself? To find your power deep within and let it bring forth the light in you?"

Rion grimaced. "Honestly? No. I'm not really a religious person. And this is a little hokey to me."

"Ah, but Buddhism is not about religion. Buddhism is about the inward, self-reliance, self-sustaining understanding of the life cycles that are continuous. But let's say you are Christian, and you believe that Jesus lives in your heart. Then, when you look inward, you are looking to a higher power. It can still align with your beliefs. There are Christian Buddhists."

"I don't have a belief in a higher power," said Rion. "Just like Ava, I've had too much shit happen to me to believe it was all for a purpose. I'm definitely not Christian. And I'm not a Buddhist either."

"But you are a human," Hagar countered. "A person with fears. Fear of flying, yes?"

Rion hesitated. "Yes."

"And what do you do to fight that fear when you are on a plane? Do you pray it all ends at some point?"

"No. I take breaths, count backward from fifty and wait until the takeoff or landing is over."

Hagar lowered herself again and touched his shoulder. "And that, my friend, is mindfulness."

She walked on and touched someone else, leaving Rion to think about what she said.

Rion couldn't find Nicholas at breakfast, so at ten minutes to 10 a.m., he grabbed his mat and went to the main meditation room with everyone else. He sat down, not having much of a clue about what he was supposed to be doing. The room filled up with at least a hundred individuals, and there was an elevated platform with one monk in front of twenty monks behind him. For so many people in a cavernous room, Rion noticed it was eerily quiet. A gong went off. The monks began to chant long, drawn-out words. It was loud and echoed throughout the entire room. Rion looked to his left and right, and both men had their eyes closed, and one was silently mimicking the words. Rion closed his eyes and concentrated on the sound like he did at the workshop. He found himself falling into a trance, the strong sound and unfamiliar words reverberating through his body. He was sleeping, but he wasn't. He was dreaming, but what about, he wasn't sure. And when the chant stopped, he barely noticed.

When Rion opened his eyes, he saw that the person on his right, along with a few others, had left, but the man on his left was still there, seemingly in his own trance. He stood up and took his mat, and walked back to his room. Nick was standing in his doorway, waiting for him. Rion stopped in front of him.

"I haven't seen you all morning."

"I saw you," said Nick. "After the hour-long meditation, I saw you still sitting there, so I decided to let you be."

"An hour-long?" Rion said in astonishment. "No way. It was like twenty minutes, tops."

Nick looked at his watch, then at Rion. "You were there for an hour and a half. We chanted for an hour, then you stayed in Zen. I've been waiting for you for about thirty minutes."

Rion's mouth dropped. "Wow. I guess I can meditate. Maybe this is for me."

Nick smiled and hugged his boyfriend. "Lunch is mindful eating, then I'm doing a silent meditation in the woods with a group of others. I'm not sure when we'll be back."

"Mindful eating?" Rion asked skeptically.

"It's eating slowly, silently, and meaningfully. Taking in every bite, enjoying every moment, thankful for every nourishment."

Rion shook his head. "I take it all back. This is not for me."

Nick chuckled. "After dinner, we'll take a walk. I found something really cool I want to show you."

Nick held Rion's hand and led him into the forest, off the path. He explained, "After my labyrinth walk, I spotted some Siamese tulips and followed them deep into the woods and accidentally stumbled across it."

"Across what?"

"You'll see."

They walked about ten minutes until Rion heard it, the rushing of water. "Oh wow," he said as they came closer. It was a waterfall, large and beautiful, that led into a river of floating pink lotus.

Rion stood on a large boulder. "Holy, holy shit. It's gorgeous. I wish I had brought my phone to take pics."

Nick stood on the boulder next to him and put his arm around Rion's shoulder. "It is. And even more beautiful at sunset than this morning."

They turned to each other and kissed. Then Rion asked, "Is sex off the table for the next nine days?"

Nicholas laughed out loud. "It's not, not off the table. But the logistics of how, when, and where will be the challenge. Plus..." Nick hesitated, then said, "Plus, I think the three of us will be on different spiritual journeys. We may not see much of each other until the ten days are over."

Rion nodded. "Ava already left us. And I'm actually appreciating being able to meditate for the first time in my life. Tomorrow my workshop is on learning how to breathe, which sounds stupid, but I have a feeling it's going to be really great. And you're leaving at the crack of dawn, doing silent meditations, labyrinths, and chanting while I'm still trying to figure out the purpose of mindful eating."

Nick smiled at him and kissed his lips again. "We can meet here every night at this same time."

Rion kissed him back. "Deal."

va plopped her tray next to Rion that afternoon. He smiled at her. "Well, look who decided to spend some time with her baby brother after eight days."

"Oh, shut up. We did the workshop together the first day," she reminded him. "Let's go outside. I want to grab my phone and text everyone, let them know I'm doing great."

"It's in the middle of the night back home," Nick reminded her.

"Oh. Well, I want my phone, anyway. As much as I enjoy being here, I'm going a little stir-crazy without it."

They grabbed their pita bread wrapped up in tissue and stopped at the lockers. Ava and Rion grabbed their phones, but Nick did not. He had no desire to be pulled back into his world. Nick steered them toward the labyrinth he had been walking daily before the sun rose. They sat in the center and talked. Rion told them all he had been learning about meditation and mindfulness and believed that he was just starting to master it. Nick talked about falling into a Zen state of consciousness for hours daily and feeling grateful to the universe for the trip. Ava caught them up on what she had been reading about Buddhism and really felt like it was for her. She also told them about her time with Amy and Sara, the sisters from Colorado, and Desdemona from Scotland, and how they planned to keep in touch.

"They're actually staying a little longer," Ava said. "They're renting an Airbnb just a few miles down the road."

"People do it all the time," said Nicholas. "It's so much to learn, and once you find your center, you don't want to let it go."

"Yeah, but I gotta get back. I have some amends to make, starting with my mama. I treated her so badly when I was detoxing," Ava said and frowned. "I said some awful things that I know hurt her."

"I still can't believe she saved you," Rion said, shaking his head. "Actually saved you. Our mama, the addict."

"Recovering addict. Mama was a superstar, Ree," said Ava. "She really has changed. I believe her this time, that she's going to stay clean. I literally threw a bag of coke at her face and she just brushed it off, grabbed my arms, and restrained me."

"You threw coke at our mother?" Rion said in astonishment.

"Oh, I was awful," Ava said sadly. "But she never gave up on me. She took all the angry words and the physical assault and just loved me through it. She's so much stronger than we think she is."

"Wow."

"Yeah. You should accept her amends, baby bro. She needs our support to keep going."

"I'll accept her amends when she tells me who my father is. That's the only amends that I need," said Rion.

"I don't know, Ree," Ava said, picking at his pita bread. "She's not telling you for a reason. I think he's a really bad person, and she doesn't want him in your life."

Rion stared at her in disbelief. "She had a baby with a fucking drug kingpin," he said, and Ava laughed loudly. Rion was also laughing as he said, "There is no worse person than that."

When the laughter died down, Nick called his name softly. "Rion?"

"Yeah?" he said, turning to his boyfriend.

Nick licked his lower lip nervously. "I know who your father is."

Rion immediately stopped smiling. "What?"

"I mean, I don't *know* know, but I ..." He trailed off, looking at the anger on Rion's face.

Rion sat up straighter. "How? Did your siblings do a background check on me?" he asked testily.

"No! I mean, *yes*... but that's not how I know," Nick tried to explain.

"What the fuck, Nick!?" Rion said angrily. "It was Emma, wasn't it?"

Nick was flustered. "Yes, Emma did run a check, but listen, she couldn't find out either. Roslyn really kept that information close to her."

"Then how the—"

"I need you to calm down," Nick said sternly. "This is going to be really emotional and hard to hear, but I need you to calm down and listen to me. When you're ready to listen, I will talk."

Rion adjusted his long tunic and resumed sitting crossed-legged on the ground. Nick sat in front of him. Ava looked at Nick expectantly, too.

"Okay," Rion said calmly. "I'm ready to listen."

Nick began to explain. "When that guy, Mus, was on the phone, he made a comment that I know you and Gabby didn't hear, because you were so shocked to know that your mother had already come to save Ava. He said something to the effect of, 'All we need is Junior to claim his son, and we'd have a family reunion.' And Maurese hung up the phone on him before he could say anything more."

Rion's lips parted slightly. "Junior?" Ava asked. She looked at her brother. "What Junior?" Rion slowly turned to her. They stared at each other. "It can't be. No." Ava shook her head. "No."

Rion didn't respond. He looked at Nick. "We only know one person associated with the 781 that they called D.J. or Junior."

Nick nodded slowly. "Maurese's older brother. Right?"

Rion looked at him in confusion. "Yes. How did you know? How can you be so sure it's him?"

Nick hesitated. "Because... because your mother confirmed it."

Rion's eyes narrowed, but he didn't speak, letting Nick continue.

"When you and Gabby went into the room to see Ava, Maurese sent me away to get a Pepsi from the vending machine. I went around the corner, but I heard them. He told her what Mus said. And then he said that Junior…" Nick hesitated again, then said very quickly, "That Junior didn't want to have anything to do with you, and your mother said, 'Because your older brother is a schizophrenic piece of shit, even when he's sober.'"

"Holy, holy shit," Ava breathed out. "So Maurese is…" She reached out and grabbed her brother's wrist. "You're blood-related to him. He's your actual uncle. And he never told you!"

Rion's expression remained calm, his scrunched-up forehead his only sign of distress. Nick was watching him. "Are you okay, babe?"

Rion stared at him as if he couldn't see him. Suddenly, he pulled his hand out of his pocket with his phone. "Are you calling Mama?" Ava asked.

"No," Rion said simply.

He pressed the call button next to Maurese's name, put it on speaker, and sat it in front of him. The phone rang a few times, and Maurese answered groggily. "Ree? You know it's like the middle of the night for me."

"Yeah, I know," he answered.

"Everything okay?"

"Is D.J. my father?"

Maurese did not speak. Rion allowed the silence. Nick and Ava also stayed quiet in anticipation.

"Why would you… why would you say that?" Maurese stumbled out.

"Is your older half-brother, the one you call Junior, my biological father?" Rion asked again.

Maurese sighed. "You have to ask your mother who your father is, Rion. I can't… It's not my place to… This is a conversation between you and Ros."

"Okay," said Rion calmly. "Let me ask the question a different way: Are you my uncle?"

Maurese sighed again. "Who told you? Nick? I thought he might have heard—"

"Yes or no, Maurese?" Rion asked, ignoring his question. "Yes? Or no?"

"I know what you're thinking," he said clearer as he sat up in his bed. "I didn't know this whole time. I suspected, but I didn't know for sure. I had no proof. They both denied it for many years. When she named you Rion I asked her. She said she just liked the name. And I asked him, and he said no. But then I watched you grow up, looking just like him. Looking like... like me. We both look like my father. Your grandfather."

Rion felt his chest begin to tighten up, the first time he felt anxious since he left San Francisco. Maurese's confession was somehow freeing him and caging him at the same time. He closed his eyes and counted back from fifty as Maurese was talking, remembering to breathe in through his nose and out through his mouth.

"And I knew it, but I still didn't want to believe it," Maurese continued. "We were together at the time, even though she just had a baby with Gabe. Ros and I were trying to have a relationship as adults. So I didn't want to believe that they would do something like that to me. But Ros admitted it just three years ago. Her amends to me was to tell me the truth, finally: She cheated on me with my brother and had his baby. I told her that she needed to do the same with you. But she said you would go looking for him, want to ask him questions, demand answers. And Junior wouldn't take kindly to being confronted, and she was afraid that he would hurt you. And not just emotionally but physically, too. He has bipolar disorder, schizo-effective disorder, some other disorders, so either he's mean and high, or he's mean and crazy. She's still afraid that he would hurt you. So I understood why she kept the two of you apart all these years. Trust me. It was better for you to grow up without knowing who your father was than to know how awful a person he is. Your mother was only trying to do what was best—"

"Reese…" Rion finally spoke, cutting him off. "Please. Stop." Rion sighed deeply. "I just needed a yes or a no."

"Okay," said Maurese. "I'm sorry. I'm sorry I didn't tell you when I found out. And yes. I'm your uncle. You are my half-brother's son."

"Okay," said Rion softly. "Okay." Rion opened his eyes and looked at Nick. "I met him once. Gabby and I were staying with Maurese in his studio apartment for a few months, so we wouldn't go back into foster care after Bones got picked up on a weapon's charge."

"You remember that? You were so young," said Maurese.

Rion cut his eyes to the phone. "I was eight. I remembered everything from that age. And I remember him." Rion turned back to Nick. "He came to the apartment and Reese tried to keep him out, but he pushed past him. He walked right up to me and Gabby and just stared at us. Stared at me. Then he started smiling. Maurese and his brother started arguing, then physically fighting. I didn't know what the argument was about. Gabby and I ran into the closet, closed the door, and put our hands over our heads until it was over and he was gone." Rion looked back down at the cell phone. "Was the fight about me?"

"Yeah, it was," Maurese admitted. "He said he just wanted to see you, see what all the hype was about. But the way he looked at you… it was like it dawned on him that Ros actually did have his baby. I told him that if it was true, he needed to do the right thing. He denied it, but in the same breath, made some sexual comments about Ros. I lost my cool. I couldn't believe that—"

Rion cut him off again. "What's his name? I searched every Rion in the entire state of California. He never came up. I would have definitely saw if a Rion Hollingsworth came up."

"He's not a Hollingsworth," Maurese confirmed. "And he's not from California. My father had an affair with a woman who lived in Arizona. She didn't even tell him that he had son until Junior was twelve and her husband died. She named my brother after her husband: Daniel Rion Whitman Junior."

"Holy, holy shit," Ava said quietly.

"Yeah. That's how my mother found out about the affair, and it almost tore my parents apart. Junior is three years older than me. So while my mother was struggling with infertility, my father had gotten another woman pregnant in a one-night stand during a trip to Vegas."

Rion had another thought. "Your parents are black."

"Right," Maurese confirmed. "My father is black. Junior's mother, Alice, is white. Junior is biracial."

"Whoa," Nick said, speaking for the first time. "So Rion is biracial, too?"

"Yeah," said Maurese. "He is."

"Wow," said Ava, also in shock. "I mean, it makes sense. He and Rel look the most alike in their features, the hair, the lips... Gabby and I always joked about Rel and Ree being the real siblings, and Mama found the two of us on the side of the road."

"Your mother loves all four of you very much," Maurese said. "Anything she did outside of her addiction, it was just to protect you. She kept this secret to protect you, Ree."

"Secrets and lies bring nothing but flies," Rion said, shaking his head. "That's the legacy of the children of Roslyn. Secrets and lies."

"Rion—"

"I gotta go. Thanks for telling me the truth."

"Okay, but Rion—"

"We'll talk soon. Get some sleep." Rion hung up before he could say another word.

Ava and Nick both looked at him, waiting for his reaction. But Rion stared off into the woods to the left of him, his face expressionless.

"Are you okay?" Nick asked again.

Rion nodded slowly. "Nope."

Nick couldn't help but smile. "This is no time for your shenanigans."

Rion's lips curved into a small smile as well. "I can't wrap my head around this right now. I'm going to the small meditation room." Rion stood up, and Nick stood up with him, but Rion said, "Alone." Nick nodded. He gave Rion a kiss. Rion's phone buzzed at his feet.

Ava took it and stood up to hand it to him. "It's Mama. Maurese must have called her."

Rion pressed the call button. "No, Roslyn." Then he hung up and turned his phone off. He kissed Nick again. "Put my phone back in the locker. I'll see you in a few hours."

Ava and Nick watched Rion walk away. "I guess she isn't Mama anymore," Ava said.

"This is going to send him off the deep end, isn't it?" Nick asked.

"It might," she said. "Not right now, but it's going to hit him hard. Just be ready for it."

"Well, I'll make sure he doesn't track Junior down and burn his father's house to the ground with him in it," Nick said with a straight face.

Avalon's mouth dropped in surprise, and she lightly punched his shoulder. "*Attempted* arson."

Nick bumped her back and put his arm around her shoulder. "Want to go for a walk? I want to show you something."

"Sure, Nicky."

Nicholas was reading *Become What You Are* by Alan W. Watts in his warm room with the soft glow of the lamplight, waiting for the time to pass so he could join the midnight meditation group. He had the small battery-operated fan to keep him cool, but he was still shirtless, thankful that the mosquitoes decided to give him a break. He heard the soft knock on the wooden door. He went to open it, and Rion was standing there. He had not seen Rion all day, since he had received the news of his father that afternoon. Nick looked at him questioningly. Rion stared back with his wide brown eyes. Nick stuck his head out of the doorway to see if anyone else was in the hallway, then quietly pulled Rion inside. He closed and locked the door behind him. Rion walked to the center of the small room and sighed. Nick came behind him and began to rub his shoulders. Rion turned around and kissed him passionately. Nick allowed it, but then stopped and gave him another questioning look. But he saw that Rion needed him. They had not made love since the hotel room in Fresno, and it was time. So Nick lifted Rion up by his thighs, and Rion instinctively wrapped his legs and arms around his boyfriend.

Nick brought Rion to his bed and gently laid him down, and got on top of him. The bed made a loud squeak with both of their weights. Nick paused, and his eyes were wide with alarm. Rion grinned. Nick grinned back. He pushed his groin into Rion, and Rion bit his lip to keep from moaning as the bed squeaked again. He grabbed Nick's face and kissed him again. Nick moved three times, and the bed squeaked every time. Nick broke off and put his face in Rion's neck. *This isn't happening tonight,* he resigned with a sigh.

Rion tapped Nick's arm for Nick to move off him. Nick did, and Rion stood up. He began to take off his long tunic. Nick laid on his back and watched him get undressed completely. Rion pulled a small tube of Astroglide out of his large pants pocket and tossed it at Nick, landing on his stomach. Nick looked down, then back up at Rion, and smirked. *I guess it is happening,* he thought happily. Why they weren't talking, he wasn't sure, but there was something sensual about it.

Rion gently came onto the bed and it squeaked, but not as loud as it did when Nick was moving on it. He pulled his pants down, not surprised that Nick wasn't wearing underwear, and sat on Nick's legs on the twin-size bed. Rion did not hesitate. He held up Nick's mostly limp cock and took him in his mouth. Nick instantly slapped his hand over his mouth to cover his small moan. He used his other hand to run it through Rion's curly hair as Rion brought him to steel. Rion took the lube off Nick's chest and coated his palm, then began to stroke Nick. Nick was going crazy with desire, and his cock ached to be inside of Rion. He pulled Rion down for another kiss. Rion stifled a moan, allowing Nick's mouth to steal his breath and sound. He, too, ached to be connected to Nick again. Rion slid his knees upward until he was on either side of Nick's hips, making minimal sound on the squeaking bed. Without breaking their lips apart, Nick reached behind Rion, took his cock, and pushed the head inside of Rion's tunnel. Rion stifled another moan. Rion sat up fully and reached behind himself, holding open his bottom, and allowed Nick to insert the rest of himself inside of him. Once fully seated in Nick's lap, Rion let out a breathy sigh. He looked down at Nick's serene face and knew he felt the same. Trying not to move his knees too much, Rion began to ride.

Rion moved slowly, then picked up speed to a moderate pace. The bed still squeaked, but not as loud as with Nick's weight on top of him. They touched; Nick rubbed his hands up and down Rion's torso gently, sensually, Rion with one hand on Nick's shoulder, the other in his hair. Instead of sounds, the men used their breaths, pushing out puffs of air instead of moaning. Nick's little black fan did nothing to combat the heat of their bodies, and soon they were both dripping in sweat. Nick closed his eyes and got lost in his own ecstasy. His hardness was hugged inside Rion's tightness, never feeling more at home. Rion watched Nick's face contort and knew he was close. He wanted to move faster to bring Nick over the edge, but didn't want to wake others with their forbidden lovemaking. So he kept his steady pace and waited. Suddenly Nick slapped his hands down hard on Rion's thighs and pulled in his lip to bite hard. Rion closed his eyes and kept moving as Nick's cock began to twitch and his felt his body get filled with Nick's semen. When he felt Nick stop twitching, he opened his eyes. Nick's eyes were still closed and a lazy smile was on his lips. Rion bent over and kissed him.

Nick opened his eyes. He moved his hands to Rion's butt cheeks and lifted up his knees, putting his feet flat on the bed. He gave a quick thrust upward. Rion's body jolted, but Nick kept his bottom steady. Nick did it again. Rion let out a low grunt. Nick smiled and shook his head. He pushed up a third time, and Rion got the hint. He was about to be fucked hard, and he needed to be quiet about it.

Rion leaned over and put his palms flat on the bed on either side of Nick's head. Nick began to pump upward, not letting his bottom half hit the squeaking bed. Rion grinded his teeth, bit his tongue, and did everything he could to keep from crying out. Nick was still hard as a rock inside of him, sliding furiously over his prostate. The pressure built up in Rion's midsection, and he knew he was going to cum. He reached one hand down and began to stroke himself at a much slower pace than Nick's quick thrusting. His body began to tremble as his orgasm seized him. His mouth opened and he let out a silent cry as cum shot out of his cock head, thick and white from the lack of release for over two weeks, right onto Nick's hairy chest. The sight and feel of Rion's cum was enough to bring Nick over the edge again. His body froze mid-stroke as he emptied out into Rion a second time. Then he fell flat onto the bed with a loud squeak as the mattress and coils protested again under both of their weights.

Rion put his head down into Nick's neck. Nick caressed his partner's sweaty back and allowed his own body to retract naturally out of Rion. Only then did Rion adjust himself and stretch out his legs. Nick began to draw the letters on Rion's back repeatedly: N.W.A.W.R. Rion understood. It was a reminder that no matter what, Nicholas would always be by his side. Rion fell into a deep sleep, feeling loved, safe, and comforted by him.

Nick could see him from the back, standing on the large rock in front of the waterfall they found on day one. Rion was staring at the river of floating lotuses with his hands in his pockets, deep in thought, his phone in his hand. The morning sun was peeking through the trees, leaving a golden glow all around. Nick took out his phone and snapped a picture.

Rion turned around, hearing the click of the photo. "Thought I might find you here," said Nick. "You were gone before I woke up." He stepped up on the boulder and stood next to him. "You okay?"

Rion shrugged. "Just thinking. We only have one more day here, and I have a lot of truths to face when we get back. And I guess I'm just not ready."

Nick sighed. "I'm not ready either. I feel at so much more peace than I have in a long time. I'm learning so much here. And so is Ava. She's really taking to Buddhism. I think this might be it for her. No turning back."

"Yeah, I noticed," said Rion. "You were right. Coming here, finding her peace and her center may have done more for her than any rehab in the U.S. ever did. She's not just clean; she's whole. Mind, body, and spirit. Shit, I think I am, too. Especially since I got the last piece of the puzzle of myself that I've been waiting to hear my whole life." He sighed again. "I just don't think I'm ready to face any of them."

"Yeah," Nick agreed. "I don't think any of us are. So I have a proposition for you." Rion looked at him curiously. "Let's just stay. The three of us can stay another month. Or longer. We're not the first attendees of the retreat who decided to stay after ten days; Ava's friends are doing it too. We can get an apartment close by and come every day to meditate, learn, and practice."

"We've got Ava with us," Rion said. "If it was just you and I, I would say yes, but Ava will want to go home. And I still haven't talked with her about moving to New York with us yet."

"I already checked with Ava before I came to find you," said Nick. "I asked her last night at dinner. Ava wants to stay. She's not ready to go back, either. She said she has nothing going for her back home and everything she needs right here. But she'll only stay if you stay."

"Oh," said Rion. "Well, you know I don't have an issue with spontaneity, so I guess we're staying for another month. Or longer."

Nick pulled Rion in for a hug. Rion took Nick's face in the palm of his hand and kissed his lips softly. He said the words he couldn't say the night before. "I love you, Nicholas."

"I love you, Rion," Nick responded.

They kissed a little more. Nick held his phone up and took a picture of them while they kissed. Rion teased, "You're putting that on your IG page?"

Nick chuckled back. But then he looked at the picture. It was the perfect scenery; greenery all around them, with rays of sunlight peeking through the trees. The waterfall was right behind them. Their lips had just touched, and their eyes were closed. There was a peace and serenity in the photo.

Nick's face became serious. "Why not?"

Rion looked at him in surprise. "Why not what?"

"Why not post it on IG? Let the world know now."

"Nick..." Rion said warningly.

Nick pulled their bodies close together. "I'm ready, Rion Matthews. I'm ready for the whole world to know about us. I've been ready for months, especially after you met both of my siblings. I need you to be comfortable with it, though. Fully stepping into my world with me by your side. And I need you to trust that I will protect you."

"Stepping fully into your world is one thing. But if you post that, your Instagram page is going to crash," Rion said, half seriously, half playfully. "Maybe we should ease me in, introduce me another way?"

"Like what, at my family's masquerade gala next week?" Nick joked. "No, we have to do it like this. Rip off the Bandaid and let the wolves come out among the sheep. It will die down after a few months after another celebrity does some crazy thing and we'll be forgotten about."

"And your parents?" Rion reminded him. "Madeline?"

"Are you afraid of her?" Nick asked. "Because I'm not. Not anymore. Let her do her worst. I'm confident nothing can tear us apart. Not after all we've been through this last year."

Rion was thoughtful. Nicholas had opened up his body and his heart in ways he had never done with anyone else. Emma and Brian were accepting of their relationship, and he had a feeling they would support them publicly, too. His sisters all loved Nicholas like he was a brother to them, too. Despite his current feelings about his mother, she was clean and had been for almost four years. And the very last secret of his life, who his biological father was, was out now. There was nothing that Madeline Highton could do to tear them apart.

Rion took out his phone and stepped closer. He held it up high to pose for the camera. Nick turned to it and he and Rion smiled. Rion snapped a few pics, then Nick quickly leaned over and kissed his cheek, surprising him. Rion's eyes were wide, his face pink, his grin infectious. Nick looked at it and said, "Send me that one, too."

Rion smiled as he did. He watched Nick set both pictures up and ask, "What's your handle on IG?"

"rdm_rdr," he said.

Nick looked at him. "How original," he said sarcastically.

Rion laughed. "You have over twenty million followers. There was no way you were going to pick me out. The page is private, and I only have a couple of scenery pictures of London, none of my face."

"Well, you're going to have to open it," said Nick, trying to decide what to write in the description. "And put up a profile pic. Throw the paparazzi all the red meat at once so it doesn't drag out." Finally, he decided, and it made him smile. "Done."

"Done?" Rion said, a wave of panic hitting him.

"Yes. Done."

Rion opened up his IG page and saw he was tagged in a post. It was the two pictures they had just taken: the first of Nick kissing Rion's cheek, the second of their actual kiss. Nick's caption was simple: "He's not English :)" He followed up with a bunch of hashtags ranging from cities like London, New York, San Francisco, to others like "MenLovingMen," "Partnered," and "OffTheMarket." Nick also created two new hashtags: #NWAWR and #NiionLitesForever. That made Rion smile more than all the others. It also connected to his Facebook account. So the word was out. Everywhere.

Rion watched it go from ten to a thousand likes in a minute, to thirty-five thousand in two minutes, and the comments were blowing up right before his eyes.

"Holy, holy shit. This is going to be crazy."

"Yup," Nick said calmly. "It's going to get crazy for the next forty-eight hours. I expect a curse-out call from Zoey at any moment about why I didn't warn her."

Rion sat down on the rock and started to read the responses. A lot of hearts, fires, and shocked-faced emojis. Some demanding clarification: "Is this him!?" "What's his name?" "Your guy back in London wasn't English?" "Who's the hottie? He's adorable" "Are you in love?" "Where are you?"

Rion decided right then and there to do his own post. He also added two pictures, one of the selfie they took so everyone could see his full face as his profile pic and the same picture of the kiss as his first real post. Then he began to write.

Nick's phone rang, and he was right. Zoey was his first call. "God dammit, Boss! You're supposed to warn me about these things!" she yelled.

"It's like 9 p.m. on a Wednesday. Don't you have anything better to do than track my social media account?" Nick teased.

"Oh, I was. I was currently finishing up a nice quiet dinner with my husband when I started getting calls from the entertainment press, wanting to know who RDM is."

"The official comment: RDM is an erotic romance writer under the pen name Ryan D. Ryder. And he's my partner."

"That's it!? The wolves are going to want to know more. Should I vet interview offers, or are you doing it in your magazine with Eddie again?"

"Not this time, Zoey," he said, watching Rion type furiously on his phone, concentrating. "No, this time, I blew up my life for me. I'm not doing any more interviews about my family or love life. I have to protect what's mine."

"Got it," Zoey said. "When you get back in a few days, we'll talk about next steps."

"We're not back this week," Nick confirmed. "We're staying in Thailand another month. Or longer. After that, we might do a bit of traveling, depending on how we feel."

"Rion's scared of flying ass is not doing a bit of traveling," Zoey deadpanned.

Nick laughed. "We'll see. I just have a feeling it will be a while before we head back to the States. For now, I'm turning off my phone again and going back into mindfulness."

As he said this, Nick received a text at the top of his phone and read it.

[Emma: Blair showed me the post. In the words of Robby, Mother is going to shit bricks.]

[Emma: #NiionLitesForever I'm so happy for you. Hug Rion for me.]

Nick grinned. "I gotta go, Zoey. You and Marcel handle the wolves for the next couple of weeks. I'm on a spiritual and emotional journey with the love of my life."

Zoey smiled. "You go do that, Boss. Have a good day."

"And you a good night," he responded.

When he hung up Rion was still typing. "What are you writing?" Nick asked.

"Shhh…" said Rion. "Trying to figure out the best way to word this…"

Nick smiled and looked at his post one more time. It was up to 725,205 likes and thousands of comments. All positive and demanding more information. He received a couple more texts, including one from Eddie with a simple "I knew it!" one from Brian with a big thumbs-up, and one from Marcel asking several questions. He sent Marcel back to Zoey for instruction. Then he received one from Parker.

[PM: #NiionLitesForever Indeed. I always knew Rion was the one, you know. I wouldn't have yanked his balls so hard if I didn't. No pressure, no diamond. And you have a diamond there. Well done, mate.]

[Nick: Thanks mate.]

[PM: Stop by London soon.]

[Nick: We just might.]

Suddenly, Nick's notifications went off with a tag alert. He looked at it and it was Rion's post. He had changed his handler to Rion_D_Writer, the same as his Gmail account, and his page was no longer private. Rion added one more picture: one of the two of them taking a selfie together at Queen Victoria's Garden right outside of Buckingham Palace. His post was long, and Nick took his time reading it:

Sixteen months ago, I had this great idea for a story: Two people from vastly different worlds fall in love at Oxford University in London. I decided to get on a plane for the first time in my life to visit the city for research purposes. It was a redeye flight from San Francisco to Heathrow, making one stop at JFK to refuel and pick up passengers. A man with dirty blond hair, blue eyes, a red shirt, and Tom Ford shoes got on and sat down across the aisle from me. He introduced himself as Nick Highton. Anyone who knows me knows I can't resist starting a conversation with a stranger, finding out more about them, what drives them, what they fear, what makes them happy. Nick opened up to me about these things as I expected he would like many others. What I wasn't prepared for was how much I opened up right back. I told him about my family history of drug addiction, gang relations, and mental health. He already knew my biggest fear—I pretty much freaked out on the plane—but I found myself telling him other fears, ones I kept inside, like not knowing who my father was, and failing my sisters who pushed for me to be the success story in our broken family. In seven hours, we discovered that we were two people from completely different worlds that craved to be loved deeply just as we were, something left unfulfilled by our individual upbringings. Nick was right: It was an instant connection. Nick and I found ourselves drawn to each other mentally, then physically, and within days, we were emotionally connected. We spent the month of June together and effortlessly fell in love. Then we went our separate ways, me back to California, him to New York. And instead of allowing the connection to grow, I cut it off and pushed him away. It will always be my biggest regret. Fast forward five months, I watched Nick blow his life up, then confess to the world his love for me, and my heart called out to him every single fucking day. So last Dec, I finally took my scared ass back on a plane to face my fear of flying, then my fear of rejection. But I didn't need to worry; the connection never left and we picked up right where we left off. And here we are. All it took was a plane and a simple connection for me to find the love of my life. And I promise you, I am never letting him go. Our souls are aligned. My heart is full. And I am happy. Love you @MrDeepStrokez #RWAWN2 #NiionLitesForever

Nicholas's eyes welled with tears, and they began to fall. He turned off his phone. Nick sat next to Rion on the boulder and noticed he also had tears on his face.

Nick took his hand. "That was very poetic of you, Ree."

"Yeah, well," Rion said and sniffed. "Maybe this is a romantic comedy."

Nick giggled and sniffed, too. "I'm so glad you got on a plane to come to New York."

"Oh, Nick," Rion said, and wiped away his tears. "I'd face my fear of flying every single day if it meant I got to spend the rest of my life with you."

"Yeah?" Nick sniffed again. "So you're ready for this journey with me?"

Rion responded by putting his head on Nick's shoulder and squeezing his hand. They sat in silence as the rushing sound of the waterfall sang in front of them and lotus petals gently floated near their feet.

1. Of all the reasons Rion has given Nicholas about why he wanted to stay anonymous as his partner, which one do you believe was the most important one for them: The paparazzi? Building their foundation? Madeline Highton?

2. Zoey made the comment after they switched positions for the first time: "Now your relationship is on equal footing." Is Zoey correct? Why or why not?

3. Describe the way Nicholas handles the press and his newfound fame in comparison with how others in real life handle the press after a scandal.

4. What are your thoughts on Emma's life and her secret partner in Seppani? What are your thoughts on Brian's life and private BDSM lifestyle?

5. In the second installment, we learn a little bit more about the relationship between Nick and Madeline and the relationship between Rion and

Roslyn. What are the similarities? What are the differences?

6. What are your thoughts on Rion's CBD/THC use?

7. Nick learns more about Rion's traumatic past and abusive childhood. Do you think it changed his opinion of Rion and his family? If so, how?

8. Maurese, who Rion had seen as a father figure in his life, neglected to tell him the truth about his parentage. Do you think he should have when he found out? Why or why not?

9. Nick and Rion both wrote Instagram posts to announce their relationship to the world, one short and sweet and one long and heartfelt. Which one did you like?

10. What's next for the two men?

Wife, mother, partner, daughter, sister, friend, social worker, life skills coach and part-time erotic romance novelist, Eskay Kabba finds the complexity of human nature and creates romantic and erotic love stories. The characters reflect the notion that no one is all good or all bad, but we are all just trying to find love in hard places. Eskay pens erotic romance novels that celebrate the LGBTQ community, people of color and interracial relationships. When not writing about the throes of passion, Eskay finds joy in spending time with her family and loved ones, reading dystopia and fantasy series, and binging popular shows from a streaming app. Eskay. Kabba@gmail.com

More books from 4 Horsemen Publications

LGBT Romance

AJ Buchannan
Orchestrated Love

Eskay Kabba
Hidden Love
Not So Hidden
Signs of Affection
Deeply Devoted to Him
Honest Love
A Plane and Simple Connection

Lucas LaMont
Roman's Reckoning: Type 6

Mikaél's Moment: Type 6
Stephan's Resurgence: Type 5
Anastasia's Arrival: Type 6

Stormie Skyes
Check Yes, No, or Maybe

V.C. Willis
The Prince's Priest
The Priest's Assassin
The Assassin's Saint
The Champion's Lord

LGBT Erotica

Dominic N. Ashen
Steel & Thunder
Storms & Sacrifice
Secrets & Spires
Arenas & Monsters
My Three Orc Dads: a Novella
Before the Storm: a Novella

Eskay Kabba
Hidden Love
Not So Hidden
Signs of Affection
Deeply Devoted to Him
Honest Love
A Plane and Simple Connection

Grayson Ace
How I Got Here
First Year Out of the Closet
You're Only a Top?
You're Only a Bottom?
I Think I'm a Serial Swiper
Lookin in All the Wrong Places
What Makes Me a Whore?
A Breach in Confidentiality
Back Door Pass
My European Adventure
An Unexpected Affair
Finding True Love
The Dr. Cage Chronicles

Leo Sparx
Before Alexander
Claiming Alexander
Taming Alexander
Saving Alexander
The Fall of the House of Otter
The Case of Armando

Robert Lewis
Someone to Love
Someone to Come Home To
Someone to Kiss

Discover more at
4HorsemenPublications.com

www.ingramcontent.com/pod-product-compliance
Lightning Source LLC
Chambersburg PA
CBHW061235310726
48971CB00007B/2080